To Train A Heart

To Train A Heart

A Victorian Romance by

SHAELA KAY

Other books by Shaela Kay

A Heart Made of Indigo
Scoundrel In Disguise
The Rodenburg Girl

Christmas at Edgewood Park
Christmas at Cartwright Manor

Only Ever Friends

Published by Blue Water Books
Richland, WA

Cover design © Blue Water Books

© 2023 Shaela Kay Odd
Visit the author at www.shaelakay.com

This book is a work of fiction. Characters and events in this book are products of the author's imagination and are represented fictitiously. Any likeness to any person, living or dead, is purely coincidental.

For Serity,
who will one day be an author
herself, I have no doubt

Chapter 1

London, England 1842

Madeline closed her eyes and pressed her hands to her stomach. She took one last, steadying breath before opening the door and stepping into the drawing room.

She was surprised to find not only her aunt within, but her uncle as well. Suddenly the summons she received seemed far more serious. Ignoring the trembling in her breast, she put a smile on her face and went to greet her guardians.

"You wished to see me, Aunt?" Madeline said, stopping in front of her.

Aunt Ellen looked up from her needlework. "Yes, Madeline. Please be seated."

Madeline's stomach twisted as she did so. Her uncle stood behind the chaise where her aunt sat, but he said nothing. His expression was stern, as usual, and beneath his withering gaze

Madeline had to fight the urge to make herself appear smaller.

Aunt Ellen finished her stitch and set her work aside. The years had been kind to the older woman, who looked as if she could have been younger than Madeline's father, rather than nearly a decade his senior. Madeline knew the lines around her mouth and eyes were from displeasure, not the passage of time.

She studied Madeline for a moment, then released a heavy sigh. "I understand that Henry has made you an offer," she said.

Madeline stiffened, and the presence of her uncle now made sense. She clasped her hands tightly in her lap. "Yes, Aunt."

"And this offer you have refused." It was not a question, but it was clear a response was expected.

"Yes."

"May I ask why?"

The stone in Madeline's stomach rolled, pushing the breath out of her. "I do not love him, Aunt! Not in that way," she amended. "Though you know I care for him."

"In your situation, love should be the least of your concerns," her uncle snapped, making Madeline flinch.

Aunt Ellen lifted a hand to her husband and he huffed, turning away. She looked back at Madeline.

"Henry is a good man," she said, "and he cares for you a great deal. Though a barrister will never make a fortune, our son would provide a comfortable home. You would want for nothing."

Madeline made no reply, and a flash of irritation warmed Aunt Ellen's eyes.

"If you will not consider your own future, at least consider your brother's. What will become of Thomas?"

Her aunt seemed to think Madeline's refusal was amendable, but it was not. Madeline had no intention of marrying her cousin, however indebted she might feel to his family. When she still did not respond, Aunt Ellen looked to her husband. He narrowed his eyes at Madeline.

"If you will not accept Henry, then I see no reason for you to stay," he said coldly.

Madeline blinked. Was she being dismissed from the room, or from the house?

"Your aunt and I were obliged to take you and Thomas when your parents died. But we have our own daughters to consider, and you are quite capable of making your own way in the world now."

"Making my own way? How? I have no money."

Uncle Richard's lip curled. "Perhaps you should have considered that before refusing our son."

Madeline flushed, her temper rising, but she knew from experience that it was better to remain silent.

Aunt Ellen looked back at Madeline. "Your father left you a modest dowry. Until such time as you find a suitable husband," she sniffed in annoyance, "I may be able to help you find a position as a governess."

If her aunt had slapped her in the face, Madeline could not have been more surprised. She *was* a governess, as well as a tutor—the fact that her charges were her younger cousins was irrelevant. Madeline had stepped in to teach them when she came to live with her aunt and uncle five years ago. It was meant to be a sort of set down, a punishment of sorts—though for what, Madeline could not say. She supposed it may have had something to do with her father marrying beneath his station, an offense which Madeline's aunt did not seem to have ever forgiven him for. But Madeline loved to teach

3

and was happy to do it, and even her aunt grudgingly admitted she was good at it. Sending her away meant that the family would have to hire someone else, and Madeline felt the sting.

She looked up at her aunt. The lines around her mouth had pulled her lips into a taut line. Her eyes, so much like Madeline's father's, were hard.

"I am sorry to have displeased you, Aunt," Madeline said.

Her uncle snorted, turning away, but her aunt sighed. "I am sorry, too," she said. "When you first came to us, I worried what might become of you. But then I saw how Henry's affections for you grew, and I felt sure you would make a match of it. We all did."

A flash of anger coursed through Madeline. Why did everyone expect her to marry Henry? He was certainly a good man, as her aunt said, and Madeline enjoyed his company. Most people were shocked or even displeased when she tried to talk of science and politics in the drawing room. But her cousin had always been patient and pleasant when she inquired after his studies or engaged him in philosophical conversation.

"I tried, Aunt, truly I did. But I have only felt the affection of a friend—or at most, of a sister—for Henry. When I consider becoming his wife, and loving him in that way..." She blushed, looking down. "I cannot do it. I cannot think of him like that."

If Madeline hoped her explanation would satisfy her aunt, she was mistaken. Aunt Ellen merely picked up her needlework again, and did not look up as she spoke.

"I see. Thank you for your candor. I will send out inquiries this week, and we shall see if we can find a position for you. Thomas, of course, will stay with us."

"But—"

"You are dismissed, Madeline," her uncle said, glaring at her.

Madeline swallowed back the retort that sprang to her lips, knowing it would do more harm than good. With a murmur of acknowledgment, she rose and left the room.

Madeline closed the door to her bedchamber and leaned against the heavy wood. How had things turned upside down so quickly? Last week she had been teaching her brother and their cousins the geography of Asia, confident and secure, and now she found herself at odds with her aunt and on the verge of being thrust out.

She rubbed a hand across her eyes and moved to sit on the bed. This was all Henry's fault. If she had only seen his intentions when they first took root, she could have gently redirected his affections. But how could she have known? Henry had always been a pleasant young man. Quiet and congenial, he had never treated her any differently than he did anyone else. It was not until his sister's coming-out ball last month that Madeline first suspected his affections for her might be more than what anyone else in the family felt. But by then it was too late. She had tried to be gentle in her refusal, but there was no way around it. She had refused, he had been heartbroken, and now she must suffer the consequences.

She lay back on the bed, staring up at the pale blue ceiling as she wondered what would happen to her and Thomas. Of one thing she was certain—she would not leave her brother in the care of their aunt and uncle if she left. Thomas was twelve years younger than Madeline's twenty years, and since the deaths of their parents had looked on her almost as a mother. Though their aunt and uncle saw to their needs, they were far from kind, and Madeline knew she could not leave him with them. Not when he had already lost his parents. Not when all they had left was each other.

She sighed, the familiar ache in her chest settling just below her breastbone. She missed her parents—her father especially. As far back as she could remember, her father had doted on her. Not in a way that left her selfish and demanding, but in a way that left her feeling loved and safe. As a girl she would climb onto his lap whenever she saw a book in his hands, and he would read aloud to her from whatever it was. Science, philosophy, agriculture, animal husbandry—his tastes were varied and his thirst for knowledge endless. Madeline was like him in that regard. She soaked it all in like a sponge.

"Theodore, you are filling her head with useless information. What need will she ever have to know Newton's Laws of Motion in her life?" her mother used to scold.

But her father would only laugh and say that no knowledge was useless. And for all her chiding, Madeline knew her mother was secretly pleased at her daughter's rather unorthodox education. As long as Madeline learned her French and needlepoint, she was allowed to study whatever else she wanted.

A timid knock on the door brought Madeline out of her reverie. She sat up, just as Thomas cracked open the door and peeked inside.

"You know you are never to open a closed door without an invitation," Madeline said, raising her brow at her brother. He slipped inside and shut the door behind him.

"I know. But I was afraid you were asleep. I did not wish to wake you."

"Why did you think I was asleep?"

Thomas shrugged. "Aunt Ellen said you went to your room when I asked where you were."

Ah. Madeline patted the bed and her brother climbed up beside her. "And why were you looking for me?"

Thomas rested his head against her arm, and she put it around him. "Maria said you are going away."

"Did she now?"

"Yes. She said because you won't marry Cousin Henry you have to go away." He looked up at her. "Do you?"

Madeline gave her brother a hug, dodging the question. "Aunt Ellen wants to help me find a family that needs a governess."

Thomas pulled away, his face clouded. "Why? You are already a governess. To Cousin Maria and Cousin Eleanor."

Madeline brushed back a lock of his curly hair. "Cousin Eleanor has just come out. She no longer needs a governess. And Maria will soon leave the schoolroom as well."

"But what about Cousin George? What about me? I don't want you to go away, I want you to stay."

He started to cry, and Madeline stroked his head. "Hush now, Thomas. I am not going anywhere at present. We shall not be parted."

He sniffed, and after a moment he looked up. "Promise?"

She gathered him into her arms, tucking his head under her chin as she held him close. "I promise."

Chapter 2

Yorkshire, England

Arthur cracked the door open and looked inside. The candle beside the bed had been put out, and the soft sounds of slumber whispered through the dark. He set his candle down in the hallway, then opened the door just wide enough to allow him to slip inside the room, leaving the door ajar. As his eyes adjusted to the darkness, the small form on the bed sighed and rolled over. Arthur crept quietly to his side. He watched his sleeping son, the familiar ache inside growing the longer he stood there. Reaching out his hand, he brushed an errant lock of hair away from his son's face.

"Sir?"

The voice was quiet but it still made Arthur jump. He turned and saw his housekeeper's anxious face peering at him from the doorway. Arthur put a finger to his lips and made his way softly to the door.

Back in the hallway, his housekeeper was holding two candles—her own, and the one he had left outside the door.

"Forgive me, sir. I saw the candle on the floor and wasnae sure who left it." Her Scottish brogue was thick, though the dim light hid her auburn hair.

"Thank you, Mrs. MacLeod. I am sorry to have disturbed you. I thought you had already gone to bed."

He took his candle from her and turned down the corridor. She walked beside him for a few moments before speaking again.

"Sir, about Augustus."

"Yes?"

"Margaret Hammil will be leaving next week."

He grunted in reply.

"Have ye made other arrangements for him, sir?"

"Not at present. But I intend to send out inquiries to a few families I know. I will find a place for him soon enough."

"Then… ye have decided to send the lad away?"

"He will be going away to school in a few years as it is. It will be better for him to be taught in someone else's home until then. Not here."

They went around a corner into another hall, where Arthur's rooms were. He turned to dismiss Mrs. MacLeod for the night, but she spoke before he could. "Mrs. Vanguard would not have liked it, sir," she said.

Arthur stiffened, as he did whenever his late wife was mentioned. The pain never failed to pierce him through, though he was getting better at managing his reactions to it. He waited for the ache to subside, letting his housekeeper's words sink in. At last he sighed.

"Goodnight, Mrs. MacLeod," he murmured.

The housekeeper bobbed a curtsy. "Goodnight, sir."

"Mrs. MacLeod?"

His voice was tired, and his face was pained when she looked up at him.

"Thank you for your concern. I will take it under counsel."

The housekeeper nodded, and Arthur entered his rooms without another word.

"Stand up straight now, and dinnae go mussing your shirt," Mrs. MacLeod scolded as a maid finished smoothing Augustus's hair.

"Yes, ma'am."

"I think your father has something important to tell ye, but if he asks your opinion, dinnae be afraid to speak up."

The boy's eyes grew wide. "Father has never asked my opinion before."

"Well, he may today. It concerns your future, and since your mother isnae here to consult on the matter, it stands to reason he wants to talk with ye."

Gus watched her with solemn, dark eyes, his pale face losing what little color he had.

"Och, dinnae worry lad. He'll not eat ye. Off we go now, come along."

She led the boy through a long corridor and down two flights of stairs. Gus knew the way to his father's study, but he was grateful for her company. They paused in front of a pair of large, carved doors.

"Ready?" Mrs. MacLeod asked.

When Gus nodded, she reached up and knocked loudly.

"Come."

With a reassuring smile, the housekeeper opened the door. "Master Augustus, sir," she called.

Gus stepped into the room and the housekeeper shut the door behind him. His father was sitting behind a large desk, bent over some papers and a few open books. "Come here," he called without looking up.

In a few steps Gus stood before the desk, nervously shifting from one foot to the other. Arthur Vanguard finished his work and sat back, finally looking at his son. It was no more than a cursory glance, before shifting his gaze once more to the papers in front of him.

"You had a birthday recently," Arthur said without preamble.

"Yes, sir."

"Did you enjoy yourself?"

"Yes, sir. Cook made all my favorite foods, and Nurse read me an extra story before bed." He paused. "I'm going to miss her when she leaves. Why does she have to go?"

Arthur cleared his throat. "Because eight is too old for a nursemaid. You are old enough to have a tutor now."

Gus blinked. "A tutor?"

"Yes. It is time you begin your formal education."

Gus shuffled his feet but said nothing. Arthur watched his son for a moment, then turned his attention back to his work.

"I have spoken with the headmaster at Eton. Your name is on the list and he is expecting you to enroll in a few years, when you turn thirteen."

Gus made no reply.

"Until then, I intend to place you with a family in London. You will have a private tutor and be taught in their home, with their own children."

"You... you are sending me away?"

Arthur flinched, hearing Lily's voice in the innocent question. "It is time you begin your formal education," he repeated, ignoring the guilt that settled in his gut.

"Can I not attend school in the village?" Gus asked, his voice timid.

"The common school? Certainly not."

Gus was silent, and after a moment Arthur went back to his work. Gus fidgeted nervously for a few minutes before quietly clearing his throat. His father looked up at him, but almost as quickly looked away.

"Have you something to say, Augustus?" he asked, searching through the papers on his desk.

"Yes, sir."

Arthur glanced up. "Well?" he said, his tone sharper than he intended. Gus shrank away from the sound. The sight of his only child cowering before him made Arthur wince. Lily would have been horrified. He sighed.

"Come, Augustus. What would you like to say?" His voice was strained, but more gentle.

"Might I have a tutor here, sir? Instead of in London?"

Arthur frowned. "There would be other children to play with, if you went to a family in London."

"Yes," Gus drew out the word into two syllables, "but... but I don't know them. I don't know anyone except you and Mrs.

MacLeod and Nurse and Cook and the other servants." He looked down. "It won't feel like home there. I'll be lonely."

Arthur studied his son, which was something he usually tried very hard not to do. Gus's features were nothing like his father's. He had fair hair and dark eyes, with a pointed little nose and chin that gave him the appearance of a nymph. He looked so much like his deceased mother, that looking at him caused Arthur physical pain. He usually avoided anything and everything that reminded him of Lily—including his son.

He turned away, the familiar grief clawing it's way up his throat. "We live quite out of the way here, Augustus. It may be difficult to find someone willing to board with us."

Gus's countenance fell, and the look of sadness on his face, so like his mother's, nearly undid Arthur. He picked up his pen and bent his face to his work. "But if you do not wish to go to London, I suppose we can find a tutor for you here," he said in a rush, anxious to end the conversation and be alone once more.

"Oh yes, please! I would much rather have a tutor here than go away."

Arthur did not look up—he merely nodded, fortifying the wall he had built around his heart. "I will not often be here," he said brusquely. "You know my business in Leeds takes me away quite frequently. You shan't see me more than you do at present, I should think."

If he had been looking at his son while he spoke, Arthur would have seen the hurt in the boy's eyes. But he did not, and after a moment he waved a hand in dismissal.

"That is all, Augustus. You may go."

"Yes, sir."

The boy turned and fairly ran out of the room, leaving his father alone once more. Arthur rubbed a hand across his face, feeling twice as old as his thirty-two years. "Oh, Lily," he murmured, "if only you were here."

Chapter 3

It had been nearly three weeks since Madeline's aunt had told her she needed to leave. Three weeks of hearing the whispers of the servants and seeing their averted eyes when she came into a room. Three weeks of the barely civil responses from her cousins and former pupils. Three weeks of enduring humiliating visits with her aunt, trying to find a suitable position for her. Three weeks that felt like a lifetime.

She returned from another unsuccessful visit one morning in terrible spirits. Her aunt seemed to think that it was somehow Madeline's fault that none of Aunt Ellen's friends and connections had need of a governess at present. But what could she do? Madeline had been at the mercy of her aunt and uncle for years. She had long since grown accustomed to their ways, and unfortunately, her aunt had a habit of placing fault where no blame was due.

Madeline huffed, removing her bonnet and tossing it onto the bed. She could not continue in this manner much longer. Henry had disappeared to a friend's country estate after her refusal, and she was almost resolved to write to him and tell him she had reconsidered, if only to satisfy her aunt and uncle and rid herself of their displeasure. But that would be unfair to Henry. Henry deserved the love and affection of the woman he married, and Madeline knew she could never provide that.

But what else could she do?

"Perhaps I could work as a companion, rather than as a governess," she said aloud. "Surely there is a lonely widow *somewhere* who might desire my company, and allow Thomas to live with us as well."

She rang the bell, and instructed her maid to bring her the *Times*, "as many copies as you can find," she said. Twenty minutes later, the servant returned with a sheaf of newspapers, leaving Madeline to peruse them alone.

Madeline turned the pages of the paper, searching for the advertisements. There were a few personal requests for lost items, a handful of employment listings that were not suitable, and one or two public apologies. She picked up another paper, and found a similar page of unhelpful news. But in the third paper, a small advertisement bordered in black caught her attention.

Live-in tutor desired for one eight-year-old boy. Must have experience. Position permanent and compensation fair.

A direction for one Arthur Vanguard in Yorkshire was listed, and Madeline's heart raced as she considered answering. She knew, of course, that tutors for boys were expected to be male. She also knew that only wealthy families employed a tutor for just one child—most others simply sent them to school.

Madeline's mind could not dispel the thought. A boy the same age as Thomas would be the perfect playmate for her brother. And though she was not a man, she was certainly qualified to oversee the child's education. She had tutored her brother and her cousins in all their subjects for years. Her Latin needed some work, but thanks to her father's own fascination, she was well-versed in mathematics and science. Did she dare write to Mr. Vanguard? Would he even consider her?

Madeline tore the advertisement out of the paper and tucked it between the pages of her most beloved book. She folded the newspapers and stacked them neatly out of sight—she would send them back downstairs with her maid later. For now, she had much to consider.

By the next afternoon, Madeline had determined to answer Mr. Vanguard's advertisement. After spending another uncomfortable morning making visits with her aunt, she knew that anything was preferable to continuing in that humiliating task. Her aunt's displeasure grew by the hour, and Madeline was tired of waiting for her patience to run out.

She sent a letter the very next day. Madeline had given up her pin money for a week in order to buy her maid's assistance, and her silence. Finally, after nearly a fortnight of waiting—and half a dozen more fruitless visits with her aunt—her maid delivered a letter to her room.

"This just came, miss," she said, handing Madeline an envelope.

"It was lucky I was there when the post arrived—such a to-do over the direction! Peterson thought it had been misdirected."

Madeline took the letter in her hand. It was addressed to *Mr. M. Crawford.* "Thank you, Hannah. That will be all."

She waited until the servant had left her alone, then she walked to the window and sat down on the bench there. She stared at the letter, her pulse thrumming, her body trembling, and closed her eyes. "Please, Lord," she murmured.

The letter was short, written in a small, tight hand. Madeline read it through twice before she allowed herself to breathe.

> *Mr. Crawford,*
>
> *I was pleased to receive your letter of introduction and would like to make your further acquaintance to discuss your services. Please send word as to when I may expect you, and bring your references.*
>
> *Regards,*
> *Arthur Vanguard*

He wanted to meet her.

The initial relief at having found a way out from underneath the thumb of her aunt was short-lived, for the longer Madeline considered Mr. Vanguard's offer, the more tightly her stomach wove itself into knots. Two things from his letter stood out to her as if written in scarlet ink: the salutation, and the word *references.*

She had been careful to sign her letter of intent *M. Crawford,* knowing that Mr. Vanguard would assume she was a man. Madeline had no wish to be openly deceitful, but neither did she wish to be dismissed simply because she was a woman. Her ambiguous signature had had the desired effect: he was clearly impressed by her qualifications, and, assuming her to be a man, desired to meet her.

Madeline felt a bit uneasy about the deception, but it would be remedied soon enough. She would send him word of her forthcoming visit, and he would see upon her arrival that she was both qualified *and* a woman.

The references he requested, however, would be more difficult to obtain, for the simple fact that she had none. Her own education, albeit a bit unorthodox, had equipped her with more than enough knowledge to oversee the primary education of any young person. And she had been serving as both governess and tutor to her brother and younger cousins for years. But she had no formal references. Her aunt had sent letters of inquiry to several of her friends and acquaintances, recommending Madeline for the position of governess in one of their homes, but those were personal letters.

Madeline paced the room, tapping the folded letter upon her open palm. What sort of man was Mr. Vanguard? Was he open-minded, like her father had been? Or would he turn her away without a second thought? She crossed to the bed and sat down, unfolding the letter once more. She read it through, noticing again how very succinct it was. The man was precise, if anything.

Well, she could be precise, too. She would present herself to Mr. Vanguard as invited, and advocate for the position. She would be clear, direct, and persuasive.

Madeline prayed it would be enough to convince the man to hire her.

Chapter 4

One week later

Madeline stepped down from the coach and moved quickly away, putting as much distance between her and the animals pulling the carriage as she could. Thomas hopped out after her, and the servant employed to help the driver climbed on top of the coach to untie their bags. Madeline was forced to draw near enough to accept them from him, her nervous eyes on the mismatched horses to her right. She took their bags and bid the man a hasty farewell, nearly running down the lane in her haste to escape the enormous creatures.

"The horses are likely more afraid of you than you are of them," her brother mused, coming to stand beside her.

Madeline shivered. "I find that quite difficult to believe," she said. She sighed in relief as the carriage started off again, grateful they were nearly to their destination.

It had been a long day of travel and Madeline was exhausted. Knowing that secrecy was imperative to their departure, she had not given Thomas forewarning, and it had been difficult to convince him to arise when it was still dark and leave the house with her. The train to York left at 7:30, and they had only just made it to the station on time.

"I'm hungry," Thomas said.

"So am I. Come along, we are almost there."

They stood at the end of a long drive, the imposing building that was their destination a mere shadow in the distance. The sun had set an hour ago, but the moon was bright and the sky was clear. Thomas slipped his hand into hers. She smiled down at him, trying to ignore the quivering in her stomach as they began walking.

"Is that where we are going to live?" Thomas asked.

"Yes."

"Are there any children to play with?"

"There is a little boy just about your age. I'm going to be his teacher."

"And will you be my teacher, too?"

"Of course."

They walked in silence for a few moments, before Thomas voiced another question.

"Does Aunt know we are going to live here?"

"I wrote her a letter before we left," Madeline said, squeezing his hand. He nodded, and they passed the rest of the walk in silence.

Madeline's confidence dwindled with every step closer to their destination. What had seemed like a good idea and an almost guaranteed position in the comfort of her room in London now seemed foolish and naïve. Would she even have a chance to speak with Mr. Vanguard? Or would they be turned away at the door? And if she did meet the man, would she be dismissed because she was a woman? Because she had brought her brother? There had been no communication whatsoever in regards to Thomas; Madeline had felt it best to ask forgiveness, rather than permission, on that front. She knew Mr. Vanguard would be upset upon her arrival, but precisely *how* upset remained to be seen.

In the dim light, it took them twenty minutes to walk from where the carriage had dropped them off at the road to the front doors. Madeline smiled down at Thomas once more, gathering courage from his answering grin, and lifted the heavy knocker. She counted her breaths, willing her heart to slow down as they waited for an answer.

Though his eyebrows rose only slightly, the servant who answered the knock must have been surprised to see them standing there. He bowed politely and showed them inside. "I would like to see Mr. Vanguard, please," Madeline said, as soon as he had shut the door behind them and turned to face her. "I have come about the tutor position for which he advertised."

The butler frowned. "Forgive me, miss, but there must be a mistake. Mr. Vanguard has already—"

"Found someone to fill the position," Madeline interjected, taking a step forward and thrusting a paper at him. "And that someone is me."

The butler, who looked old enough to be her father, took the paper and glanced over it. It was the letter from Mr. Vanguard which Madeline had received the prior week. He looked up at her, then back down at the paper. "You are Mr. Crawford?"

Madeline flushed. "Yes. Well, not *Mr.* Crawford, of course. My name is Madeline Crawford. I answered Mr. Vanguard's advertisement with a letter indicating my qualifications and merely signed it M. Crawford. Mr. Vanguard must have assumed I was a man." Her cheeks flared, but she lifted her chin and tried to stop her knees from trembling.

"And this is?" the servant asked, nodding at Thomas.

"My brother."

The man looked at her solemnly, then read the letter once more. At last he shook his head.

"Please wait here. I will inquire of Mr. Vanguard whether he wishes to see you."

"Thank you." Madeline's shoulders sank in relief as he walked away. She looked down as Thomas squeezed her hand.

"What if he will not see us?" he whispered.

"Hush, all will turn out right."

The butler did not return for nearly ten minutes, and Madeline was sick with worry by the time he reappeared. "Please follow me," he said without preamble, then turned and started back the way he had come.

Madeline tugged on Thomas's arm, hurrying to catch up. He led them down a dark hall to an open set of double doors. He stepped through them and announced their arrival. "Miss Crawford and her brother, sir."

Madeline and Thomas stepped inside the room—a study, from the looks of it—and the butler shut the doors behind them.

The only light in the room came from the large fireplace on the wall to her left, and an oil lamp on the desk in front of her. The lamp illuminated the face of the man sitting on the other side, and he did not look at all pleased to see her. Madeline cleared her throat.

"Mr. Vanguard, thank you for being willing to meet with me. I am Madeline Crawford, and I—"

"Forgive me, Miss Crawford," the gentleman said, standing and coming around the desk. He was tall—much taller than Madeline had anticipated, and she took a step back as he drew closer. "What I have to say may be best said to yourself alone. Your brother, is it?" he asked, nodding at Thomas, who was half-concealed behind her.

"Yes. His name is Thomas," Madeline said, cursing the quaver in her voice.

Mr. Vanguard rang a bell, and a few moments later the small door in the back of the room opened and a middle-aged woman stepped inside.

"You rang, sir?"

"Yes, Mrs. MacLeod. Please take Mr. Crawford to the kitchen and find him something to eat."

If the woman was surprised, she did not look it. Stepping forward, she held an arm out to Thomas, who looked to Madeline for direction. She nodded at him to follow her. They left through the same door at the back of the room, and Madeline cast an encouraging smile at her brother when he turned to look back at her before it closed behind them.

The silence was broken only by the crackling of the logs on the hearth, but before Madeline could gather her courage to speak, Mr. Vanguard strode swiftly to the main door and jerked it open. He returned to his seat behind the desk scowling, and Madeline heard him mutter something that sounded like "dashed nuisance" as he sat down.

"Miss Crawford," he said, sounding very much like a disgruntled schoolteacher, "I do not know what possessed you to respond to my advertisement in the first place, but I assure you that had I known you were a woman, I would never have replied to your inquiry."

"Which is precisely why I signed my letter as I did," Madeline said, her temper rising. "Your advertisement requested only a tutor with experience, of which I have in abundance. As stated in my letter, I have been employed as a governess and tutor to both young ladies and young gentlemen for several years."

"A female tutor? Preposterous. My answer is no."

His rebuttal stung, but Madeline did not back down. "Aside from my being a woman, what disqualifies me for the position?"

Arthur narrowed his eyes at her. "I do not make it a habit to engage employees prone to deception, *Miss* Crawford."

Madeline swallowed. Letting her temper get the better of her would get her nowhere. She needed to be as professional and dignified as possible. She cleared her throat, striving for composure. "I confess, I was not clear as to my sex because I was afraid you would not consider my services if you knew I was a woman. But I made no deception—I merely signed my initial, rather than my address."

"Which you knew would be construed as mister."

Madeline said nothing.

Arthur closed his eyes, pinching the bridge of his nose. "Miss Crawford, what I cannot fathom is why you answered my advertisement in the first place."

"I need a position, sir."

"You would be more suited to the position of a governess than a tutor."

Madeline was again silent.

"And then there is the matter of your brother. What makes you think that I—or anyone, for that matter—would allow a child to accompany a paid tutor? Why on earth did you bring him with you?"

"I thought he might be a welcome playmate for your son."

"You mean an unwelcome guest and an additional burden, I think."

Mr. Vanguard had not invited her to sit down, but Madeline lowered herself into the chair across from him and clasped her hands in her lap. "Mr. Vanguard, allow me to be frank with you."

His eyebrows shot up. "That would be refreshing, indeed."

Madeline ignored the barb and took a deep breath. "My brother and I have been living with relatives since the deaths of our parents five years ago. My own education prepared me for the responsibility of tutoring my younger cousins as well as my brother in that time, but we now find ourselves in need of a new home. My cousins are grown up, and my aunt has encouraged me to find a position elsewhere."

Mr. Vanguard narrowed his eyes. "She knows you answered my advertisement?"

Madeline pressed her lips together and made no reply. Mr. Vanguard scowled.

"More secrets, I see." He rubbed a hand across his face, not looking at her. "Miss Crawford, even if you are qualified, you must see the impropriety of such an arrangement. You are a single young lady, traveling without protection, and I am a widower in need of a tutor for my son—a *male* tutor. As a gentleman, I cannot have a single woman in circumstances such as yours living under my roof. Your residence would jeopardize both our reputations, and I cannot be inconvenienced with your presence here." He stood abruptly, and

Madeline scrambled to her feet. "I am sorry for your plight, Miss Crawford, but my answer is no. You may see yourself out."

Desperation made the anger simmering in her breast suddenly burst into flame, and Madeline's eyes flashed. "You would turn out a helpless woman and child, with nowhere to go, in the middle of the night?"

Mr. Vanguard looked amused. "Helpless is not at all the word I would use to describe you, Miss Crawford."

"And gentleman is not a word I would use to describe you, Mr. Vanguard."

Madeline saw him rear back as if he had been struck, but she was so angry she did not care. "Your reply to my letter indicated that my qualifications were acceptable and our meeting was merely a formality to seal the offer of employment. My brother and I have nowhere to go. I came with the hope of finding a *gentleman* who would care more for compassion than convention, who would honor the letter he sent to a qualified applicant. A *gentleman* who would take pity on us, but I can see that there is no *gentleman* here to meet with me."

She turned and stormed out of the room, marching back the way she had come, searching for a servant. Her eyes stung, but her anger kept the hopelessness she felt at bay. She saw a footman standing in the entrance hall and bluntly asked him directions to the kitchen. He looked startled at her sudden appearance, but gave her directions. In a few moments she found herself in the cozy kitchen of the manor house, watching her brother finish a large cup of milk.

"Maddie! You should try one of these buns, they are the best I've ever had," Thomas said when he saw her standing in the doorway.

Seeing him there, looking at her with such innocent joy, made all of her anger evaporate. He trusted her to take care of him—how would she tell him they must leave? Where would they go? Where would they sleep? Madeline swallowed past the lump in her throat, trying desperately not to cry as she walked over to him.

"Where is Mrs. MacLeod, Thomas?" she asked. "The woman who brought you here from the study?"

Thomas shrugged. "I don't know. A bell rang a short time ago and she left to see what was needed. What did Mr. Vanguard say?"

Madeline crouched down, running a hand through her brother's unruly curls. She waited until she trusted her voice not to break, but before she could answer him Mrs. MacLeod bustled back into the kitchen.

"I'll show ye to your rooms, if ye'll follow me," she said, smiling at them.

Madeline stared. "Our rooms? But, Mr. Vanguard said…"

"I dinnae ken what the master said to ye when ye was alone, but he just ordered me to set ye up in the guest wing for the night. I expect he'll have words for ye in the morning, but it can wait until then. Follow me."

She turned to go, and Madeline, still stunned, followed woodenly behind her, pulling Thomas along with her.

Arthur grumbled to himself as he sat on the edge of his bed, pulling off his cravat. Why in heaven's name had he allowed Miss Crawford and her brother to stay the night? "She insulted my honor," he muttered to himself, "and I cannot very well call her out, since she is a woman. A woman! Here, in this house!" He growled at his bedclothes. "Preposterous. And the very idea that she could be a tutor to Augustus—her! A tutor, for my son!"

He lay back against the pillows, glaring up at the ceiling. He could almost hear his late wife's laughter, teasing him, as he shut his eyes.

Arthur, darling, what has being a man to do with being a tutor? If she is qualified, what harm can it do?

"A great deal of harm, I assure you," he grumbled, opening his eyes. But what harm could it do to *him?* Any harm done would be to the young lady—Miss Crawford—and her reputation. She would be ruined if he allowed her to stay, surely she must know that. And yet, she seemed completely unconcerned with such matters. Arthur assumed it was because of her brother. She certainly appeared to need the position, as she had said. But did *he* want the burden and responsibility for the both of them?

Despite his better judgment, he found himself pondering question after question about his unwelcome guests. What happened to their parents? What had occurred to cause their aunt to throw them out? They were not destitute—Miss Crawford's clothing and mannerisms landed her solidly within the middle class. Had she no desire to marry? A new thought suddenly accosted him: perhaps she had already been involved in a scandal, and that was why she had been thrown out and needed work. He smirked. It would explain why she seemed to care so little about her reputation as well.

Arthur rolled over and snuffed out the candle at his bedside. The darkness helped to clear his mind, and he drew a deep breath, considering his options.

One night. He told Mrs. MacLeod to let them stay one night, and gave instructions that they were not to leave the next day until he had spoken with Miss Crawford again. But what would he tell her? Would he let her stay and tutor his son, throwing convention and propriety to the dogs? Or would he turn them away, and wash his hands of any and all responsibility towards them?

Chapter 5

Arthur Vanguard was no closer to a decision when he awoke the next morning than when he had fallen asleep the night before. His dreams had been full of his late wife's sparkling laughter but not her face, which left him feeling sad, and in turn, irritable. He came downstairs like a thundercloud, ready to strike at whomever blocked his path. As he passed by the breakfast room, his steps slowed, and he stopped, stunned.

His wife's laughter filtered through the doorway like a breath from the past.

The door stood ajar, and Arthur pushed it slowly open until he could see inside the room. His son, Augustus, sat at the far end of the table across from another lad—Miss Crawford's brother, Thomas. The boys looked to be of similar age and size, and judging from the grins on their faces, of similar mind as well. They were chattering about something when suddenly Augustus laughed—the same sparkling sound Arthur had heard in his dreams all night long.

Had his son's laughter always sounded like Lily's? Arthur tried to remember the last time he had heard Augustus laugh, but it was so long ago he could not remember. The realization filled him with shame.

His eyes landed on Miss Crawford, who sat beside her brother at the table, watching the two boys with an affectionate glance. She was turned away from him and had not noticed his entrance, but when Gus caught sight of his father, his face turned pale. Madeline noticed his stare and turned to see Arthur standing in the doorway.

Arthur cleared his throat and stepped fully into the room. "I see you have met our guests, Augustus," he said, not meeting Miss Crawford's eye.

"Yes, sir," Gus replied. "I am glad you invited them to stay."

"Yes, well... we must always be hospitable."

Miss Crawford raised an eyebrow at him, but looked away the next instant. Arthur did not know what, if anything, she had told his son of their meeting the night before, and not knowing annoyed him. Whatever she had said, Augustus was clearly smitten with both of them. How was he to send her away now, if she had already made a conquest of the boy? And why did that tilt of her chin annoy him so?

"Will they be staying with us, then? Will Miss Crawford be my new teacher?"

The eagerness with which his son asked the question irritated Arthur even further. "It is not necessary for you to know anything at the moment except that they are here as our guests for the day, and I expect you to be on your best behavior." His voice was sharper than he intended, and once more he saw his son's face pale.

"Yes, sir."

Arthur withdrew, and by the time he had reached the end of the hall, the laughter in the room behind him had begun once more. He glared at the floor as he walked. It appeared his decision had been made for him.

Madeline watched Mr. Vanguard withdraw from the corner of her eye. She blew out her breath, surprised at how tense she had felt in his presence. Both her brother and Augustus must have felt it as well, for as soon as he left the room they began speaking once more.

"What shall we do today?" Gus asked, swallowing a bite of toast.

"It is too cold to go out," Thomas lamented, glancing at the windows.

The sky looked ominous, threatening to rain at any moment, and Madeline sighed. February was such a dreary month at times. "How about a tour?" she said, directing her question to Gus. "Your father said you are to treat us as your guests today, and what could be more natural than a tour of the house?"

"We can start in the kitchen!" he replied. "That is my favorite place to be, although Father does not like me down there much."

Madeline hid a smile. "Why is it your favorite place, Gus?"

He grinned. "Because Cook keeps a tin of biscuits, just for me. And she lets me help with the bread on baking day. I like to put raisins in the dough."

Thomas and Gus were soon deep in conversation about their favorite foods, and Madeline shook her head as she finished her tea. She had hoped, of course, that her brother and Mr. Vanguard's son would get along well, but even she had not anticipated how quickly the boys would take to one another.

They finished their breakfast, and Gus led the way through the house and down a short flight of stairs to the kitchen. It was clear from the warm welcome they received that Gus was a favorite with the staff.

"And who are your friends, Master Gus?" the cook asked. She was as round as she was jolly, with silver streaks in her hair and laughter lines around her eyes.

"This is Miss Crawford and her brother, Thomas," Gus said. "She might be my new teacher."

"Welcome to Milford Manor, Miss Crawford. Would you like some tea?"

"No, thank you, Mrs....?"

"Whittecombe, miss. But I answer to 'most everything."

The cheery woman gave her a saucy wink, then turned her attention to the two young boys. "Now then, Master Gus, are you after some biscuits for you and your new friend?"

"Yes please!"

"Go on then, take the lot—'tis baking day tomorrow and I'll have more soon enough."

The boys whooped and emptied the tin of biscuits, splitting them up between them. Madeline laughed.

"You would think they had not eaten in ages, rather than having just come from breakfast," she mused.

"Ah, but biscuits find a way into any belly, even full ones," Mrs. Whittecombe replied. "I'd wager you could put away your fair share of biscuits when you were their age, eh, Miss Crawford?"

"Maddie likes scones more than biscuits," her brother announced, his mouth full.

"I like scones, too," Gus said. "With clotted cream and strawberry preserves."

"And don't I know it!" the cook said with mock severity. "Go on now, best be on your way, Master Gus. Miss Crawford, a pleasure to meet you. You're always welcome for a bite to eat and a cuppa in my kitchen, so don't be a stranger, now."

Madeline murmured her thanks while the boys finished off their treats. "Come on," Gus called, leading them back the way they had come. "I'll show you the rest of the house."

It was an interesting thing, Madeline found, to be given a tour of a grand country manor from an eight-year-old boy. He and Thomas kept up a steady stream of talk as they walked down the hall, passing over many rooms that Madeline was curious about. She poked her head into a few whose doors stood open, admiring the fine furnishings and plush carpets of each. She would have to ask Mrs. MacLeod for a proper tour if they were invited to stay.

If. Madeline sighed. The idea of going back to London and facing her aunt and uncle made her stomach churn.

The second floor of the house consisted of less formal rooms, but most of the doors along the hallway stood closed, so Madeline was not able to catch more than a glimpse inside one or two. They passed several rooms before Gus stopped and opened a door.

"This will be the school room," he said as they followed him inside.

Madeline looked around. It was a long, narrow room, with low windows all along the far wall. A fireplace stood at each end of the room, with a cluster of chairs in front of both. An oblong table sat directly in the center of the space, surrounded by simple but sturdy wooden chairs. Madeline walked across to the windows and looked out over the back garden.

"When will we begin our lessons?" Gus asked.

"I am not sure," Madeline hedged, trailing her fingers along the edge of a bookcase. "Your father and I have not discussed the details of the arrangement."

"I hope it is soon," Gus said. "I like to learn."

"What have you learned from your previous tutors?" Madeline asked.

Gus shrugged. "You are the first. Before now, I was just with Nurse Maggie. She taught me my numbers and how to read and write. But Father said I'm too old for a nursemaid any longer, so he hired you."

"Is your mother dead, then?" Thomas asked. Madeline gasped.

"Thomas! That is none of our business, and quite an impertinent question. Apologize at once."

"I don't mind," Gus said, more subdued. "My mother died a few years ago. I remember her some, but not much."

"My mother died, too," Thomas said softly. "And my father. I was three years old, so I don't remember them well. But I remember them a little."

A pang of loneliness swept over Madeline at her brother's words. "And I will always be here to tell you more about them, to keep their memory alive," she said, speaking around the swelling in her throat. Thomas smiled at her.

"I wish I remembered more about my mother," Gus said, sounding wistful.

"Perhaps your father can tell you more about her," Madeline offered. But Gus shook his head.

"Father never speaks about my mother. And he does not speak

much to me anymore, either," he said. "I think he blames me for my mother's death."

"Blames you! Whatever do you mean?" Madeline asked.

"Mother died because she was taking care of me." Gus said, his eyes filling with tears. "I got sick a few years ago, and she tended to me until I was better. But then *she* fell ill…" He sniffed loudly, wiping his nose with his sleeve.

Madeline produced a handkerchief and gently dried his tears. "That is a terrible coincidence, Gus, but it is not your fault that your mother died. And I cannot think that your father would blame you for such a tragedy."

Gus said nothing more, and after a few moments of silence Thomas perked up. "Do you have any toys?" he asked. "Can I see your room?"

Madeline was grateful for the change in conversation. They left the schoolroom and made their way to the third floor. At the top of the stairs they met Mrs. MacLeod.

"Master Augustus! I've been searching high and low for ye. Are ye minding your manners?"

"He has been a perfect gentleman, and an excellent host," Madeline said with a smile. Gus beamed at her.

"I was just showing them the schoolroom. Now I'm going to show them my room—Thomas wants to see my toys."

"Well go on with ye, then, but only take young Thomas—Miss Crawford will come with me."

The boys took off down the hall while Madeline's stomach squirmed. "Mr. Vanguard would like a word with ye, miss," the housekeeper said.

Madeline was not sure whether she felt more gratitude or dread at the thought of knowing her fate. She took a deep breath and nodded at the woman beside her. "Of course."

They went back to the main floor, and Mrs. MacLeod led her to the study. The door was standing open, so with a reassuring smile, she left her there and went about her business. Madeline took another deep breath, smoothed the skirt of her dress, and rapped on the door.

"You wished to see me, Mr. Vanguard?"

Arthur looked up from his desk to where Madeline stood in the doorway. "Miss Crawford, yes, please come in."

Madeline walked into the room and stood in front of the desk, her hands clasped before her. Arthur noted his place in the ledger before him, then stood and walked around the desk. Madeline watched him, her eyes growing round as he shut the door firmly behind her, leaving them most decidedly alone. As he turned back towards her, she dropped her gaze, but before she averted her eyes she thought she saw him smirk.

"Please, Miss Crawford, be seated."

Madeline sat in the chair she had occupied the night before, and Arthur sat in his own chair. He laced his fingers together and leaned forward upon the desk.

"Miss Crawford, there is one thing upon which I must make myself absolutely clear."

"Yes, Mr. Vanguard?"

"If you choose to accept the position I will offer, you are also accepting full responsibility for any and all difficulties that should arise due to your being in my employ."

"Difficulties, sir?"

He scowled, and Madeline noticed a deep cleft in his cheek when he did so. "Your reputation, Miss Crawford. I saw you flinch when I shut the door. If you are to be my son's tutor, I wash my hands of any obligation with regards to your person and reputation. You will be willfully choosing to put yourself in jeopardy by accepting such a position in my home."

Madeline understood the gravity of this statement, but she could not help the reply which sprang to her lips. "And will I *be* in any such jeopardy while under your employ, Mr. Vanguard?"

Arthur's ears turned red. "Of course not, I am a perfect—" He saw the teasing glint in her eyes, and let out a huff. "—gentleman."

"Of course," Madeline said with a quick nod, not daring to smile. After a moment she cleared her throat and looked him directly in the eye. "I appreciate your concern, Mr. Vanguard, but I assure you, I have no reservations in that regard. I believe you to be an honorable man, and feel safe in your employ. Nothing else concerns me."

"Nothing else?" Arthur exclaimed. "You are not concerned about your future prospects—particularly those regarding marriage—that such an arrangement would surely destroy?"

Madeline shook her head. "If marriage is in my future, Mr. Vanguard, my prospective husband will have to trust in the honor of myself and my employer over the wagging tongues of what society may say about either of us."

"You know that is not how things are done."

Madeline shrugged. "Nevertheless, that is my resolve."

Arthur sat back. Her answer astonished him, and not only because he believed her to be in earnest. He did not think such indifferent ladies existed in society.

"How old are you, Miss Crawford?" he said at length, narrowing his eyes at her.

Madeline flushed. "Sir, you know it is most improper to ask a lady's age."

Arthur waved a hand dismissively. "But we have already established that you care not a whit for what society deems proper, do you?"

Madeline's lips twitched, hiding a smile. "I am not yet one and twenty, Mr. Vanguard."

"Mm. And when you reach your majority? What then?"

She frowned. "I suppose I will be another year older."

"Will you have no inheritance to come into? No change of fortune to consider?"

Madeline was thoughtful for a moment. "I do not think so," she said. "My uncle never shared the details of my father's will with me, and my aunt has only inferred that I have an appropriate dowry, if I should ever marry. But nothing of that matter should affect my employment. I intend to remain as long as my services are needed."

"You would not wish to leave my employ and establish your own home somewhere else?"

Madeline shook her head. "I have my brother to consider, Mr. Vanguard. While I should like to have a house of my own someday, this position would offer me all that I need at present: a home for my brother and myself, a consistent wage to set aside for our maintenance, and the ability to continue to teach him until it is time for him to go to university. Not to mention the companionship your son would provide."

"Ah yes, your brother," Arthur said, leaning back in his chair. "That is another point we must discuss. It was quite high-handed of you to presume he would be welcome."

Madeline made no reply.

"However, this entire situation is turning out to be quite unorthodox, so he may as well stay. But if he is to remain here, you are to be fully responsible for him. I will not have him disturbing my household or preventing you from fulfilling your duties, is that quite understood?"

"Yes, sir. Of course"

"And your wages will be less, to accommodate his room and board."

Madeline nodded. "Naturally. Please withhold whatever amount you feel is appropriate."

Arthur tapped his fingers on the edge of the desk, thoughtful. "You do not even know the wage I plan to offer you."

Madeline smiled. The truth was, even if he did not pay her at all, she would be willing to stay. But of course she could not say as much. "I am sure that whatever you decide will be agreeable to me."

He took a sheet of paper from a drawer and wrote something along the top of it. He turned it around and slid the paper across to her. "As a weekly wage, this is what I am prepared to pay you."

She swallowed. The sum was far greater than she had anticipated, and more than enough for their needs. Nodding, she pushed the paper back towards him. "That is perfectly acceptable."

Arthur nodded curtly. "Good. I travel for business quite frequently, and I will be leaving in a few days' time. I trust you to begin at once and carry on in my absence."

Again she nodded.

"Then seeing as we are agreed upon all points, I propose a trial period of one month. If, in that time, your work and Augustus's progress is found to be acceptable, I will employ your services indefinitely. But if I am not satisfied at the end of thirty days, you will accept your wages and take yourself and your brother off at once. Are we agreed?"

Madeline swallowed. How would she know if her work was acceptable? How much progress did Mr. Vanguard expect his son to make? She looked across the desk at him, meeting his steely gaze, and nodded. "Agreed," she said.

"Good." Arthur sat back. "You will begin tomorrow. The schoolroom is equipped with everything you should need for now, but if you find it lacking, speak with Mrs. MacLeod—she will see to whatever you need."

Arthur got to his feet, clearly a sign that she was dismissed. Madeline stood as well, once again struck by how tall he was.

"I hope I will not be disappointed in you, Miss Crawford," he said.

"I hope so too, sir."

He gave her a nod, which Madeline returned with a curtsy before turning and leaving the room.

Chapter 6

Madeline's hands were trembling as she shut the door behind her. *He is going to let me stay. We are* both *going to stay.* She closed her eyes and leaned back against the door, pressing a hand to her cheek. The coolness helped to calm the whirlwind inside her.

After a moment, she pushed herself away from the door and made her way up the stairs to her room. Once there, she unpacked the few items still in her valise. There was not much—she wore the only other gown she had been able to bring with her, and besides her nightdress, stockings, and underthings, there was only a silver-plated hand brush and mirror, a few treasured books, and her reticule full of money. Not that it contained a grand sum, but since she and Thomas had been required to travel so light, she brought everything she had, which would hopefully be enough to replenish their wardrobes. Soon enough she would be earning wages and able to save for Thomas's education.

Wages. It was a curious thing for Madeline to consider, that she would be employed as a tutor and earning money for herself. It was a good thing, too, because she had not been able to pack much for Thomas, either. He was growing so quickly his trousers would soon be too short.

She lifted her reticule and counted the money inside. Good—there was enough and to spare for some cloth to make herself a few more dresses, as well as some more clothes for Thomas. She went to the wall and pulled the bell cord, tidying up her few possessions as she waited for a maid to answer her summons.

In a few minutes there was a knock on the door. "Come in," Madeline called.

A young lady with red hair and freckled skin opened the door. "You rang, miss?" she asked, stepping into the room.

"Yes—Sarah, isn't it?"

The maid smiled as she bobbed a curtsy. "Yes, miss."

"Sarah, I would like to acquire some fabric suitable for making clothes. Does the town have a place to make such purchases?"

"Not in the village, miss. But 'tis only six miles to York, and Mrs. MacLeod sends a cart every week for supplies."

"Wonderful, I will speak with her and perhaps I can accompany the servants when next they make the trip."

"Very good, miss. Was there anything else?"

"No, thank you, that is all."

After she left, Madeline sat down at the small desk. She found a sheet of paper and began to write.

Dear Aunt Ellen,

*I hope this finds you well. I am writing to inform you
that I have found a position and a home for Thomas*

and I, with a respectable family that has need of my services. We are settled quite comfortably and shall be well taken care of, so you may be easy on that account.

I apologize once more for leaving as suddenly as we did. Please know that I acted in the manner I saw best for my brother and I. Thank you for giving us a home when we had none.

With affection,
Madeline

She read the letter through twice before she was satisfied with it. She knew her aunt and uncle would wish to know where they were situated and with whom, but Madeline also knew that they would very likely insist that Thomas return to them if their whereabouts were known. For now, Madeline thought it best to leave their location a mystery.

After folding and sealing the letter, she went in search of her brother. Her room was situated in the guest wing of the house, but she knew the family wing to be on the same floor, on the other side of the grand staircase. She walked slowly down the corridor, admiring the rich wood and the artwork on the walls as she went. There were a few gaps between paintings where surely something else had hung. She wondered idly what had occupied the space, but did not think much else about it. When she reached the family wing, she could hear the voices of her brother and his new friend drifting down the hall. She approached the open door with a smile.

The two boys were lying on their stomachs on the floor, a handful of small tin soldiers scattered between them. They were making noises of battle as only small boys can, and Madeline paused in the doorway to watch them.

"Watch your left flank, my soldiers are coming in!"

"Oh no, 'tis an ambush! Soldiers, advance!"

"I've been captured, help!"

"Ha! Now I've got you."

Gratitude blossomed in Madeline's heart as she watched them. What a blessing to have found such a home for them both! Madeline now had employment, and Thomas had a new friend. She hoped it would prove to be a blessing for Gus as well.

Gus finally spied her standing in the doorway, and he grinned up at her. "Hello Miss Crawford! Come to play soldiers with us?"

Madeline smiled. "No, I was only looking for my brother. Thomas, may I speak with you a moment?"

Thomas stood up from the floor. "Of course. Is something wrong?"

"No, not at all."

"You can stay here," Gus said, getting to his feet as well. "I am going to run down to the kitchen and see if I can nip a couple of apples."

He scampered off, and Madeline sat down on the edge of a chair. Thomas came and stood in front of her.

"Mr. Vanguard has agreed to take me on as Gus's tutor," she said.

"So we can stay?" Thomas asked with excitement.

Madeline smiled. "For now, yes."

Thomas frowned. "What do you mean 'for now?'"

"Mr. Vanguard is not sure about the idea of a woman teaching his son," she said. "He has agreed to let us stay for one month, and then reevaluate the arrangement."

"What if he sends us away?"

Madeline reached up and smoothed down one of his curls. "Then we will find a new place to live."

"Will we go back to Aunt Ellen's house?"

"I hope not. I hope we can stay here."

"I hope so, too," Thomas said. "I like it here. And I like Gus. I always wanted a brother!"

Madeline smiled. "I am so glad you like it here. I shall do my best to please Mr. Vanguard so that we may stay."

"I will do my best as well. And I'll tell Gus—he wants us to stay, too, he told me."

Madeline gave her brother a hug. "Then hopefully between the three of us, we shall win over Mr. Vanguard."

Gus was elated when he heard the news, and agreed to be a model pupil to help ensure the Crawfords were not asked to leave Milford Manor. When the three of them gathered in the schoolroom the next morning, a buzz of excitement filled the air.

"Now, Gus, can you tell me what you have learned so far? Where are you at with your studies?"

Gus went to one of the shelves and pulled out a few books. He showed her the primers he had finished and the books he had read.

"And are you studying any languages at present?" Madeline asked.

"My nurse taught me a little French, and my father would like me to learn German, but Maggie did not know any."

Madeline nodded. "My Latin is a bit rusty, but I can teach you

German easily enough."

"Father does not care if I learn Latin," Gus said with a shrug, returning the books to their places.

Madeline arched an eyebrow at him. "Really? That surprises me."

"Father says it is too old-fashioned, and that German will serve me better."

Madeline was intrigued. "I suppose that is true. What else does your father say?"

"Not much. He plans to send me to Eton when I'm thirteen. He was going to send me to a family in London to be taught in their home, but I did not want to go. So father hired you." His voice and face lifted at the pronouncement, which caused Madeline to smile, though inside her heart ached for the lad. What kind of man would send away his only child, after already losing his wife?

"I gather you do not spend much time with your father?"

"Not anymore. He used to take me for outings and play with me in the afternoons. But since Mother died he hardly ever spends time with me. Sometimes I see him at breakfast, and we have dinner together when he is home, but he is often away."

"That sounds rather lonely," Madeline said gently.

Gus lifted a shoulder. "I am used to it now. And I always had Nurse Maggie." His eyes grew excited as he turned to Thomas. "But now that you are here, I shall never be lonely!"

Madeline smiled, then told the boys to quiet themselves and sit at the table. She set Thomas to the task of copying one of Tennyson's poems, while she picked a book from the shelf and sat beside Gus. "I would like to hear you read, Gus," she said. "That will give me a good idea of where to start your formal lessons."

He nodded. Thomas pulled the ink set towards him and started writing on a sheet of paper as Gus began sounding out the words on the page before him. It was clear after a few minutes that he was terribly behind where she expected him to be. She stopped him and pulled out the latest primer he had finished.

"I thought you had made it through this last primer?" she asked gently. Thomas glanced over at them, but quickly put his head down when Madeline frowned at him. Gus slumped in his seat.

"I did," Gus said. "But Nurse Maggie did a lot of the reading for me."

Madeline nodded, slowly turning the pages. "Very well, let us see how your writing compares."

Gus fetched a slate and piece of chalk.

"Now, I want you to write out the sentence I dictate to you," she said. Gus nodded. "The sentence I want you to write is: *There is a cat by the fire.*"

Gus giggled. "Father won't let us have a cat."

Madeline smiled indulgently. "That is unfortunate, but I'd still like you to write the sentence."

He sighed, screwing up his face in concentration. It took him several minutes to complete the task, and, as Madeline suspected, his handwriting and spelling were atrocious. She smiled at her pupil, but inwardly she sighed.

"Very good effort, Gus. There are some spelling errors, but I can tell you were sounding out the words and did your best."

Gus nodded glumly, glancing at Thomas seated a short distance away. He had finished his copy work and was now working through a German primer. "When will I get to learn German?" he asked, looking back at Madeline.

"Not until you can read and write in English a little better," Madeline said gently. "But we are going to work on that, starting right now."

Chapter 7

Normally the evening meal between father and son was quiet and formal, with only a few words exchanged between them and Arthur dismissing his son the moment Gus finished eating. That night, however, Gus's soup sat untouched while he chattered on about how he had spent the first day of his formal lessons.

"And after we finished, Miss Crawford took me and Thomas outside to play in the garden. She said we will need daily exercise if we are to grow healthy and strong."

"Miss Crawford is quite right," Arthur said, the moment he could get a word in. "But tell me, why did you not study German along with Miss Crawford's brother? Did you not tell her I wished you to learn the language?"

"I did," Gus said, picking up his spoon for the first time and slowly drawing it through the bowl. "But Miss Crawford said I must get better at reading and writing in English before she can teach me any German."

Arthur frowned. "What do you mean? You already know how to read and write in English, do you not?"

"Yes, sir," Gus said meekly, not looking at his father, "but..." His voice trailed off, and he took a spoonful of soup.

"But?"

"But not very well."

Still frowning, Arthur turned to the footman stationed at the door. "Bring me a book from the library."

The servant bowed and left the room, returning a few minutes later with a slim volume. He handed it to Arthur without a word and went back to the door, standing at attention once more. Arther turned the book in his hand to read the title. It was a collection of essays by Charles Lamb.

"Here," he said, opening the book and placing it beside his son. "Read me this page."

Gus had gone pale, and his voice trembled as he started to speak. Carefully, painstakingly, he sounded out a few words, only to have his father snatch the book back after a few moments.

"Confound it child, I thought you could read!"

Gus began to cry, which distressed Arthur even more. He felt ashamed—of his son for his illiteracy, and of himself for his lack of concern. Lily had seen to such things when she had been alive, but since her passing Arthur had done virtually nothing. He had taken it for granted that the nursemaid he'd employed for eight years would teach Augustus how to read and write legibly, and never once did he bother himself to see if she was. A flash of anger coursed through him, but whether it was directed at the nursemaid he no longer employed or at himself, he could not say.

His son was still crying quietly, and Arthur shifted

uncomfortably. "Augustus, there is no need to carry on so. I am not angry with you, I was merely surprised, and disappointed."

Gus sniffed loudly, and Arthur sighed.

"Have you not a handkerchief? There—that will do." He handed the boy his own handkerchief, glancing at the ceiling as Gus blew his nose loudly. When he heard no more sniffling, he looked over at his son. Gus's eyes were red, and he stared glumly at his water glass. Arthur picked up his spoon and resumed eating, and soon Gus did the same.

Nothing else was spoken between them until after the main course had been consumed, when Gus asked to be excused. Usually Arthur was happy to send him on his way as soon as possible, but tonight he felt the prick of guilt in his gut, and he cleared his throat instead.

"Before you go, I must apologize. I did not mean to upset you earlier. Forgive me."

Gus nodded mutely.

"I will be leaving tomorrow. I hope you will devote all your energy into improving yourself while I am gone."

"Yes, sir."

Arthur gave him a curt nod. "Good. Then you are excused."

Arthur left before noon the following day, and Madeline was surprised that he did not call for his son to say farewell before departing.

"How often is your father away?" she asked Gus, who was copying out his letters onto a slate.

"More often than he is here," he said, not bothering to look up.

"I wonder what he does that takes him away so frequently," Madeline murmured, more to herself than to anyone in particular.

"He has many tenant farmers," Gus said. "And he has to check on the horses."

"Horses?"

"Yes. Father has a horse farm outside of Leeds. He spends most of his time there."

Madeline shuddered. Her fear of horses went back several years, the result of a riding accident she suffered when she was young. Though she had not been severely injured, since that time she had been completely terrified of the animals.

"Well. Your father will want to check your progress when he returns, so today I would like you to write out the Lord's Prayer on a sheet of paper. In a month's time, you shall repeat the exercise so that we may note the improvement."

"But I don't know the Lord's Prayer," Gus said.

Madeline stared. Thomas looked up, eyes wide. "You don't know the Lord's Prayer?" he said.

"No."

"'Our Father which art in Heaven, hallowed be thy name...?'" Thomas prompted. But Gus just shook his head.

"Sorry. I never learned it."

A shocking thought crossed Madeline's mind, and she sat down next to her young pupil. He was watching her anxiously, so she put an arm around his shoulders and gave him a gentle smile.

"Augustus," she said, her voice soft, "do you attend church with your father?"

"No," he said. "Father does not attend church."

"Do you attend with anyone else?"

Gus shrugged. "Mrs. MacLeod has taken me a few times, for special services. But I have not been for years. I don't remember much about it."

Madeline gave him another hug, striving to compose herself. Her opinion of Arthur Vanguard was not high to begin with, and this new revelation sank him even further in her esteem. How could he be so neglectful of his son that he did not even care for his spiritual welfare?

"I will help you with the Lord's Prayer today, and beginning this week you will attend church with Thomas and I so you can learn it yourself."

"Really? I can go to church with you?"

The eagerness with which he spoke pained her, but Madeline summoned a smile, nodding. "Of course. Starting this Sunday."

Thomas and Gus both gave a whoop, and Madeline laughed, wondering what she had gotten herself into.

Chapter 8

Mrs. MacLeod informed Madeline at supper that she would be sending a couple servants into town the next day. "Sarah told me ye had need of some material," she said. "If ye tell me what ye'd like, I can add it to the list for Carver and Jane to collect."

"Would it be possible for me to accompany them? I will need a few other things as well, and I should like to see what York has to offer."

"O' course. Will your brother be going with ye?"

Madeline hesitated. "I believe that would be for the best. Mr. Vanguard made it clear that he is to be my sole responsibility, and while he is a good child, I would hate to have him fall into any mischief while I am away."

Mrs. MacLeod gave her a knowing smile. "Aye, and two young lads can find themselves in plenty o' mischief sooner than ye can shake a stick at." She nodded. "I'll let Carver know to expect ye both."

But Thomas was not happy when Madeline told him the news that evening before bed. "I don't want to go to town, I want to stay here and play with Gus!"

"Dearest, I know you do," Madeline said. "But I cannot leave you unattended, and I shall surely be dismissed if anything should happen with you while I am away."

"Nothing will happen, I'll just be with Gus all day."

Madeline tousled his hair. "That is precisely what concerns me."

Her brother scowled. "If I am to accompany you, cannot Gus come as well?"

Madeline considered for a moment. "I suppose so. I shall ask Mrs. MacLeod about it."

In the end, there was not enough room in the cart for the three of them and both servants, but the boys raised such a fuss about being parted for the day that it was decided that Jane would stay behind to make room for both boys.

It had rained in the night, but by the time they set off the next morning the wind was chasing away the clouds. Madeline climbed up onto the bench seat, nervously eyeing the matching bays harnessed to the cart. She was uncomfortable being so close to the animals, but unless she wanted to sit in the bed of the wagon, there was no help for it. She shivered in the damp air, grateful for the hot bricks at their feet.

Gus and Thomas were sandwiched between Madeline and Carver on the long bench seat. The young man drove the wagon without saying much, but the two boys seated beside him more than made up for his lack of conversation. They chattered happily with one another, leaving Madeline free to admire the countryside.

She had heard, of course, of the famous moorlands in Northern

Yorkshire, but there was very little of the scrubby wilderness she had been expecting this far south. Instead, there were fields of farmland spread out in swathes of green and brown, with long, low hills cutting in and around them. Shrubs and brambles lined the road, broken here and there by low stone walls. They passed field after field of rich brown soil, neatly plowed in uniform rows, ready to be sown.

"Carver," Madeline asked, turning to the young man driving the wagon, "what do the farmers grow around here?"

"Corn and sugar beet, mostly. Wheat and oats as well," he said, his gaze still on the road ahead of them.

"And sheep?" Madeline asked as they passed a cluster of the grazing animals.

Carver glanced at her and grinned. "Lots of sheep. My father has a sheep farm the other side of the village."

"But you work at the manor?"

The young man shrugged. "I help on the farm as well. I work at the manor off-and-on as needed, when things are slow on the farm. But lambing season has just begun, so this will be my last week for a while."

Madeline nodded as they passed another pasture dotted with sheep. She noticed a few lambs wandering among the others, their new white fleeces a stark contrast to the older, darker color of the ewes.

Eventually Madeline pulled out a book to read. Mr. Vanguard had given her permission to use the library, and she had chosen a slim volume of Shakespeare's sonnets to read on the ride. She hoped to find a few suitable verses to have the boys memorize.

It took them just over an hour to reach the town of York. Milford

Village had a small church, a blacksmith, and a public house, but for anything else that was needed, a trip to York must be made. They passed through the massive Micklegate Bar and into the city, the ancient stonework dark and discolored in many places. Madeline had passed through the same gate when she and Thomas had arrived a few days prior, but since the railway station was only a short distance away, she had not seen much of the city.

Carver drove the cart through town and over the River Ouse. The shops and houses of York passed by in quick succession as they made their way into the heart of the city. Soon the magnificent Gothic towers of St. Peters came into full view, stretching heavenward. Madeline craned her neck as they passed, noting the missing roof and blackened shell of the nave and south tower.

"Was there a fire in the cathedral?" she asked.

"Aye, about two years ago," Carver said.

He said nothing else, and soon pulled the horses to a stop in front of a large haberdashery on Petergate. Madeline climbed down from the wagon with his help and bid the boys to follow her.

"If you mind your manners inside," she said, "I'll buy you each a piece of stick candy for the ride home." They eagerly agreed, and the three of them entered the shop together.

A middle-aged woman looked up from the counter as they came in through the door. "Good morning. May I help you find something?"

"Yes, thank you. I would like to purchase some fabric, if you please."

"Right over here."

Madeline left the boys looking through a large basket of buttons and followed the woman across the room. She spent her time selecting a few different bolts of cloth for herself and for Thomas, as well as needles and thread. She also purchased another pair of gloves and a Sunday bonnet, though she felt guilty for the extra expense.

"That color sets off your hair quite nicely," the woman said, holding up a mirror for Madeline to see herself.

"It is certainly becoming." She turned her head this way and that, trying to see it from all angles. "It reminds me of one I had at home."

"And where is home, miss?"

Madeline removed the bonnet, placing it on the counter next to her other purchases. "London. Though I suppose Milford is my home now."

"Indeed?" The woman's brow lifted. "And what brings you to Yorkshire?"

A nagging little voice in Madeline's mind told her not to say much, but she pushed it aside. Gossip traveled quickly in a small community, and word would spread eventually—she may as well ensure it was the truth from her own lips. "I have taken a position with a family here."

"You are a governess, then?"

"A tutor."

"A tutor?" The woman frowned. "You mean a teacher? At the village school?"

"No, a private tutor. Employed by Mr. Arthur Vanguard."

The woman stared. "Mr. Vanguard! Of Milford Manor?"

Madeline inclined her head.

"He has only one child, does he not?" The woman glanced at the two boys across the room, her eyes large as windowpanes.

"Yes, a son just my brother's age. He is staying with me there."

The woman's eyes swept over Madeline in a way they had not before. Madeline flushed, knowing she was being judged but not ashamed of what the woman would see: a young lady of good breeding, with chestnut hair and fine clothing—not a poor, destitute orphan she may have expected Mr. Vanguard to take on as a charity case. It occurred to Madeline that the woman might think she was Mr. Vanguard's mistress, and the thought darkened the blush on her cheeks. But she held her chin high, and met the woman's scrutinizing look with as much careful grace as she could manage.

"Well," the woman said at last, her eyebrows still high on her face, "I suppose Mr. Vanguard may hire whomever he wishes for such a position."

It was clear the woman disapproved of Madeline as a tutor, if not of Madeline herself. Her disapproval only sharpened Madeline's manners, and she thanked her kindly for her help before asking that her purchases be wrapped. Giving the proprietress a smile, she turned to go.

"Thomas, Gus, come along," she called, heading for the door. The boys fell into step behind her, and together they left the shop.

Carver was waiting for them with the cart when they emerged, having completed his errands while Madeline did her shopping. He placed her parcels in the back of the cart and offered her his hand to help her mount the seat.

Madeline hesitated. "I promised the boys a treat if they behaved themselves, which they did. Do you mind if we run inside the mercantile for a moment?"

"Not at all," he said. "I'll just wait for you here."

"Thank you."

Madeline, Thomas, and Gus crossed the street to a mercantile a few doors down. A small bell jingled merrily over their heads at their entrance, and a young lady looked up from her seat behind the counter. She set the book she was reading aside and stood to welcome them.

"Good day," she said. "May I help you?"

"Good day," Madeline replied. "I would like a penny's worth of candy for each of the boys, and a sack of lemon drops for myself, please."

The young lady nodded, and the boys began talking over one another in an attempt to tell her what sweets they wanted. An older woman, similar in coloring and complexion to the younger one, bustled in from the back of the shop. "Eloise, have you seen—" Her voice cut off in surprise. "Oh, pardon me, I did not know we had customers." She glanced at Madeline, then nodded to her daughter. "You help those rascals and I'll wait on the lady." She winked at the boys, then approached Madeline with a smile.

"Good day to you, miss. How can I help you?"

"Good day. We just want a bit of candy for the road. I'll take a small bag of lemon drops, please."

"Where are you off to?" the woman asked, filling a small paper bag with the tart yellow candies.

Madeline's stomach twisted, anticipating another exchange like the one at the haberdashery. But she smiled and said, "Milford Manor. I have recently taken a position there."

The woman frowned. "Not another nursemaid for the child, surely? Hasn't he grown old enough for a tutor?"

"He has," Madeline said with a nod. "And I am that tutor."

Instead of disapproval, the woman's face lifted in delight. "Are you now! Well, I'm glad to hear it. That child needs mothering more than teaching if you ask me, and you'll be there to do both, I'd wager."

Warmth spread through Madeline's middle at her words, and tears sprang to her eyes. She laughed, wiping at them with her handkerchief. "You have no idea how badly I needed to hear that," she said. "Everyone else seems to think I'm daft."

The woman waved a hand dismissively. "There will always be naysayers, in my experience. Best to ignore them, I say." She smiled and held out the bag to Madeline, who took it gratefully.

"Thank you, Mrs....?"

"Martin. Abigail Martin."

"Madeline Crawford."

Mrs. Martin nodded her head in acknowledgment. "I hope to see you again, Miss Crawford."

"And you as well, Mrs. Martin."

Madeline paid for the sweets, and with mouths full of candy the boys followed her back to the wagon.

Chapter 9

Usually Arthur rode his horse, Xerxes, to Leeds, which took a full day of riding to reach from Milford Manor. This time, however, Arthur took one of his carriages, on account of the often unpredictable spring weather.

He arrived without incident on Thursday evening, and settled himself into the guest room he always occupied at Harley Hall. He was more comfortable there than in his own bedchamber at Milford, for one simple reason: there was no trace of Lily within its walls.

He went down to breakfast the next day, and was soon joined by his host and business partner, William Harley.

"Arthur! I was wondering when we would see you next," he said, coming into the room. "How were the roads?"

"A bit damp in places, but not terribly so."

"Did you come down on Xerxes?"

"Unfortunately not. I did not want to make you jealous," Arthur said with a wry grin.

"You know my offer stands, if you are ever willing to sell him."

But Arthur shook his head. "Not a chance. You shall have to wait for one of his colts to grow up. But even then, I doubt Xerxes will ever sire his equal."

His friend groaned, and Arthur chuckled. He turned back to his breakfast while William helped himself to some cold cuts from the sideboard. "How are things at home?" he asked, sitting beside him.

Arthur took a sip of his tea, not looking at his friend. "Unusual."

"Unusual? What do you mean?"

Arthur sat back in his chair, considering the man beside him. They had been friends at school, and he was the first person Arthur had thought of when he decided to invest in a stud farm. William was a good man and a good friend, and Arthur was grateful to be in business with him.

"Do you remember," Arthur said at last, "when I told you I was expecting a visit from a man in London who was interested in tutoring my son?"

"Yes."

"He came. Or rather, *she* came."

William blinked. "You mean it was a woman who answered your advertisement?"

Arthur nodded.

His friend stared at him for a moment before throwing back his head and laughing. "A woman! As a tutor?" He shook his head, still chuckling. "I hope you sent her packing."

Arthur took another sip of his tea, and when he said nothing in response, the smile faded from William's face.

"You *did* send her away, did you not?"

"No."

"What do you mean, no?" His friend was incredulous. "You do not mean to say you have given her the position?"

"That is precisely what I mean," Arthur said, getting to his feet. "Temporarily, at least." He downed the last of his tea and headed for the door. "Have any of the mares we purchased been delivered yet?"

William followed after him as Arthur made his way towards the stables. "You cannot be serious, Arthur."

"I am perfectly serious."

"Why did you not send her away?"

"I certainly tried," Arthur said wryly, remembering the fire in Madeline's eyes.

"Not hard enough, it seems."

Arthur barked a laugh. "If you had met the lady, you would think differently. Besides, what else was I supposed to do? Send her away in the middle of the night? No one else had shown an interest, and Augustus needs a tutor."

They reached the stables and Arthur strode past the doors, heading for the main pasture. He could feel his friend's gaze on his face, but he ignored the impulse to ask what he was thinking. Arthur had a good idea what it could be, and it was not something he wished to discuss.

They arrived at their destination and Arthur stopped, placing his hands on his hips as he surveyed the pasture. A dozen horses grazed beyond the fence, each as beautiful and varied as the flowers in the field beyond.

"How many are we looking to breed this season?" Arthur asked, indicating the horses.

"Well, that depends," William said, crossing his arms and giving his friend a pointed look. "How often will you be around?"

Arthur looked surprised. "No less than usual. Why?"

"You won't wish to stay at home with your new houseguest?"

"She is *not* a houseguest. She is my employee."

William ignored him. "Is she young? Is she handsome?"

"What has that to do with anything?"

"Just a simple question," William said, holding up his hands innocently. "Although," he said a moment later, a cheeky grin spreading across his face, "if she was *not* handsome, you would have said so at once."

"You are an incorrigible brute, do you know that?"

William feigned a heavy sigh. "So my wife tells me."

Arthur could not stop the smile that pulled on his lips. William had always been able to do that—make Arthur smile, even when he did not want to.

"You know," William said, rubbing his jaw, "plenty of lonely widowers have fallen in love with their daughter's governesses. Perhaps this tutor will—"

"No."

"You did not even hear what I had to say!"

"I do not need to. The answer is no."

William scowled. "Arthur," he said, "it is high time you put yourself out there again. Lily would have wanted you to."

Arthur shot him a look, but William ignored it. "Do you honestly believe she would have rather had you shut yourself up at home? You went to town each year for the Season, both before *and* after you were married, and yet you have not returned once since your mourning officially ended."

"I have no reason to go."

"You have *every* reason to go!" William said, throwing his hands in the air. "Solitude is not good for you, my friend. It has turned you bitter. You need society, Arthur. You need companionship—and more than just the kind Frances and I provide. Going to town for the Season is the most logical thing to do in your present situation: you are young, handsome, rich, and in need of a wife."

"I am *not* in need of a wife," Arthur growled.

"This is precisely my point," William said, thrusting his finger into his friend's chest. "You have become a sour old dog since Lily died, and I am tired of seeing you so miserable."

Arthur ground his teeth together. "If I had known I was to receive a lecture upon my arrival, I would have stayed at home."

"Arthur, old friend, it gives me no pleasure to censure you thus," William said. "But I care about you. Frances cares about you, too. It is depressing to see you so melancholy."

"You will forgive me, Will, but I am not concerned about whether or not my situation depresses your spirits," Arthur said caustically.

"You may not be concerned for my welfare," William said, his look and his voice earnest, "but I care about yours."

Arthur made no reply, and the men lapsed into silence. Arthur would not meet his friend's gaze. He stood looking out into the pasture, his jaw tight, his eyes hard.

After several minutes, William sighed. "How long has it been, Arthur? Two years? Three?"

"An eternity."

"I know it feels that way. But don't you think it is time to—"

"No."

"Think of your son, Arthur."

"I *am* thinking of my son!" Arthur said. "Why do you suppose I went looking for a tutor in the first place?"

William frowned. "Could he not go to school?"

Arthur shook his head. "He is too young for Eton, and I refuse to send him to the common school. Besides, he is positively smitten with Miss Crawford and her brother."

"Her *brother?*"

Arthur sighed. "Yes, her brother. She brought him along, supposedly as a playmate for Augustus. They are nearly the same age."

William grinned. "Better and better."

Arthur scowled. "Enough, Will. I am done talking of this."

His friend shrugged, and Arthur turned back to enter the stables. William returned to the house while Arthur busied himself inspecting the stalls and discussing the expected arrival of the new horses they had purchased at auction. He tried to shake off the conversation with Will, but something his friend had said struck a nerve. *I am tired of seeing you so miserable.*

"I'm not miserable," Arthur muttered to himself.

The groomsman standing nearby cocked his head. "What was that, sir?"

"Nothing," Arthur said. "Carry on."

He walked back to the house and made his way to the study, just as William's wife, Frances, was leaving the room.

"Why, Arthur!" she said, her face splitting into a smile at his approach. "William was just telling me you were back."

"Yes, although I am not sure how long I will be staying on this visit."

She raised her brow, a slight twinkle in her eye. "Indeed! I understand you have some new residents at Milford Manor. I expect you are anxious to return to them."

Arthur groaned inwardly, but he managed a tight smile. "No more anxious than normal, I assure you." He gave her a short bow and went past her into the study, where he shut the door. William looked up from the desk.

"Is something wrong?" he asked.

Arthur pinched the bridge of his nose. "Did you *have* to tell your wife, Will?"

His friend chuckled. "Sorry, Arthur. She could tell something had me riled up when I came in, and would not rest until she had the whole of it."

"I told you I no longer wished to discuss it."

William held his hands up in mock surrender. "You are the one who brought it up, Arthur. I was simply looking over the accounts."

Arthur sighed. "How do we stand?"

"Better than expected," his friend said, getting excited. "I've just received word that the two yearlings we sent to auction sold for nearly double what we were hoping. And the new mares are due to arrive today."

"Excellent."

They spent the rest of the morning going over the horses and ponies they hoped to breed in the coming months, and discussing the training of the younger animals they had at hand.

"We could stand to hire another trainer," William said. "Jackson and Burroughs have their hands full, and if we have as many foals this year as we hope, we will need all the help we can get."

"Why don't I work with Jackson while I'm here?" Arthur said. "You know I'd rather be out there with the horses than in here with you. Although I'll admit, you do smell better."

William chuckled. "I should hope so. And that is not a bad idea. If you can take over some of the training, that would certainly help. How long do you plan to stay on this visit?"

"A fortnight at least—maybe longer, if I am needed."

William lifted his brow, but Arthur folded his arms and glared at him. His friend shrugged.

"Very well—I believe Jackson is in the far paddock. He is working with the two-year-olds today."

Arthur nodded, then turned and left the room.

Chapter 10

The day following Madeline's excursion to York was Saturday. She was eager to begin work on their new clothes, and decided to cancel lessons for the day. The boys spent the morning playing with Gus's toys, and Madeline began cutting out a new dress from the material she had purchased in town. Her funds were nearly depleted, but she knew that with weekly wages she would soon fill her reticule again. For the time being, she and Thomas wanted for nothing, and for that she was glad.

Madeline had to drag the boys away from their game of checkers when it was time for the midday meal, and afterwards she insisted that they go outside for some fresh air and exercise. She donned her bonnet, coat, and gloves and followed after them.

The day was cool and damp, and Madeline took a deep breath, filling her lungs with the fresh, clean air. It smelled of earth and grass, and every so often the breeze would bring a reminder that sheep and cows were grazing in nearby fields. Madeline made her way through the carefully tended gardens to the wilderness beyond. Passing over a low stone wall, she found herself in a small meadow of grass and shrub. The grass was long and unruly, with brambles and bushes springing up wherever they had a mind to.

It was beautiful.

Madeline spread her arms wide, smiling up at the sky as she turned in a slow circle. Dropping her arms, she let out a contented sigh, then turned and made her way back to the gardens.

She found the boys following a beetle on the lawn near one of the side doors. Thomas jumped up when he saw her coming and ran to meet her.

"Maddie! Will you play tag with us?"

She brushed a piece of grass off his coat. "Only if I do not have to be 'it.'"

Thomas grinned. "I can be it!"

He ran off to tell his friend, and soon the three of them were running pell-mell through the gardens. First Thomas was it, then Gus, then Thomas again. After twenty minutes Madeline collapsed on a bench, laughing.

"I can hardly breathe!" she gasped, clutching at a stitch in her side. "Thomas, you and Gus play by yourselves for a while. Let me sit here and catch my breath."

Gus looked concerned. "Are you well, Miss Crawford?"

She smiled and touched his arm. "I am perfectly well, Gus, I only need a bit of rest. Thank you for your concern."

His face relaxed, and he and Thomas scampered off to play. Madeline watched them go, wondering at the course of events that had led them to one another. If her parents had not died, she and Thomas would never have gone to live with their aunt and uncle.

Her cousin Henry would never have fallen in love with her, and Madeline would never have sought a position which led her to answer Mr. Vanguard's advertisement. Gus and Thomas would never have met, and Mr. Vanguard…

Madeline paused. What about Mr. Vanguard? She did not know him well, and what she *did* know of him was tainted by her own prejudice. He was stern and aloof, but had he always been so? Or had he once been a doting husband and father? From something Gus had said, she believed he had. That must have changed when he lost his wife, and Gus lost his mother. But why had it driven him away from his son? Surely their shared grief would have brought them closer together, would it not? That is how it was for Madeline and Thomas. She could not even imagine turning away from her brother when her parents died. He was all she had left.

A brisk wind blew through the garden, clearing away her troubled thoughts and making the bare branches of the trees sway. She shivered, standing from the bench and calling to the boys. They made their way over to her, their cheeks and noses red from playing in the crisp air.

"Shall we go inside for some tea?" she asked.

"With biscuits?" Thomas asked.

"Of course."

They trooped back inside with Madeline leading the way. "Go wash up," she told the boys, "then meet me in the schoolroom for tea. And don't run!" she called out as they took off for the stairs. She sighed and shook her head, turning towards the kitchen.

Madeline was now quite familiar with the layout of the house, having asked Mrs. MacLeod for a more thorough tour once she knew they would be staying. After popping into the kitchen to ask

Mrs. Whittecombe to send tea to the schoolroom, Madeline went up to the second floor by way of one of the servant's stairs. It brought her out at the end of a short corridor, just around the corner from the school room.

There were only two doors in the short hallway: one led to a closet, and another belonged to a room that was always locked. Mrs. MacLeod had said nothing about the room during their tour, gesturing only to the closet door before heading down the stairs. At the time, Madeline had been too timid to ask after it, but her curiosity had since got the best of her. She stepped forward and knocked on the door. When there was no answer, she tried the knob and found it locked. How strange, when all the other rooms on the floor remained unlocked.

Madeline wondered again what stood behind the door. Another closet, perhaps? Continuing on to the schoolroom, she resolved to ask Gus about it and see what she could learn.

After removing her things, Madeline settled herself into her favorite chair near the east fireplace. She had all the pieces cut out for a new dress, and now had only to sew them together. Soon a maid came in bearing a heavily laden tea tray, and Gus and Thomas arrived shortly after.

Mrs. Whittecombe had outdone herself. There were fresh scones with cream and jam, two types of biscuits, some meat-filled pastries, and savory herb buns. Madeline sipped her tea while the boys ate as if they would never have another meal.

"Gus," Madeline said, pouring herself another cup of tea, "do you know all the rooms in the house?"

"Oh yes," Gus said, swallowing a mouthful of biscuit. "I know all the rooms and corridors by heart, even the ones in the attic for the servants."

Madeline picked up her sewing. "There is a room down the corridor, to the east, that has a locked door. Do you know what it is?"

"Around the corner? By the back stairs?"

Madeline nodded. "Yes, across from the closet."

Gus picked up a pastry and put it on his plate. "That was my mother's room."

"Your mother's room! All the way down here?"

"Not her bedroom," Gus said, taking a bite. "Her painting room."

"Painting room?"

"Yes. My mother loved to paint. That room was where she did most of it."

"Oh, I see," Madeline said, resuming her work. "Like a private study, or a studio."

Gus nodded, and he and Thomas picked up their conversation again. Madeline continued her sewing, mulling over the new information. His mother had been an artist! Madeline could sketch fairly well, but she had never had the knack, or the patience, for painting. She wondered what sort of art Mrs. Vanguard had created. Were any of the paintings in the house her handiwork? What medium did she prefer?

The evening passed pleasantly in much the same fashion. The boys played, Madeline sewed, and when it was time for bed she tucked them in and kissed them goodnight. She was tired when she climbed under her own covers, but in spite of her exhaustion she found she could not sleep. Her mind was full of questions, and long after she had extinguished the lamp she lay awake, wondering about the lady artist and the man and boy she left behind.

"Quickly now, we don't want to be late."

Madeline pulled on her gloves and smoothed down a lock of Thomas's hair. Gus stood beside them, bouncing on the balls of his feet.

"Are we really going to walk there?" he asked.

"Of course. The fresh air will do us good, and besides, it will help the both of you to burn off some energy so you will be still for the sermon."

Thomas and Gus looked at each other and grinned. They followed her out the door and started down the drive. The ground was damp but not muddy, for which Madeline was grateful. The last thing she wanted was for them to appear in church for the first time with soiled hems.

The village of Milford was little more than a rough street with a handful of houses and buildings surrounding it. It served only the tenant farmers' immediate needs, and it took only twenty minutes for them to arrive at the small, stone church. Madeline's cheeks were flushed and her eyes bright as she made her way inside, anxious to see their new spiritual home.

She was not expecting Westminster, but she certainly did not anticipate the derelict building she entered. A cracked window near the front of the chapel whistled whenever the wind blew through it. The pews were old and well-worn, and the entire place smelled of dampness and decay. Stunned, Madeline stood in the doorway until her brother nudged her from behind. Mentally shaking herself, she led the boys to one of the sturdier-looking pews and sat down.

There were only a handful of people in the church, and an

ancient vicar stood at the front to address them. A few hymnals were scattered about, and many appeared so shabby the pages were coming loose. Madeline's lips pressed into a thin line at the sight of such disregard. Why had the church been permitted to fall into such disrepair? She glanced up at the vicar, who did not look in much better condition than that of his surroundings. He looked well past the age of retirement, but perhaps there was not another candidate able or willing to take the living.

Madeline tried to ignore her disappointment and focus on the sermon, which was on the beatitudes. She let the familiar words wash over her, closing her eyes and imagining she was at home in London, attending church with her parents. But the length of their walk and the monotone voice of the vicar were not a good combination so early in the day, and Madeline found herself in danger of falling asleep. She opened her eyes and tried to concentrate on the words of the sermon.

"Blessed are the meek," the vicar read, "for they shall inherit the earth. Blessed are the merciful, for they shall obtain mercy. Blessed are those that mourn, for they shall be comforted."

Tears sprang unbidden to Madeline's eyes as a wave of grief hit her. How dearly she missed her parents! Even after five years, sometimes the pain felt as fresh and raw as when she first lost them. She fumbled in her reticule for a handkerchief, trying desperately not to sniffle in the silent chapel.

"Maddie? What is wrong?"

Thomas's whisper caused a few heads to turn in their direction, and Madeline shook her head, placing a finger to her lips. She dabbed at her eyes and nose, breathing deeply to keep from dissolving into tears. When at last she felt in control, she offered

Thomas a quick smile and folded her hands in her lap. Thomas scooted a bit closer, reaching out his hand to take hers. He squeezed it three times: *I love you.*

The lump she had at last managed to swallow once again filled her throat, and Madeline squeezed his hand back four times: *I love you, too.* She then turned to face the pulpit, letting the tears slide down her cheeks as the grief rose and fell in waves within her.

Chapter 11

They soon settled into a routine. Madeline taught Gus and Thomas in the mornings after breakfast, they took a break for luncheon, and spent the afternoon outdoors whenever they could. If the weather prevented them from enjoying the garden, the boys would play games while Madeline sewed or read nearby.

Thomas and Gus had been inseparable from the start. One was never without the other in play, work, or mischief, and the only time they were ever parted was at supper. Gus usually took supper with his father, or alone, if his father was absent, and Madeline and Thomas dined together in the schoolroom or the kitchen. But one afternoon, a fortnight after their arrival, Gus shyly asked if he could eat his supper with them.

"Of course you may," Madeline said. "But only until your father returns. Then you must dine with him as usual."

Gus's face fell. "I would rather dine with you and Thomas all the time."

Madeline smiled. "I'm sure you would. But you are with us all day long. Won't your father be lonely without you to talk to?"

"He hardly ever speaks to me, even at supper. He would not care."

Madeline's heart nearly broke at his words. She opened her arms and Gus stepped into her embrace. She held him tightly, wishing with all her heart she could take away his pain. After a few moments he stepped back, and Madeline released him. She gave him a gentle smile.

"As I said, you are welcome to dine with Thomas and I while your father is away, but you will need to spend your evenings with him once he returns," she said softly.

Gus nodded glumly, but a moment later he grinned. "Never mind," he said, a mischievous gleam in his eyes. "Father is gone more often than he is home, so I will be dining with you most of the time anyway."

He scampered off before Madeline could reply, though what she would have said to him she did not know.

The days followed after one another in quiet succession. Gus was an eager pupil, and soon he was reading and writing with far greater proficiency, which was a relief to Madeline. She had been at the manor for nearly three weeks, and knew that her accounting with Mr. Vanguard was fast approaching.

In her spare time, Madeline sewed like she had never sewed before. She managed to finish her first new dress just in time for worship the following Sunday, and was pleased to see how well it matched her new bonnet.

As usual, Madeline and the boys walked to the village for services and back again after they were finished. The sermon had been enlightening, and Madeline was musing on the vicar's interpretation of Psalm 139 as they made their way back to the manor. The day was warm and dry, which was a blessed relief from the rain they had received earlier in the week. Gus and Thomas were seeing how far each of them could throw a stick: one of them would throw it as far as he could up the lane, then count the paces until they reached the spot where it lay. Then the other boy would throw it and count the paces, and so on.

Suddenly a carriage turned onto the lane behind them, and Madeline turned to see two horses pulling a coach, heading directly for them. She let out a cry and stumbled off the road, desperate to escape the beasts she felt sure would trample her in a moment. It passed only a few rods from where she stood, her heart pounding as she looked frantically around for the boys. They were safely off the road on the other side, and she breathed a sigh of relief at their quick thinking.

Madeline was shaking as she stepped back onto the drive, following the carriage with her eyes as it approached the manor, which was less than a quarter mile away. It did not stop at the front doors but drove directly around the house to the back, which could mean only one thing: Mr. Vanguard had returned.

"Come along, boys, quickly now." Madeline's heart was still beating rapidly as she called the boys to her and picked up the pace. "Your father may like to see you when we arrive," she said to Gus.

Gus only shrugged. "He hardly ever calls for me when he gets home. I only see him at supper."

"Nevertheless, we should hurry. I want you both to get cleaned up right away."

But Gus was right. Instead of calling for his son, Madeline was informed by the butler that Mr. Vanguard wished to see *her* as soon as possible, in his study.

A sliver of unease pierced her at his words. "Is anything wrong?" she asked, removing her bonnet and gloves and handing them to him.

"I know not, miss," he said. Then, with a glance at the children, he lowered his voice and said, "But Mr. Vanguard did not looked pleased when he asked."

Madeline's heart sank. Her month was not even up and she feared she would already be dismissed. She brushed at her skirts and drew a deep breath, then turned and walked resolutely down the corridor.

Arthur had not been paying much attention to the drive home until he heard the driver pull up the horses and felt the carriage slow. He glanced out the window just in time to see Miss Crawford's terrified face flash past. Stunned, he glanced out the back window and saw two small boys standing off the road across from her.

What on earth was she doing with Augustus and her brother in the middle of the drive?

Mrs. MacLeod was waiting to greet him as soon as he entered the house, but before she could say anything he asked after his son. "Miss Crawford took him to church, sir," she said.

Arthur blinked. "To church?"

"Yes, sir."

"Is today the first time they have gone?"

"No, sir, he has been attending with her every week since her arrival."

Arthur scowled. "I want to speak with Miss Crawford the minute she gets home," he said, stomping away from the housekeeper.

Once in his study, Arthur paced back and forth in front of his desk. What the devil did she mean, taking his son to church without his permission? What else had she been doing in his absence?

A brisk knock on the door brought Arthur's head up. "Come in," he barked.

Madeline opened the door and stopped just inside the room, her face calm.

"Close the door, Miss Crawford."

She shut the door and turned around to face him. "You wished to see me, sir?"

"Yes, I did."

Her eyebrows lifted slightly in that maddening way of hers, and Arthur scowled. "I understand you have been taking my son to church with you."

"Yes, sir, I have."

She answered him plainly, without any hint of remorse or regret in her voice. Arthur's eyes narrowed.

"Did it never occur to you that you should ask permission before taking such a liberty?"

Madeline's lips pressed together. "If I had been aware before you left that neither you nor your son attended worship services, I certainly would have asked permission. But since I was not, I felt it best to act in accordance with my conscience. Augustus told me that he had attended church with Mrs. MacLeod on occasion, so I assumed you would not mind if he attended with Thomas and I. I beg your pardon if I have caused offense by my actions."

Her tone was civil, but Arthur could see that her hands trembled. He strode to the desk before turning to face her once more.

"And what, pray tell, were you doing out on the lane just now? Can you not receive your exercise in the garden?"

Madeline looked surprised. "We were returning home from church, sir."

Arthur stared at her. He opened his mouth, then closed it with a snap. "Are you telling me," Arthur said, pinching the bridge of his nose, "that my son has been *walking* to church, like a servant?"

"Yes."

"That is outrageous. I forbid it from happening again."

Madeline's eyes flashed as she strode forward. "It is better for him to walk to church like a servant than to miss church altogether, like a heathen."

Ah, there it was, that temper of hers. Oddly enough, it set him more at ease to see her getting riled. "Are you calling me a heathen, Miss Crawford?"

Madeline raised her brow. "When was the last time *you* attended worship services, Mr. Vanguard?"

He scowled at her to hide a grin. "That is not the point. The point is that I will not have my son walking into the village any longer, is that quite understood?"

Madeline drew a deep breath, briefly closing her eyes. "Mr. Vanguard," she said, her voice even once again, "you hired me to tutor your son, and it is a responsibility I take quite seriously. I feel it my duty to teach not only letters and languages, but also morals and principles. Did you know that your son had never heard the Lord's Prayer before?"

Arthur's eyes narrowed. "If you want to take him to church, fine. But I will not have him walking. Why have you not ordered the carriage?"

She blanched. "I… enjoy the exercise."

Her abrupt change in demeanor gave Arthur pause. She had gone pale—what had he said to unnerve her?

"You do not like riding in carriages?" he asked. "Do you become unwell?"

Madeline flicked her hand dismissively, the color returning to her cheeks. "Of course not. Carriages don't bother me."

Arthur arched an eyebrow, waiting. She huffed, and abruptly sat down. "I do not like horses."

He blinked. She did not like horses?

"The horses merely pull the carriage, Miss Crawford. You do not have to ride them."

"I know," she said. "But I do not like them all the same."

All the fight seemed to have gone out of her, and for the first time Arthur saw a glimpse of the woman underneath her careful façade. She was frightened and lonely, thrust into adulthood far sooner than most young ladies ever were.

The silence stretched between them, thawing Arthur's heart, and the longer no one spoke, the more curious he became. He knew very few details about her life before coming to the manor—only that she and her brother had lived with relatives after her parents had died. What had their home been like? Had she been happy there? Or had she been ill-treated? The longer he watched her, the more questions filled his mind until at last he spoke.

"How old were you when your parents died, Miss Crawford?" he asked.

Madeline blinked. "Pardon?"

"When your parents died—how old were you?"

"I hardly see how that is relevant to the conversation," she said tersely, her walls coming up once more.

Arthur shrugged. "Humor me."

Madeline studied him, but Arthur kept his face impassive. "I was fifteen," she said. "Thomas was only three."

Arthur nodded slowly. "I see. And you went to live with your aunt after that, yes?"

"Yes."

"Had you already come out?"

A faint blush touched her cheeks as Madeline responded. "No, I was put straight to work, teaching my younger cousins. I never had a proper coming-out."

Arthur frowned but said nothing. The tension between them slowly evaporated, and after a few minutes' silence Arthur cleared his throat.

"If you wish to take Augustus to church with you, you have my permission. But I will instruct that the carriage is to be ordered for you each week, and I insist that you use it. Are we agreed?"

Madeline nodded, getting to her feet. "Yes, sir. Thank you."

Arthur could not help the wry grin that sprang to his lips. "I take it you are more afraid of becoming a heathen than you are of horses, hm?"

A smile spread across Madeline's face. It brightened her eyes and heightened the color in her cheeks, and Arthur was surprised to find himself thinking she was rather pretty.

"Yes," she said, with a mischievous gleam in her eyes. "I am far more afraid of fire and brimstone than of horses and hooves."

Chapter 12

Arthur had enjoyed his time in Leeds. Working with one of their trainers, Arthur had learned more about the various types and methods of horse training, of which there were a surprisingly large amount. Whether a horse was destined for the races, the plough, to pull a carriage or carry a rider, knowing how and when to go about their training was essential. While Arthur had hoped to take on some of the duties himself, it took only a few days before Arthur told William to place an advertisement and begin the search for an additional trainer—there was simply too much to learn.

Arthur had always been interested in breeding horses, but it was not until three years ago that he had pursued it in earnest. Desperate for a distraction from his grief, he had approached William shortly after Lily's passing. His friend had been anxious to help, and they started the venture on William's estate within the year. It proved a success almost from the very start, and since Lily had never been involved, it held no painful memories for Arthur.

If only that were true in Milford.

It was always an adjustment for Arthur when he returned home. Where nothing in Leeds reminded him of Lily, everything at the manor did. The park, the house, the very walls caused him pain, because they all held memories of his late wife. And his son—so like Lily in appearance and manner—caused him some of the sharpest pain of all.

Usually the meals he shared with Augustus were quiet, solemn affairs; more painful duty than enjoyable connection. But something was different this time. His son still did not say much, but when he did speak, there was contentment in his voice, a joy which had not been there before. Arthur noticed the change, and wondered at it.

"Father?"

Gus's voice broke into Arthur's reverie. "Hm? My apologies, Augustus, what did you say?"

"I asked if Thomas and Miss Crawford could join us for supper some time."

The question caught Arthur by surprise. "Why do you want them to join us for supper?"

Gus shrugged. "I just… thought it might be nice to have some company."

Company. The word felt almost foreign to Arthur, connected as it was to earlier, happier memories with Lily. There was once a time when the manor had been full of company. Full of music and laughter. House parties and card parties and supper balls—Lily had a large circle of friends and was always extending invitations to the manor. Of course, the Vanguards had also gone to town for the Season, and that was where his wife had really blossomed. Though he was more reserved than Lily, Arthur had enjoyed having company and the never-ending social invitations they received. But it had been years since Arthur had gone to London during a session of parliament, and ages since anyone had come to dinner. All of that ended with Lily.

"Perhaps," Arthur said at last. Gus smiled and returned to his meal.

"Tell me," Arthur said, "what has Miss Crawford taught you while I've been gone?"

"We learned a poem by William Wordsworth, and she's had me writing down the Lord's Prayer every day."

Arthur raised his brow. "Every day?"

"Yes. She said it will help my penmanship as well as my memory."

"Mm. I spoke with her earlier—she said you've gone to church with them the last three Sundays. Have you behaved yourself?"

"Yes, sir."

"Good. What do you think about Sabbath services?"

Gus made a face. "I find it awful dull."

Arthur laughed, startling his son as well as himself. He coughed to cover it up, but Gus's face was full of delight.

"I've not heard you laugh for ages, Father," he said.

Arthur instantly sobered. "Yes, well, there has not been much to laugh about since—" His voice abruptly cut off, and Gus's face fell.

"Since Mother died," he said slowly.

Arthur gave a curt nod, and the meal continued in silence. When he was finished, Gus asked to be excused, but instead of leaving the room, he stood and went over to his father. Without a word, he put his arms around his neck and hugged him. Stunned, Arthur did not move.

"I miss Mother," Gus said quietly. "But I am glad you asked Miss Crawford to be my tutor. It makes me miss her less."

He let his boyish arms drop, gave his father a small smile, and scampered off. Arthur stared after him for a long moment, trying to hold the pieces of his heart together.

"Remember now, I want you to use your very best penmanship," Madeline said, placing a sheet of paper in front of Gus.

"Why?" he asked.

"Because your father told me that after one month he would judge whether or not I was a suitable choice to be your tutor. I have seen great improvement in your schoolwork since I arrived, but I don't want to give Mr. Vanguard any reason to dismiss me."

"Me neither," Gus said. "I'll make it my very best, Miss Crawford."

Madeline smiled. "I know you will."

Mr. Vanguard had been home for a week, but she had seen very little of him since their argument over walking to church. Each day she awoke with a stone in her breast, wondering if today she would be called to his study and made to defend her position. She tried to ignore the feeling, tried to look at things objectively and measure her success that way, but to no avail. Each day she fretted and worried, and each night she fell into bed, exhausted by the anxiety.

The door to the schoolroom opened, and Mrs. MacLeod stepped inside. Madeline immediately tensed, but the housekeeper's air was cheerful as she addressed her. "Good day to ye, Miss Crawford," she said. "Mr. Vanguard would like a word, if ye please."

"Of course," Madeline said, striving to calm the fluttering in her breast. "I shall be right down."

She gathered some books and papers together, bid the boys to continue in their work until she returned, and started for the stairs. She counted the steps to keep her mind from flying into a panic, and found herself standing in front of the study doors far sooner than she anticipated. Saying a silent prayer, she rapped on the door, then entered the room when she was bid to.

"Ah, Miss Crawford, please come in."

The room was bright and cheery, due in part to the opened drapes, but also owing to the smile Mr. Vanguard gave her. Madeline watched him curiously, noticing that this was the first real smile she had seen from him. Not a smirk, not a leer, but a genuine smile. It was probably meant to put her at ease, but instead, it unnerved her even further.

"You wished to see me, Mr. Vanguard?"

"Yes, I did. Please, have a seat."

Madeline took the chair he indicated, and was surprised when, instead of sitting behind the desk, he took another chair nearby. She arranged the books and papers neatly in her lap, and then cleared her throat.

"It has been a month since my arrival, and I assume you would like an account of the progress I have made with Augustus."

Arthur's brow lifted slightly. "Indeed."

"I admit to being surprised at my arrival that he could hardly read or write, so I felt it best to strengthen that foundation before forging ahead." She paused, and Arthur nodded. "He has since finished McGuffey's First Reader and memorized the poem *I Wandered Lonely As A Cloud* by William Wordsworth. Here is a sample of his handwriting from one of our first lessons," she held out a piece of paper, which Arthur took, "and here is a sample from his work yesterday."

She handed another piece of paper to him, and Arthur nodded, looking them over. When he said nothing, but merely glanced up at her, Madeline began to panic. "We have only just started arithmetic, since—as I mentioned before—I wanted him to have a more solid understanding of letters before we began sums. And I have plans to teach him German," she said, her voice now coming in a rush, "but again, foreign languages are much easier to learn if one already has a firm grasp of English, and I thought it best to—"

"Calm yourself, Miss Crawford, please," Arthur cut in. "There is something I would like to say."

Madeline swallowed, clasping her hands together to prevent them from shaking.

Arthur glanced at the papers she had given him, then handed them back to her. "We agreed on a trial period of one month, after which time I would assess your skills as a tutor and determine whether or not I would like to employ your services permanently." He paused, and Madeline held her breath. He seemed to notice the tense way she held herself, and again he offered her a smile. "Hearing your report, and seeing these samples have served to solidify my decision."

"Which is?"

But instead of answering her, Arthur stood and strode calmly to the window, his hands tucked behind his back. Insufferable man! Did he mean to torment her in such a way?

"I am not sure that you can see the change in Augustus the way that I can," he continued, his gaze on the west lawn out the window, "not having known his disposition before your arrival. But I can assure you, the change in him is most astonishing." He turned abruptly, and the smirk Madeline had grown accustomed to seeing crossed his face. "Although I am not sure whether I have you or your brother to thank for that."

Madeline let out a startled laugh. "Well, you cannot have one without the other, so I suppose you can thank us both."

"I do. Most heartily." Arthur came back to the chair but did not sit down. "And I would be most pleased if you will stay and continue in the position of tutor to Augustus."

Madeline jumped to her feet, clapping her hands together in joyous delight. "Oh yes, I would like that very much!" She blushed at the startled look on Arthur's face, and cleared her throat. "My apologies, sir. I did not mean to react so... exuberantly."

Arthur chuckled. "No apology necessary, Miss Crawford."

Madeline once again gathered the books and papers in her arms and made her way to the door.

"Miss Crawford?"

She turned, and Arthur gave her a bemused smile. "There was one other thing."

"Oh!" Madeline flushed. "Oh, forgive me Mr. Vanguard, I should have waited until I was dismissed."

"No matter, it will only take a moment." He paused, and Madeline saw with some surprise that he looked uneasy. "Augustus has asked—" He stopped, cleared his throat, and began again. "That is, I understand you and your brother have been taking your meals in the schoolroom, is that correct?"

"Or in the kitchen, yes."

"Well, then. We—that is, Augustus and I—would like to invite you to dine with us in the evenings."

Madeline's eyebrows shot up in surprise. "You would like me to have supper with you?"

"And your brother, of course," he said hastily. "With both of us. For supper. Yes."

His answer amused her, and she ducked her head, hiding a smile. "We would be honored, sir. Thank you."

"You are most welcome."

He offered her a small bow, which Madeline returned before leaving the room.

Chapter 13

At seven o'clock, Madeline and Thomas went downstairs for supper. "May I sit next to you, Maddie?" Thomas asked, slipping his hand into hers as they crossed the entrance hall.

"I'm afraid I don't know what the seating arrangements will be," she answered.

"I hope I'm not sitting next to Mr. Vanguard," he said.

"Hush!" Madeline said as they entered the drawing room. Gus looked up at their entrance, his face lighting up at the sight of them.

"You came!" he cried, rushing over to greet them. Madeline laughed.

"Of course we came—had you any doubt of our accepting your father's invitation?" She glanced around, but Arthur was not in the room.

"Father said he invited you, and I thought you would come, but then I worried it might all have been a dream," Gus said.

"Ah, we are all here. Good."

Madeline turned at the sound of Arthur's voice, and was immediately struck by how handsome he looked. Startled, she pushed away the thought, telling herself she was merely surprised at the sight of him in dinner attire—she could not recall ever having seen him dressed so formally before.

Before Madeline had time to fret about her own appearance, dinner was announced, and Arthur offered Madeline his arm. She took it with some surprise.

"I did not expect so formal an event, Mr. Vanguard," she said as they left the room. "Forgive me for not dressing appropriately. I will do so in the future."

"There is no need," he said. "I am only standing upon ceremony for your sake, but it sounds as though we both prefer less formal gatherings."

"Do you not dress for dinner on a regular basis, then?"

"Not here at the manor, no," he said as they entered the dining room. "But I can, if you would like."

"No, thank you," she said as he led her to her seat. "As you said, I prefer to eat more casually."

He held her chair for her until she was settled, then gave her a small bow. "Miss Crawford."

"Mr. Vanguard."

The formality of it all was such a stark contrast to the verbal sparring she had grown accustomed to experiencing between them, that Madeline could not help the grin that spread across her face. Arthur took his seat, raising an eyebrow at her.

"What is so amusing, Miss Crawford?"

"I was only thinking of all this in contrast to our first meeting," she said.

Arthur chuckled. "I see. Would you have imagined then that we would be sitting down together like this?"

"Not in a hundred years," she said.

"Nor I," he said, his own eyes alight with amusement.

The meal was pleasant, and any awkwardness Madeline had imagined disappeared within the first few minutes. Children were never permitted at supper parties, so the presence of Gus and Thomas naturally helped to relax the atmosphere in the room. Arthur made an effort to engage her in conversation, and she was pleasantly surprised that he was not put off when she inquired after his feelings on the Mines and Collieries Act that passed the previous year. By the time they had finished the meal, Madeline was almost sorry to see it end.

"I believe it is time for bed, children," she said, after they had finished their pudding. They nodded and rose from the table. She rose as well, turning to Arthur with a smile. "Thank you for the meal and the conversation. I shall see the boys to bed and then retire myself."

"Thank you for joining us," Arthur said, getting to his feet. "Augustus was right."

She looked at him curiously. "Right?"

He smiled, and a hint of color touched his ears. "It is nice to have some company," he said.

Their first dinner together was so pleasant that Madeline decided to plan an evening of entertainment. Her birthday was in a fortnight, and while it had never been celebrated a great deal, having a recitation after dinner would help to make the day feel special, as well as give Augustus a chance to show his father some of the things he was learning.

He was nervous when Madeline first shared the idea with her young pupils, but Thomas's excitement soon rubbed off on him.

"Can I pick anything I want to recite?" Thomas asked.

"Within reason, yes," Madeline said with a smile.

"I want to recite a war poem," Thomas said, brandishing a fake sword. "Full of battles and conflict."

"Do I have to recite in front of everyone?" Gus asked, looking at Madeline with wide eyes.

"If by everyone you mean your father and Thomas and I, then yes."

Gus looked thoughtful. "Then I would like to recite a love poem."

"A love poem! Whatever for?" Madeline asked.

"If Thomas is to recite a poem about battle and war, I want to recite something about love and peace," he said with a solemn nod.

Madeline gave him a quick squeeze. "I think that is a wonderful idea, Gus. And there are plenty of poems for you to choose from."

Their lessons for the next week focused on their selections—a portion of Homer's famous *Iliad* for Thomas, and Robert Burns's *A Red, Red Rose* for Gus. They copied them, read them aloud, and worked on memorizing the stanzas. Madeline copied out the poems onto pieces of paper for them, with only the first letter of each word, to help them in their memorization. It took Gus longer to master his poem, but after ten days both boys knew them by heart.

Madeline awoke on her birthday to silver sunlight streaming through her curtains. The April morning was misty and cool, with the promise of a fine day. White cotton clouds chased each other across the pale blue sky, gathering into a fleecy mass along the horizon. Madeline opened her window and leaned out, breathing in the clear air and feeling grateful she was alive.

As she drew back inside, a flash of white on the floor across the room caught her eye. She went over to investigate, and found that Thomas and Gus had slipped notes under her door sometime early that morning. Thomas had drawn a picture of him and Madeline holding hands, along with the words *I love you Maddie* and a cascade of hearts. Gus's note was a small card upon which flower petals had been pounded. The violet blossoms had lent their color to the paper and were arranged in a pretty pattern. The words *I am glad yore my teechur* were scrawled underneath in Gus's hand. Madeline smiled. It was going to be a wonderful day.

"Happy birthday!" Thomas shouted as Madeline entered the breakfast room. "Did you get our notes?"

"I did, thank you so much," Madeline said.

"One of the maids helped me with the flowers," Gus said, "but I did all the writing myself."

Madeline gave each boy a hug. "How did I get so lucky, hm? Two wonderful boys, helping to make my birthday special. Thank you."

After breakfast they settled themselves in the schoolroom as usual. Both boys worked cheerfully on their lessons in the morning, and in the afternoon practiced their pieces for the recital that night. When tea time finally arrived, Madeline was delighted to find that Mrs. Whittecombe had made all her favorite treats—including a tangy lemon pudding. She and the boys had a picnic on the lawn to celebrate, and afterwards went inside to rest and prepare for the evening.

Though their meals together were relatively relaxed and Madeline and Arthur had agreed to forego the typical change of dress, Madeline wanted tonight to be special. She had recently finished a new gown which she intended for church and other more formal events, and she was excited to wear it. It was a beautiful cornflower blue, with delicate embroidery along the hem and sleeves and bodice. A maid helped her pin small white flowers in her hair as she dressed for supper, excited for her two young pupils to recite. When she entered the drawing room before dinner, Arthur looked her over with some surprise.

"Why, Miss Crawford," he said, "you look quite lovely this evening. What is the occasion?"

Madeline's cheeks turned pink with the praise, but it was Gus who answered for her.

"It is her birthday!" he said, grinning widely.

Arthur raised his brow, looking from his son to Madeline. "Is it? Well, many happy returns, Miss Crawford. I wish I would have known—I could have dressed as well."

"It is no matter," Madeline said quickly. "I only wanted a reason to wear my new gown, as I only just finished it."

Arthur nodded, looking thoughtful. "Well, then," he said. "Shall we?"

Madeline was grateful that he did not escort her into the dining room. Especially tonight, all dressed up and with flowers in her hair, she felt it would have been awkward and presumptuous to take his arm. Instead, they walked together without ceremony into the dining room, though Arthur did hold her chair for her.

Supper was a repeat of tea, with all her favorite foods, and

Madeline was almost embarrassed at all the attention. Thomas must have told the cook that Madeline's favorite meal was braised lamb, for it graced the table after the soup course. Arthur shook his head, his signature smirk playing about his lips.

"I do not believe I have ever been treated so royally by my staff on my *own* birthday, Miss Crawford," he said. "You have indeed made an impact on Milford Manor."

Madeline flushed, sending a little frown across the table to Thomas, who ducked his head to hide a grin. "Yes, well, I assure you that I am not the one responsible for all this," she said. "I believe my brother must answer for that crime."

"When is your birthday, Father?" Gus asked.

"December," Arthur said.

His son's face lit up. "Only a month after mine! Why do we never celebrate it?"

Arthur shrugged. "When you get as old as I am, you will find that birthdays do not matter very much. Time passes whether we celebrate or not. Although I must say," he added, as the servants came in bearing two different kinds of pudding, with glazed berries atop one and some delicious-smelling sauce poured over the other, "I am beginning to wish we did."

Madeline flushed again, but whether from his remark or his teasing look she was not sure.

When the meal had finished and their bellies were full, Madeline turned to the boys, her eyes bright. "Are you ready?" she asked them. Both heads—one curly and dark, the other fair and straight—nodded in excitement. She smiled, turning to Arthur.

"We have prepared some special entertainment for tonight," she said. "A recitation, by Thomas and Augustus."

Arthur looked surprised. "Indeed! Well, this is a treat. I am most eager to hear what they have prepared."

They retired to the drawing room, and after Arthur had poured himself a small glass of brandy, Madeline encouraged Thomas to stand and begin. The lad stood tall and proud before them, and began to recite.

"An excerpt from Homer's *Iliad,* book five," he said.

He began in the second paragraph, his voice clear and strong as he related the story of the gods joining in the battle of Troy. It was evident how much Thomas was enjoying himself, and Madeline wondered (not for the first time) if he was destined to become a soldier. She hoped not.

After Thomas, Gus stood and faced them, but he was quite pale and a great deal more timid than his friend. Madeline gave him an encouraging smile, and at last he opened his mouth.

> " 'O my love is like a red, red rose
> That's newly sprung in June;
> O my love is like the melody
> That's sweetly played in tune.' "

Gus kept his gaze on Madeline, who gave him smiles and nods whenever he hesitated. He grew more sure of himself as the poem went on, and by the end he was speaking as clearly and confidently as Thomas had. Everyone clapped heartily when he had finished, and he ducked his head and blushed at their praise.

"Well done, boys, well done," Arthur called. Then, turning to Madeline, he gave her an appraising look. "And now it is your turn, Miss Crawford."

Startled, Madeline shook her head. "Me? Oh, no. This was just a little assignment and exhibition I set for the boys. I did not prepare anything myself."

"Nonsense," Arthur said, his smile pulling up on one corner. "An accomplished young lady such as yourself is *always* prepared to perform for company."

She gave him a sour look, and he chuckled.

"Oh yes, please, Maddie," Thomas said. "You don't have to recite, like me and Gus did. You can sing. Or play the pianoforte. I haven't heard you play or sing for ages."

Gus joined his friend in begging for a song, and at last Madeline relented. "But only one," she said, narrowing her eyes at them in mock severity, "and then you must both go up to bed, understand?"

They chorused their agreement, and Madeline positioned herself at the instrument. She sat on the bench for a few moments, gathering her thoughts, before finally placing her hands on the keys.

Arthur wondered whether or not it was right of him to tease Madeline about performing as she started to play, but once she began to sing all remorse left him. Her voice was soft but clear, a lilting soprano he had not been expecting. As she sang, the woman before him seemed to transform, revealing the carefree young lady she surely must have been once upon a time. It was clear she was enjoying herself, and the realization both surprised and troubled him. Why had she never mentioned her love of music before?

The song she sang was well known to him, but Arthur listened as if he were hearing it for the first time. He sat, entranced, as the music of her fingers and voice blended together in beautiful harmony.

> *What made the assembly shine?*
> *Robin Adair.*
> *What made the ball so fine?*
> *Robin was there:*
> *What when the play was o'er,*
> *What made my heart so sore?*
> *Oh! it was parting with*
> *Robin Adair.*

An image of Lily, sitting at the very same instrument, drifted into Arthur's mind. Her alto voice had been deeper and richer than Madeline's, but in his memory it was missing. He could see her face and her delicate hands as they danced over the keys, but the song in his mind was not sung by Lily's voice—it was Madeline's that he heard.

Arthur was so caught up in his wonder and confusion that he did not realize Madeline had finished the song until he noticed that three pairs of eyes were staring at him. He cleared his throat, realizing too late that he had not applauded her performance, and gave a curt nod.

"That was lovely, Miss Crawford," he said. "Thank you for indulging us. Now, if you will excuse me, I bid you all goodnight."

Without another word, he turned and left the room.

Chapter 14

Madeline did not know what had happened to offend Mr. Vanguard, but it was clear he was upset after her song. She assured the boys they had done a marvelous job on their recitations, and pronounced the evening a great success, in spite of Arthur's abrupt departure. Satisfied, the boys went off to bed in high spirits, leaving Madeline alone to worry and wonder.

She awoke the next morning, still concerned about Mr. Vanguard and his reaction, but she could not dwell on it for long. The boys were more energetic than usual throughout their lessons, and after the midday meal Madeline practically dragged them out the door for some exercise. They had not been outside long before a footman arrived to tell her she had a visitor.

"A visitor?"

"Yes, miss. He said his name is Mr. Gillingham."

The name sparked something in her memory, but Madeline could not recall why it felt familiar. Where had she heard it before?

She followed the servant back into the house, brushing at her skirts to ensure there were no bits of grass stuck to the fabric. Soon they arrived at the drawing room, and the footman bowed, leaving her to enter the room alone.

Madeline was surprised to find that Arthur was also there, standing stiffly near the window. Another man, more slight of build than Arthur and with a large, foxtail mustache, stood from the sofa at her entrance.

"Ah, Miss Crawford, I presume?" he said politely.

"Yes."

"Wonderful. My name is Samuel Gillingham. I hope you will forgive the liberty of my calling upon you in this manner, but since I am already acquainted with the family, I hoped you would forgive the intrusion."

Madeline froze, suddenly recalling why the name sounded so familiar.

Gillingham.

Her father's solicitor.

With her pulse racing, Madeline merely nodded. "Of course." She took a seat on a nearby chair, and Mr. Gillingham sat back down on the sofa. "Would you care for some tea?" she asked.

"That would be lovely, thank you."

Her heart sank at his words. Accepting refreshment meant he planned to stay at least a quarter hour. What on earth could he want to speak to her about? Had her aunt sent him to find her?

As if he could read her mind, the gentleman chuckled. "You were not easy to track down, Miss Crawford, though by no means the most difficult of my clients to locate."

"Did my uncle send you?" Madeline asked bluntly. From his

place across the room, Arthur made a sound in his throat. Madeline glanced over at him, but he was staring out the window and she could not see his face. Clearly he was still upset.

Mr. Gillingham raised his brow. "No, actually. I sought you on a matter of business. I confess, I was not even aware you were no longer under the care of your uncle until I called on him last week."

Oh. Madeline could feel Arthur's eyes on her face, but she did not look over at him. Instead, she cleared her throat. "I see. And might I inquire as to what business that might be?"

He looked surprised. "Why, your inheritance, of course."

"My... what?"

"Your inheritance." Mr. Gillingham pulled a sheaf of papers from a leather satchel at his side. "Your father stipulated in his will that if you were unmarried, your dowry was to be released to you upon the advent of your twenty-first birthday, which I understand you recently celebrated."

Madeline's eyes flicked to Arthur's face. He was watching her intently.

Clearing her throat, she turned back to Mr. Gillingham. "Yes, I have. Only yesterday, as a matter of fact."

"Excellent. My initial search did not turn up any marriage contracts, and when I visited your uncle, he could not conceive of you having entered into such a union without his knowledge, but perhaps..." His voice trailed off, and he glanced briefly at Arthur, who scowled.

Madeline, her face aflame, answered quickly. "No, there has been no union. I am employed by Mr. Vanguard as a tutor for his son."

"I see," Mr. Gillingham replied, though his face registered mild surprise. "Well then, there is nothing to prevent you from claiming your inheritance. I have some papers for you to sign, after which the bank should be able to release the funds to you."

Madeline felt numb. Her uncle had handled the money affairs after the deaths of her parents, and all she had been told was that she had a small weekly allowance and an appropriate dowry for when the time came for her to wed. Surely her uncle had known that the money was to be released to her when she reached her majority— why had she never been told as much?

A young maid came in bearing a tea service, and Madeline poured out for herself and Mr. Gillingham. She looked over at Arthur. "Would you like some tea, Mr. Vanguard?"

"No, thank you," he said, though he came and sat on the chair opposite hers. She raised her brow at him, but he said nothing.

"Here is the contract, Miss Crawford," the solicitor said, handing her some papers. "I have marked where you are to sign on the last two pages."

She took them from him and began to read, sipping her tea as she did so. From the corner of her eye she saw Arthur fold his arms across his chest. What he meant by sitting in on their conversation she could not say, but his presence rattled her.

"You are a long way from London, Mr. Gillingham," Arthur said abruptly.

"Indeed," the gentleman said, surprised at being addressed. "I came up on the train yesterday, and spent the night in York."

"And how long do you plan to stay in town?"

Mr. Gillingham smiled. "Considering that Miss Crawford is the sole reason I came this far, I plan to return to town as soon as my business with her is concluded."

"Two thousand pounds!" Madeline suddenly exclaimed, causing both men to look over at her. She flushed.

"Is there a discrepancy in the amount?" Mr. Gillingham asked, frowning.

"No, it is…" Madeline swallowed, and tears pricked her eyes. "I had no idea my father had set aside such a sum for me."

"Did your uncle never tell you what your dowry entailed?"

"No, only that it was 'appropriate.'" Madeline pressed a hand to her breast. Dear Papa! Even from his grave, he was still looking after her.

The gentlemen were silent until she had turned the last page and signed where indicated. Mr. Gillingham took the papers back from her with a smile.

"It has been a pleasure, Miss Crawford," he said. "Let me know when you next come to town, and I shall attend you to the bank to withdraw the funds."

"I do not know when that may be, sir. May I leave them there at present?"

"Certainly."

"Thank you." She cleared her throat. "Mr. Gillingham, might I ask you a question?"

"Of course."

"You said you called on my uncle last week, is that correct?"

"Yes, I did."

"And that is when you learned I was no longer living there?"

"Yes."

"And will you call upon him again when you return, now that you have discovered where I am?"

Mr. Gillingham cocked his head to the side. "I will, yes, at the request of your aunt."

"I see. Thank you."

Mr. Gillingham looked from Madeline to Arthur and back again. "Surely there is no reason to keep your whereabouts a secret, Miss Crawford?"

"No, of course not," Madeline said quickly. "Only... well, my brother is also here. He came with me."

Mr. Gillingham frowned. "Without your uncle's permission?"

Madeline nodded.

"Ah." He looked thoughtful. "How did that come about, if I may ask?"

Madeline took a steadying breath. "My aunt and uncle wished to separate my brother and I. After I—" She caught herself, glancing quickly at Arthur, who raised a single eyebrow at her. "That is," she continued, more carefully, "after certain events occurred, my aunt insisted that I leave the house and seek employment elsewhere. Only they planned to keep Thomas with them. But we could not be parted, Mr. Gillingham. Neither of us could bear it."

"Of course. So your brother was invited to accompany you when you came to work for Mr. Vanguard, is that correct?"

Madeline glanced at Arthur before nodding slowly, and Mr. Gillingham looked to Arthur for confirmation, who shrugged. "More or less," he said.

Madeline stifled a groan.

"Well," Mr. Gillingham said, "your father's will states quite clearly that in the event that both parents should die, yourself and your brother were to be left to the guardianship of Mr. Richard Dennison."

"Yes, I understand. But can anything be done to transfer care of my brother to myself, now that I have come of age?"

Mr. Gillingham looked thoughtful, but it was Arthur who answered her question, with one of his own.

"Does your brother hold any property, Miss Crawford?" he asked abruptly.

Two sets of eyes turned to face him, but he only met the gaze of Madeline. She frowned. "I do not believe so."

Arthur turned to the other gentleman. "Mr. Gillingham?"

"There is a small sum set aside for young Mr. Crawford, yes. It is not as substantial as yours, Miss Crawford, but it is a fair amount."

"Hm." Arthur was thoughtful. "It is almost a shame your parents had the foresight to consider your futures, Miss Crawford," he mused. "If they had died penniless, no guardianship would be needed."

Confused, Madeline looked to the solicitor. "Quite true," he said. "Guardians are only appointed for children who have an inheritance."

Madeline's mind was reeling. Her father had provided a good life for them, but they had been by no means affluent. How he must have scrimped and saved to put away such a substantial sum for his children! Madeline's heart ached at the thought. How she wished she could thank him, now that she knew.

"Could Miss Crawford petition the courts for guardianship, now that she is of age and means?" Arthur asked.

Madeline looked up, hope blossoming inside of her.

"She could certainly try," Mr. Gillingham mused. "But an unmarried woman, with no home of her own, would be unlikely to be granted guardianship, especially when the current guardian is of much better means."

Madeline's heart sank as quickly as it had risen. "And if my uncle demanded that my brother return to him, he would be within his rights?"

Mr. Gillingham shrugged. "Yes and no. His guardianship really only pertains to your brother's inheritance, not your brother's person. Though since he is still a child, I'm sure your uncle would have the support of the court if he were to pursue legal action."

Madeline nodded glumly. After a moment, Mr. Gillingham cleared his throat. "Was there anything else you wished to discuss with me, Miss Crawford?"

"No, thank you," Madeline replied, getting to her feet. "You have been most helpful."

"Thank you for your hospitality, Mr. Vanguard," Mr. Gillingham said, as both gentlemen rose from their seats.

"My pleasure," Arthur said with a nod. "I'll show you to the door."

Mr. Gillingham gave a bow and a smile to Madeline, who returned the courtesy. Arthur followed him to the door, but before stepping out, he paused, looking back at Madeline.

"You and I have some things to discuss, I think," he said before withdrawing from the room.

Madeline went to check on Thomas and Augustus in the garden after the gentlemen left, and when she returned to the drawing room, Arthur was waiting for her.

"There you are. I thought I'd frightened you off," he said as she entered.

Madeline could not help the quip that sprang to her lips. "I have not been frightened off by you before—what makes you think I shall start now?"

Arthur chuckled, shaking his head. "My pride, I suppose," he said. "Please, be seated."

"I'd rather stand, if you don't mind," Madeline replied. Her nerves were frayed after the visit with Mr. Gillingham, and she did not wish to be kept any longer than was absolutely necessary.

Arthur shrugged. "If you like. Now, Miss Crawford," he said, his brow furrowed and his tone suddenly business-like, "would you care to explain to me what you meant when you told Mr. Gillingham that your aunt had planned to separate you and your brother? Why did you not tell me this before?"

"Oh," Madeline said, deflated. "That."

"Yes, that," Arthur said, crossing his arms.

Madeline sat down with a sigh. "As I told you before, my brother and I went to live with my aunt and uncle after our parents died. I acted as governess and tutor to my younger cousins, until such time as my aunt wished me to find a position elsewhere."

"She wanted you to leave, and Thomas to stay?"

"Yes."

"But she did not know about this position."

Madeline shook her head.

"Why not?"

Madeline let out a humorless laugh. "For the same reason you verbally lambasted me upon my arrival. 'A female tutor? Preposterous.'"

She quoted his words back to him with a sad smile, and Arthur

114

frowned. "So you ran away."

"Yes. It was the only way Thomas and I could stay together."

Arthur nodded slowly and began to pace in front of the chaise. He stopped and looked at her. "Surely not all of your younger cousins had left the schoolroom, Miss Crawford. Yet I gather your departure was a hasty one." Madeline flushed, and he smirked at her. "Ah, there it is, the tell-tale blush. Come now, Miss Crawford, confess. What happened?"

Madeline narrowed her eyes at him. "There was no scandal, if that is what you are inferring."

"Not at all."

But his look was too innocent, and Madeline pressed her lips together. "I shall only confess the reason if you will confess that the thought of my being involved in a scandal had crossed your mind."

Arthur glared at her, but the longer their eyes stayed locked, the more smug Madeline's smile became. At last he huffed, throwing his hands in the air.

"What else was I to assume? A young lady shows up at my door in the middle of the night, and insists that she does not care a whit about her reputation?"

Madeline calmly ran a hand down the length of her skirt. "Thank you for your confession. Now I shall confess."

Grumpily, Arthur crossed his arms again, waiting.

"I refused to marry my cousin, Henry, and my aunt and uncle were displeased." She lifted her chin, meeting Arthur's eye and daring him not to believe her.

He merely stared at her. After a moment his face relaxed. "I am sorry," he said.

Madeline turned away. "As am I. I am sorry that I could not feel for him what he, and all the family, wished me to feel." She shrugged. "It would have been most convenient."

"Yes, but—" Arthur abruptly closed his mouth, turning towards the window.

Madeline frowned. "But?"

Arthur was silent for a long time before he finally spoke. "But then Augustus would not have a tutor. Or a playmate." Arthur lifted a shoulder but did not turn around, and a strange feeling filled Madeline's stomach. It was almost like being filled with cotton— she felt soft and light and a bit queasy.

He was glad she was there.

Madeline did not know how to respond, so she asked the question that had been on her mind since Mr. Gillingham's departure. "Do you think it would be worthwhile to pursue a petition to the court? About transferring Thomas's guardianship to myself?"

Arthur did not respond right away. "Perhaps," he said at last, turning around. His brow was furrowed. "Let me think on it."

Something in his manner was... strange. He seemed distracted, and it made her feel uneasy. She stood and squared her shoulders, anxious for solitude and the opportunity to consider everything she had learned. "Was there anything else, Mr. Vanguard?"

"Yes, in fact."

He moved from the window and came to stand before her. She folded her arms across her middle, trying to hold herself together.

"Why did you not tell me how much you enjoyed music?"

His unexpected question surprised her. "Pardon?"

"Anyone who heard you last night would have drawn the same conclusion," he said, crossing his arms. But his look was gentle, curious even. "You love music."

His words caused a strange stir within her. "Yes, I do," she said.

"Why have you never said as much?"

She lifted a shoulder. "You never asked. And it was never relevant. Young men do not need to learn to play or sing for company as young ladies do, and my responsibility is to Gus, and Thomas."

"I suppose," Arthur murmured, though he did not look convinced. Madeline felt raw and exposed, and it frightened her. "Will that be all, then?" she asked.

Arthur studied her for a moment longer. "Yes, that is all. But please, consider the pianoforte at your disposal while you are here. You are welcome to play at any time."

He turned and walked back to the window as Madeline left the room, wondering what to do with all the new intelligence—and feelings—the last hour had afforded her.

Chapter 15

"I will be going to town tomorrow," Arthur announced at supper one evening, a few nights after Mr. Gillingham had come to call.

Madeline looked up from her plate, but it was Gus who spoke first. "You are going to London?"

"No, just to York," Arthur said. "I have business with my solicitor." He cleared his throat. "I would be glad of your company, Miss Crawford, if you would care to join me."

Madeline's jaw nearly dropped open, and the boys glanced at one another and then at her. Arthur gave an uncomfortable laugh. "Am I really so terrifying as all that?"

"Of course not," Madeline hastened to say.

"You never ask for company," Gus said, giving his father a curious look.

"Yes, well, solitude has its place," Arthur said, looking uncomfortable. "But so does company." He gave his son a pointed look, and Gus's face split into a grin.

Madeline hesitated. "I would not mind a trip to town for a bit of shopping, but I cannot be ready to leave until after our morning lessons. Would that be agreeable to you?"

Arthur nodded. "Of course."

"What sort of shopping do you need to do?" Thomas asked.

His sister smiled. "I have a few small errands. And as I understand it, someone else will be having a birthday soon." She winked at him, and he giggled.

"That's me! What are you going to get me?"

"Now, why would I tell you that? Birthday gifts are meant to be a surprise, you know."

"Father, can Thomas and I come with you as well?" Gus asked, and soon both boys were clamoring for the chance to accompany them.

"Certainly not," Arthur said, silencing their pleas. "Miss Crawford has already said she will be acquiring items to which neither of you should be privy. I think it best that you stay here at the manor."

The boys grumbled a bit but soon moved on, and Madeline turned her attention back to the meal.

Lessons the next morning went smoothly, and soon the dinner hour approached. After putting the school things away, she dismissed the boys and went in search of Mr. Vanguard.

She found him leaving his study just as she came down the hall. "Mr. Vanguard?"

He turned at the sound of her voice. "Ah, Miss Crawford. I was coming to find you. Are you finished with your lessons?"

"Yes. Would you like to leave for town now, or after the midday meal?"

"I'd rather leave sooner, if it is all the same to you," he said.

"Of course."

"Good. Let me settle a few things with Mrs. MacLeod and I'll meet you out front in a quarter hour."

Madeline nodded and went to her room to collect her things. The morning had been gray and damp, and she opted for her long coat rather than a short one. She put on her gloves and bonnet, attached her reticule to her wrist, and went downstairs. Her stomach felt uneasy; she was nervous about spending an hour shut up in a carriage with Mr. Vanguard—would he wish to talk, or did he expect her to leave him to himself? Awkward silences were no more pleasant than awkward conversations. Turning back, she collected a book from her room and felt a bit easier. There could be no objection to her reading during the drive, surely.

Arthur was waiting outside with the carriage when she stepped out the front doors. Thomas and Gus came to see them off, and she gave each of them a quick hug, a few raindrops darkening the fabric of their coats. "You two behave yourselves while I am gone," she said, planting a kiss on top of Thomas's head. "Listen to Mrs. MacLeod, and don't get into any mischief."

"Will you be back for supper?" her brother asked, anxiety coloring his tone.

"Of course. We shall probably be home before dark, even. Can you keep yourself out of trouble until then?"

Thomas smiled wanly at her. She bent down and gave him another hug. "I shall return in a few hours, I promise," she whispered in his ear. He nodded and quickly wiped the moisture from his eyes.

Arthur helped Madeline into the carriage, then climbed inside and shut the door. Madeline waved to the boys until they went back inside the house, then sat back with a sigh.

"Do you regret coming along?" Arthur asked.

"No," Madeline said, though perhaps a little too hastily. The half-smirk Arthur wore so well told her that he did not believe her, but she ignored him. "I only regret being parted from my brother."

"It is only for half a day, Miss Crawford."

"I know. But since my parents died, we have rarely been parted from one another. There were times I went to social functions in the evening, of course, but he was always home with our cousins."

"York is only an hour's drive from the manor."

"Yes, I know. But it makes him anxious all the same. And I as well."

Arthur was quiet for a moment. "Forgive me for asking, but how did your parents die?"

Madeline looked out the window at the glowering sky, feeling the familiar tightness in her chest as she answered. "They went to visit some relatives, and contracted cholera while they were away. My mother fell ill very quickly and died shortly after. My father sent us word, but by then he was sick as well. We never saw them again."

"I am sorry to hear that."

Madeline nodded, keeping her eyes on the view outside. By the time the ache in her breast had subsided, she noticed that Arthur had pulled out a book. She relaxed, grateful that he did not want to talk anymore at present.

Madeline pulled out the novel she had brought, and the rest of the drive continued in silence. She was so absorbed in the story that she did not even notice they had arrived in town until the carriage pulled to a halt an hour later. She looked up in surprise, and found Arthur watching her.

"You are quite entertaining to watch while you read," he said without preamble.

Madeline blinked. "I cannot imagine what you mean."

"You make faces. I wonder what on earth you could have been reading."

"Faces!" She flushed. "I most certainly do not."

Arthur sat back, crossing his arms and smirking at her as the carriage pulled forward once more. "Indeed you do. What were you reading?"

"I do *not* make faces," Madeline huffed.

Arthur leaned forward, tilting his head to read the spine of the book she had placed in her lap. She snatched it up, holding it close.

"It was likely more entertaining than my own reading material," Arthur said, almost lazily. He held up a book. "*The Economics of Horse Breeding in Modern Europe.* Even I, for whom the subject is of great interest, found it rather dull. It reads like a sermon."

"I did not know you had attended many sermons," Madeline quipped, still annoyed.

Arthur's eyes narrowed a bit, his smile growing smug. "You have an exceptional wit when you are angry, Miss Crawford, I'll give you that."

Madeline said nothing.

"Well? Are you going to tell me what you were reading?"

She glared at him. *"Notre-Dame de Paris."*

Arthur's eyebrows shot up. "A French novel?"

Madeline lifted her chin. "You sound surprised."

"I am."

He said no more, and Madeline grumpily looked out the window. After waiting their turn to enter the gates of the city, the carriage started off again, moving steadily through the cobbled streets. Soon they crossed one of the many bridges in town, and the familiar towers of York Minster cut through the sky.

"Carver said there had been a fire in the cathedral," Madeline said as they passed.

"Yes, about two years ago."

"Do you know if it will be repaired?"

"When sufficient funds are raised, I'm sure. Services have been suspended for now."

Madeline sat back, her curiosity making her brave. "Have you attended services at the minster, Mr. Vanguard?"

His brow lifted with mild surprise. "I have. I could not find anyone to fill the position in Milford when the last vicar retired, so we closed up the church and began attending services here."

"We?"

"My late wife and I."

Madeline was silent for a moment. "When did the last vicar retire?"

Arthur shrugged. "Ten, twelve, years ago. I do not recall exactly."

He was silent then, and Madeline said no more. They stopped just south of the church, and Arthur cleared his throat. "Would you like to have use of the carriage, Miss Crawford?" he asked. His cool indifference had returned.

"No, thank you. I believe all my business can be conducted on Petergate. I would rather walk."

"Very well. I shall leave you at the mercantile and call back for you when my business is concluded."

Madeline nodded. They did not speak again until the carriage pulled up in front of the shop. She was surprised when Arthur stepped out to hand her down instead of letting the footman help her.

"I expect my business to take an hour or more, but not upwards of two," he said.

"Very well. I shall be ready."

Arthur nodded and climbed back inside the carriage. It started off down the street as Madeline went into the shop.

The bell above the door announced her arrival, and the same woman she'd encountered on her first trip to town, Abigail Martin, looked up from her place behind the counter. She smiled in recognition.

"Why, hello again," she said. "Miss Crawford, is it not? What brings you to town?"

Madeline smiled. "You remembered my name."

"We don't get many new faces around here," Abigail said cheerfully. "Besides, I was hoping to see you again."

"Thank you, Mrs. Martin."

Abigail's face lit up. "I see I am not the only one with an excellent memory." She came out from behind the counter. "Is there something I can help you find?"

"Yes, please. I need a gift for my younger brother. Do you have any toys?"

The other woman smiled. "Ah yes, the one who was with you the last time. How old is he?"

"Turning nine."

"My youngest just turned seven. Such a fun age." She led

Madeline to a small collection of toys across the room on a shelf near the window. "We have a few items here if you would like to take a look."

"Thank you."

She left Madeline to browse and went to organize some books and ribbons a short distance away. Madeline looked through the assortment of dolls and wooden toys until she found what she was hoping for: a small box of tin soldiers. They were not as elaborate as Gus's, nor were there as many, but Thomas would not care. He'd had a set at their uncle's house in London, but it had been left behind when they came to Yorkshire. She knew how much he enjoyed playing with Gus's soldiers and was certain he would like these.

She took the box to the counter and selected some penny candy for both boys as well. She glanced around as Abigail drew near.

"Do you perchance have any luggage for sale?" Madeline asked.

"We have a small selection of valises, but for anything larger you will likely need to visit Hatfield's. What are you looking for?"

"A new trunk," Madeline said.

Abigail nodded. "Hatfield's will have what you need, then."

"Where is it located? Is it close?"

"Yes, just around the corner on Goodram Gate."

Just at that moment, Madeline's stomach rumbled loudly, reminding her that she had missed her midday meal. She flushed. "Thank you, Mrs. Martin. And do you perhaps know of any tearooms nearby?" she asked, pulling out her reticule.

"Theodore's Tearoom is just down the street. 'Tis not far, and their fare is very nice."

"Thank you."

"I'm feeling a bit peckish myself," Abigail added. "Would you care for some company? I can take you to Hatfield's on the way, if you'd like."

Madeline smiled warmly at her. "That would be lovely. But I do not wish to trouble you…"

"No trouble at all. Just let me get my things and fetch my daughter to mind the shop."

She retreated through the door leading into the back, returning with the young lady who had helped Madeline before. "This is my daughter, Eloise."

"How do you do?" Madeline asked.

"Ellie, I'm going to take Miss Crawford to Hatfield's and then we are going to stop in at Theodore's for a bit. Will you please take care of things until I return?"

"Of course."

"Thank you." Abigail pulled on her gloves and a short jacket before taking her bonnet in hand. "Shall we?"

The ladies exited the shop and turned down the lane. Mrs. Martin kept up a steady stream of chatter while they walked, punctuated here and there with called greetings and pleasant responses to the acquaintances she met along the way. Before long, Abigail stopped in front of a shop and indicated the sign hanging above the door.

"'Hatfield's Fine Luggage,'" she read, then turned to Madeline. "We have been very pleased with their quality, and they are quite affordable."

The ladies entered, and after browsing the selection Madeline chose a medium-sized trunk. She paid the salesman and arranged to pick it up later, before she and Arthur left town for the day. Soon the two women were on their way to the tearoom.

"Here we are," Abigail said when they arrived a few minutes later. "They have the best cakes in the neighborhood."

Inside was warm and inviting, which was a pleasant change from the chill and damp outside. Two or three chairs were clustered around each of the small tables, which were laid with a cheery cloth and a small menu. Abigail led them to a place in front of the main window and sat down.

"There now!" Abigail said, removing her gloves. "We shall enjoy a nice chat and a lovely cup of tea, and you can tell me all about yourself and how things are faring for you at the manor."

Abigail Martin had a warm, generous nature, and Madeline soon found herself conversing easily with her as they dined. She told her all about the boys' lessons and what she hoped to teach them in the coming months.

"Augustus has been attending church services with us as well," Madeline said, taking a sip of her tea.

"Is he now? And does Mr. Vanguard likewise attend?"

"No, he does not."

"I expect he is away at his stud farm more often than not at this time of year," Abigail mused.

"His stud farm?"

Abigail raised her brow. "Aye, he invested in a large farm outside of Leeds after his wife died. Were you not aware of it?"

"Now that you mention it, I think I had heard something to that effect," Madeline said, remembering what Gus had said, and Arthur's earlier comment about the book he had been reading. "He is often away, but I had not given much thought to where or why."

"I would imagine that is where he spends most of his time. I suppose it was an opportunity to manage his grief at her passing.

Horse breeding was always of interest to him, as I understand."

Madeline shuddered at the thought of being surrounded by dozens of horses. She was grateful the farm was nowhere near the manor.

"And what interests do you have besides teaching, Miss Crawford?"

Abigail's question brought Madeline out of her thoughts. "I enjoy reading, mostly. And sewing. Music as well, though my talent is modest. I have tried to take up sketching or painting a time or two, but I have not the patience for it."

"My daughter Eloise loves to read," Abigail said with fondness. "Her nose is always in a book."

Madeline smiled. "Yes, I noticed she was reading the first time I came in."

"She has read everything we own multiple times over," Abigail said, "and I often catch her reading the books we have for sale in the shop. I ought to get her a subscription for the local lending library."

"I have a few books," Madeline said. "I will bring one or two with me when I next come to town. She would be welcome to borrow them, if she wishes."

"That is very kind of you, Miss Crawford, but won't you need them for your work?"

Madeline smiled. "I doubt my brother or my pupil would care to read the books in my private collection. Besides, there is a large library at the manor, and Mr. Vanguard has given me permission to borrow anything from it that I need. I can certainly spare my own for a week or two."

"Thank you," Abigail said with feeling. "Ellie will be overjoyed."

The ladies finished their tea and paid the bill. "This was a lovely way to pass the afternoon, Mrs. Martin," Madeline said. "Thank you so much for your company."

"Please, call me Abigail. And the pleasure was mine. I have long been wanting to make your better acquaintance. I'm so glad you came to town."

"As am I. And if I am to call you Abigail, then you must call me Madeline."

The older woman smiled, the fine lines around her eyes gathering together like the points of a star as she did so. Madeline felt a warmth of feeling for her as the two embraced. Abigail was closer to forty than twenty, but Madeline did not mind. It was nice to have another woman to call her friend.

They returned to the mercantile and Madeline collected her parcels. "Thank you again for your help and hospitality, Abigail," she said.

"You are most welcome. I look forward to seeing you again when you are next in town."

"And I you. Good day," Madeline replied, leaving the shop.

Madeline was strolling down the street a short time later, looking in at the shop windows, when she saw the Vanguard carriage come around the corner. She hailed the driver, who pulled the carriage to the side of the road. Madeline stepped back, her heart pounding as the horses passed near her.

The carriage door opened and Arthur stepped down. "What fortuitous timing," he said. "Miss Crawford? Are you ready to depart?"

"Yes, I've finished my shopping. But we must collect my new trunk from Hatfield's before we go."

"Of course, let us go there now."

Arthur helped Madeline into the carriage, then climbed in after her and shut the door. He seemed to be in a better mood. They collected her luggage and were soon on their way back to the manor.

The sun was an hour from setting when they once again passed through the city gate. The morning rain had rendered the damp road muddy, and it clung to the wheels like thick, black, glue.

Madeline looked out the window. "Do you think it will rain again?"

Arthur shook his head. "No—see how high the clouds are now? They shall blow away before they fill up with rain again."

Madeline sat back, her gaze still on the view outside. "It is beautiful country here. So different from London."

"Have you always lived in town?"

"Yes. My father was a tradesman, and my aunt and uncle also lived in town, although in a much nicer neighborhood. My uncle is in parliament." She turned from the window. "And you? Have you always lived in Yorkshire?"

"Yes. Milford Manor has been in my family for generations. One day it will belong to Augustus, though that is still a long way off."

The mention of her pupil made Madeline smile. "He is such a dear boy. I am very fond of him."

"He is fond of you, too. As well as your brother."

"Oh, yes. Those two are inseparable. If they looked anything alike, most would mistake them for siblings."

Arthur smiled. "They make quite a peculiar pair, don't they?"

"Indeed they do."

"Where does Thomas get his curly hair from?"

Madeline grinned. "My father. Only his hair was red." She paused for a moment. "Gus seems to favor his mother, I think."

Arthur made no reply, though Madeline saw his jaw tighten.

"I wish I could tell him more about her," Madeline said after a few moments, when it was clear Arthur would not speak. "Gus often mentions how he is afraid he will forget her." She peeked at the man sitting across from her, wondering how he would react.

Arthur's face was pale. He sat rigid as a statue, except for the bobbing of his Adam's apple when he swallowed. Madeline said nothing, waiting for him to respond. At last he seemed to thaw. "Lily," he said, almost like a prayer.

Suddenly he sat up, crossing both his arms with a glare. "I do not wish to talk about my late wife, Miss Crawford."

"Not even to your son?" Madeline asked gently. "I know it can be painful, but perhaps—"

"You know nothing of pain," he spat at her.

Madeline drew back, her nostrils flaring. "My parents died within a week of each other, Mr. Vanguard. I certainly know about pain."

Arthur glared at her, but Madeline met his gaze, refusing to back down. Finally he looked away, and Madeline sat back, her heart pounding.

Why must every conversation between them end in an argument? She knew he could not be all prickles and burs, but any time she tried to draw him out he snapped, sharp and tight, like a trap. Madeline sighed. Perhaps she would simply stop trying.

The inside of the carriage grew darker as the miles slipped away, and the silence between them went unbroken. Madeline only realized she had fallen asleep when a heavy lurch jolted her awake, throwing her across the carriage into Arthur.

"Oh!" she cried, unable to stop them from colliding.

"Good heavens!" Arthur shouted, catching her before she fell to the floor. "Are you all right?"

Her face aflame, Madeline tried to extricate herself from his grasp. "Yes, yes, I am well. Forgive me."

"Not at all," Arthur said, helping her up. She tried to sit down in her seat again, but the carriage was tipped so dramatically that she slid right into the wall.

"Something must have happened to the wheel," Arthur said.

Thankfully, the carriage was angled so that the door was facing towards the ground instead of up to the sky, and after only a little difficulty Arthur was able to open the door and climb out. Madeline followed after him, unassisted, since he had moved around to the other side of the carriage in order to assess the damage.

"Broken, clear through," she heard the driver say.

Arthur swore under his breath, but upon seeing Madeline he clamped his mouth shut.

"Is the wheel broken?" she asked.

"Not the wheel—the axle," Arthur said. "Snapped clean in half." He looked from the driver to the footman. "How far are we from the manor?"

"Hard to say," the footman answered. "Probably as far from the manor as from town, sir."

Arthur groaned, and Madeline's stomach twisted. It was nearly dark, and it would take the servants a half-hour or longer to reach anyone who could help, and that long again to return to them. "Thomas will be worried," she murmured.

"What was that, Miss Crawford?" Arthur asked, turning to face her.

"Thomas," Madeline said, her voice rising in pitch as her anxiety increased. "I told him we would be home by dark. I promised him. He has never been apart from me as long as this, not since our parents died. He will be worried sick. I have to go to him, we must go on!"

Madeline wrung her hands, and Arthur put a hand out to soothe her. "Calm yourself, Miss Crawford, there is no cause for alarm."

"But there is! I cannot leave Thomas alone, I have to go to him!"

Arthur stepped forward, gently placing his hands on her arms. "Thomas is not alone, Miss Crawford. Mrs. MacLeod is there, and Augustus. The house is full of servants. Thomas is perfectly safe, as are you."

His voice was quiet and deep, and as Madeline turned her stricken eyes to him, he gave her a reassuring smile. She took a shaky breath and nodded.

"Yes, of course. You are right. I apologize, I just—" She took another deep breath. "Is there no way we can continue on? I will walk, if I must."

Arthur considered for a moment, then turned to the other two men. "Unhitch the horses, please," he called.

The servants began unharnessing the animals, while Madeline nervously watched. She could feel Arthur's eyes on her face but she would not meet his gaze. She felt embarrassed and exposed—firstly from falling upon him in the carriage, and then nearly falling into hysterics a few moments ago.

With the horses unhitched, the driver put together some makeshift reins and attached them to their bridles. Madeline frowned. "What are those for?" she asked.

"So we can hold on to them more easily."

"Hold on to... we are going to *ride them?*"

"If you would like to get to the manor, yes. It will be too dark for us to walk before long."

Madeline shook her head, backing away from the beasts. "No, no, I cannot. I cannot!" She swallowed. "They are so... large."

To Arthur's credit, he did not laugh. "Miss Crawford," he said, his voice soft but stern. "This is the fastest way to get to Thomas. If you want to get to him quickly, we must ride the horses."

Madeline's eyes were wide, but at last she nodded her head. The driver walked one of the horses towards her, but she stumbled back in fright. Arthur shook his head, blowing out an exasperated breath.

"This will never work," he grumbled. "Miss Crawford? Miss Crawford, do you know how to ride?"

Madeline shook her head.

Arthur sighed. "Very well, we shall have to ride double."

"Double?"

"Yes. You will ride aside, and I shall ride astride behind you."

"Oh, dear," Madeline wrung her hands, glancing between Arthur's solemn face and the horse snorting a few yards away. "Is there no other way?"

Arthur shook his head.

Drawing a deep breath, Madeline gritted her teeth. "Very well. I shall do it."

Arthur held his hand out to her, and timidly she took it. Slowly, he walked with her towards the horse held by the driver. Madeline could not stop herself from trembling, but the thought of Thomas gave her strength. Soon they were standing beside the horse, and Arthur reached out to pat its neck. Madeline shuddered.

"They can sense fear, so it would be best if you can try to calm yourself, Miss Crawford," Arthur said gently. Madeline barely nodded, breathing deeply and speaking quietly to herself. "I'm going to put you on the horse now, are you ready?" he asked.

Again she nodded, and Arthur put his hands around her waist. A swooping sensation filled her belly as he lifted her easily and set her on the horse. She tensed, grasping its coarse mane to steady herself.

With the help of his footman, Arthur swung himself up behind her and took the makeshift reins from the driver.

"I'll send someone along as soon as we get back to the manor," Arthur called, swinging the horse around.

Chapter 16

Arthur had not been as close to a woman as he was now to Madeline since the death of his wife. It felt strangely foreign, but at the same time there was something familiar about having her tucked close to his chest. He held the reins loosely, letting the horse set the pace and praying that it would not trip on anything in the growing darkness.

Madeline's shoulder was tense where it pressed up against him. "Breathe, Miss Crawford," he said. "And try to relax. I won't let you fall, I promise."

He felt her shift, though she still held herself stiffly.

The clouds parted for a brief moment, sending slivers of rose-colored sunlight slanting across the countryside. In the distance, a small flock of birds climbed into the sky, disappearing from view as they flew off to their nests for the night. Madeline turned and glanced briefly at Arthur's face, then squeezed her eyes shut and snapped her head back around.

"Are you…" Arthur watched her curiously. "Are your eyes closed, Miss Crawford?"

"No," Madeline said, though a bit too quickly. Arthur coughed to hide a laugh.

A few minutes passed before Madeline broke the silence. "Thank you," she said quietly, "for taking me to my brother."

"Of course."

The quiet fell between them once more, broken only by the soft footfalls of the horse. The sky darkened and the air around them grew colder. Arthur urged the horse into a trot, anxious to get them back to the manor.

"May I ask you a question, Miss Crawford?"

"I suppose so."

"Why are you afraid of horses?"

She shifted. "I fell off during my first riding lesson, when I was a girl. I was not seriously injured, but it frightened me so badly that I never tried again. I've been terrified of them ever since."

"Did the horse step on you after you fell?"

"No, thankfully. But they are so… large. And powerful. They frighten me."

Her voice was small, and she trembled where she sat. An urge to wrap his arms around her and hold her close suddenly swept over Arthur, and he nearly dropped the reins in surprise. Madeline felt him stiffen and she glanced back at him.

"Are you well?" she asked.

The feeling lingered, and Arthur shook himself, trying to rid his mind of the thought. "Perfectly so," he said, looking ahead at the road rather than meeting her gaze.

A quarter hour had passed since they left the broken carriage, and Arthur began looking for the turn they would take that led past the village. It was difficult to make out much in the fading light, but Arthur could see a dark shape in the distance that might be the stand of trees he was searching for.

"May I ask *you* a question, Mr. Crawford?"

Madeline's voice was soft in the darkness, and Arthur felt a strange trembling inside at her words.

"I suppose so."

He counted three breaths before she spoke again. "Why do you avoid your son?"

Arthur's first reaction was surprise, followed almost immediately by anger—how dare she suggest such a thing! But starting an argument with her while they were both seated on the same horse did not seem a good idea, so he bit his tongue. He seethed in the silence, striving to slow his racing heart. Much to his surprise, the feeling morphed and changed the longer he sat with it. He realized that beneath the simmering anger was a fair amount of shame, and underneath the shame was an even greater amount of grief.

Minutes passed without either of them speaking, but at last Madeline's voice broke the stillness. "Forgive me, Mr. Vanguard. It was a presumptive question. You do not need to answer me."

Arthur cleared his throat. "I do avoid my son. But I hope you will acquit me of neglect towards him."

"Of course, I did not mean to imply—"

He cut her off before she could finish the apology. "Good. Because I love my son. And I want to do right by him." He hesitated. "But I will admit that it is more difficult to be near him since—" He swallowed. "He looks so much like his mother."

Arthur could feel that Madeline had gone very still. A voice inside seemed to shout at him to stop, to end the conversation and prevent the pain that was surely coming. But another part of him—a stronger, hungrier part—wanted him to keep talking. It pushed and pulled at him, begging him to open his heart just a tiny bit—not to let the hurt out, but to let the healing in. At last he gave in.

"Lily was a beautiful creature. She had light hair and a fair complexion, and the darkest eyes I had ever seen. We met during her second season in London, and I was amazed that no man had snatched her up yet. It was not until much later that I learned she had refused two previous proposals." He paused, and his voice grew soft. "She told me she was waiting to fall in love."

The clouds were thinning, and a few stars peeked out at them through the gaps. Arthur looked over to the east, where the moon was due to rise, but there was no sign of it yet.

"We were married before Michaelmas that year," he continued, "and I brought her home to Milford Manor. I was afraid she would miss life in town, but she brought life and light to the manor. I told her we could change or remodel the house to better suit her tastes, but the only change she requested was the installment of an art studio, where she could paint." Arthur smiled to himself in the dark. "She was everything that is good and beautiful in this world, and she brought goodness and beauty into the world through her art. I wish we'd had more time together."

"Gus told me she was an artist," Madeline murmured. "Are any of her paintings hanging in the house?"

"No. I had them all taken down after she died."

Madeline nodded. "How long has it been since…?" Her question hung unfinished in the air, but Arthur knew what she was asking. His voice was a whisper as he replied.

"She died nearly three years ago."

Madeline said nothing, and Arthur let the pain swell inside him. It filled his chest and pressed against his throat, making it nearly impossible to breathe. He swallowed—once, twice, thrice—before he finally felt himself in control.

"I am so sorry for your loss," Madeline said. Arthur nodded, even though she was turned away and could not see him. He did not trust his voice enough to speak.

Ten minutes later they turned down the long drive that led to the manor. Madeline breathed a sigh of relief.

"I expect you are anxious to get off this horse," Arthur said.

"No," she said slowly. "I mean, yes, of course. But... well, I suppose I am getting more comfortable up here. I don't feel as afraid as I did before."

"Brave enough to keep your eyes open?"

Madeline turned her head, giving him a sideways glance. "I've had my eyes open almost the entire time, I'll have you know."

Arthur could not keep the smile out of his voice. "Oh?"

"Yes." She paused. "That is, I have since you teased me about keeping them closed."

"Teas— I would never, Miss Crawford!"

"Oh, no?" This time she turned her head far enough to glare at him, though he could hear a playful note in her voice. "I heard you snicker when I told you I had my eyes shut."

"I don't snicker."

Madeline sighed, shaking her head, and said nothing more. A slow smile spread across Arthur's face, and he was glad she could not see it.

Arthur stopped the horse at the base of the front steps. He slid off their mount and then held his hands up for Madeline. She grabbed his arms and he lifted her down, setting her softly on her feet. His hands stayed at her waist after she had released him, and she looked up at him in surprise. "Yes, Mr. Vanguard?"

Suddenly Arthur could find nothing to say. He should tell her something—how brave she had been, and how sorry he was for the inconvenience and discomfort with which they'd had to return to the manor. But looking down into her upturned face, he could not find the words. He opened his mouth, shut it again, and then cleared his throat.

"Arthur," he said gruffly, finally pulling his hands away and tugging at the hem of his coat. "You may call me Arthur."

Chapter 17

As expected, Madeline found Thomas in a state of great agitation. He calmed down rather quickly once Madeline arrived, but Mrs. MacLeod said he had been crying and wailing since sundown. "I am glad ye were not detained," she said.

"We were," Madeline said, hugging her brother to her chest. Thomas had not let go of her since her arrival. "The axle on the carriage broke while we were driving home—we had to ride one of the horses back to the manor."

"Merciful heavens," the housekeeper cried. "I better see what has been done about it." She bustled off, leaving the siblings to themselves.

"You rode a horse?" Thomas asked, looking up at her with wide eyes.

"I did."

"Were you not frightened?"

"Terribly so," Madeline said, stroking his hair. "But I was more frightened of not returning home to you." She pressed a kiss to his forehead, and he snuggled closer. "Now come—it is time you were in bed."

Madeline awoke the next morning aching all over. She stretched, rubbing her sore arms and wondering if the horse felt as awful as she did. The events of the previous evening slowly filled her mind, like spilled tea seeping across a tablecloth. The carriage accident. The horseback ride. And Arthur. *He asked me to call him Arthur.*

A rush of feeling filled her breast, but she could not identify exactly what it was. Embarrassment? Camaraderie? Friendship? Whatever it was, it was new and unexpected; not altogether unpleasant, but a bit unnerving nonetheless.

She dressed and went down to breakfast, but found that the only other person in the breakfast room was Arthur. A flutter of nerves settled in her stomach as he looked up at her entrance, and she forced herself to smile.

"Good morning," she said, making her way to the side table spread with food and drink.

"Good morning," he replied. "I trust you slept well?"

"Yes, thank you. Although I feel as if I had been hit *by* a carriage rather than riding inside one."

Arthur chuckled. "Yes, I thought you might, having never ridden a horse before. Ask Mrs. MacLeod if you can have a lavender bath drawn up—it helps relieve some of the ache."

Madeline nodded. "Thank you, Mr. Vanguard, I will."

"Arthur."

She glanced over at him. He was not smiling, but his look was mild. "Please, call me Arthur," he said.

She nodded again but said nothing. Sitting down with her tea and toast, Madeline tried desperately to think of something to say. Did he expect her to give him permission to call her by her Christian name as well? That felt far too intimate, and Madeline balked at the idea. She was not even sure if she could call *him* by his first name. He was her employer, after all, and doing so would remove the safety their respective addresses and positions afforded. It would move their relationship from one of business to one of friendship, and she was not sure how she felt about that. The ride back to the manor had changed things between them, but whether the change was a welcome one had yet to be seen.

"Did your men arrive home safely?" Madeline asked, when she could think of nothing else to say.

"Yes, and the carriage is being repaired today. Another will be available for your use tomorrow as usual."

"Thank you."

Arthur cleared his throat. "I... was hoping I might accompany you."

She blinked. "To church services?"

"Yes. If you do not mind."

Madeline did not know what to say, but he was obviously waiting for a response. "Of course," she said. "That is, of course I do not mind. You are certainly welcome to accompany us."

Arthur looked back down at the paper he was reading. "Thank you. I was not sure whether you would welcome the presence of a heathen beside you on the pew."

Madeline choked on the bite of toast she had just taken. She coughed and sputtered, stealing sips of tea to calm the spasms as quickly as she could. Arthur sat and watched her with a bemused smile. She glared at him.

"You did that on purpose," she croaked, as soon as she had breath.

He shrugged and stood from his place. "Perhaps. Good day, Miss Crawford."

He left the room, and Madeline glared at his retreating figure before returning to her breakfast.

After the meal she went in search of Thomas and Gus. Their lessons were finished for the week, but she was surprised not to see them at breakfast. Maybe they had dined earlier and were playing in Gus's room.

But she could not find them in any of the bedrooms or the schoolroom. Perplexed, she glanced outside. The sky was still overcast and gray, but perhaps they had gone to play in the garden?

She grabbed a shawl from her room and went down the servant's stair to the main floor. Just as she was turning to head out a side door, the tantalizing aroma of cinnamon and nutmeg hit her nose. She paused, smiling.

She knew exactly where to find the boys.

Turning instead towards the kitchen, Madeline made her way through the back passages and down a short flight of stairs. With every step, the air around her grew warmer and the smell grew stronger. Finally she entered the large kitchen, and instantly spied two small heads bent over the main table.

"Now, don't be puttin' too much cinnamon on the dough, Master Gus, or they'll end up tastin' like dirt," she heard Mrs. Whittecombe say. "That's it. Hold on Thomas, let me help you, your twist is fallin' apart."

Madeline smiled at the scene before her. Both boys had their sleeves rolled up and voluminous aprons tied around them like giant, floury sailcloths. They were concentrating on the dough rolled out in front of them, which Madeline gathered was being made into cinnamon buns. Gus looked up and caught a glimpse of her. He grinned, nudging Thomas with his elbow, who looked up as well.

"Maddie! Look, we are making cinnamon buns!" he cried.

"I can see," Madeline said, drawing closer. "Although I think you may have more flour on yourself than on the table." She reached out and rubbed at a smudge on his cheek. He turned away, making a face.

"How do you do, Miss Crawford," the old cook said, dusting off her hands. "Can I get you anything?"

"No, thank you, Mrs. Whittecombe. I was only looking for these two. Are they causing you any trouble?"

"Not at all, though they be eatin' all my raisins and dates." She winked at Gus, who giggled. "I'll send them along after we get these buns in the oven and I've cleaned them up a bit. Don't worry yourself at all, they'll be fine."

Madeline thanked her and retired to the sitting room to sew, where the boys joined her a half-hour later. They were no longer sticky and covered in flour, and Madeline was grateful the cook had made them wash up before presenting themselves to her.

"I cannot wait to eat our cinnamon buns!" Thomas declared, dropping himself on the sofa next to his sister. "I put raisins in mine."

"They sound delicious," Madeline said. "Will we have them with our tea later?"

"As long as they turn out," he said.

"Mrs. Whittecombe said she won't serve unsightly buns," Gus added, and Madeline laughed.

The rest of the day passed without incident. Madeline read and sewed and watched over the boys, and when the dinner hour came, they were able to sample the boys' creations. Madeline declared them the most delicious cinnamon buns she had ever tasted, and Thomas declared her the best sister in the world. Arthur did not join them for the meal, for he had sent word that he was busy with work and would be dining alone.

When it was nearly time for the boys to retire, Madeline told them that Arthur would be joining them for worship services the next day. Their reactions were what she had expected: Thomas was wary, but Gus was overjoyed.

"Father has never been to church before!" he declared as Madeline tucked him in.

"Of course he has," Madeline said, "but it *has* been a long time. Which means you must be on your best behavior so he knows what is expected of him." Gus giggled and Madeline tousled his head. "Go to sleep now. I shall see you in the morning."

Sunday morning dawned beautiful and bright. Madeline wore her second-best dress and her favorite bonnet. She made sure the boys were dressed and ready to go, then took them downstairs at half past nine. Arthur came down a few minutes later.

The carriage was ready and waiting, and the four of them climbed inside. Madeline sat beside her brother and Arthur sat across from her, next to his son.

It was a short carriage ride to the village, and they arrived just as the bell started ringing to call everyone to the service. Arthur stepped out of the carriage and offered his hand to Madeline, then helped the boys down as well. An older woman whom Madeline recognized from past Sundays came up to them, her wrinkled face beaming.

"Upon my word!" she said in a shaky voice. "Mr. Vanguard!"

"How do you do, Mrs. Cole," Arthur said, touching his hat.

"I never thought I would see the day you came back to church," she said, shaking her head. "'Tis been too long, sir; far too long." She took his arm even though he had not offered it, and turned him towards the door. Madeline hid a smile at the surprise on Arthur's face, but to his credit, he fell into step beside the old woman and escorted her into the building. Madeline and the boys followed after them.

"Where have you been all these years? Why have you not come to call?"

Arthur cleared his throat. "Pray forgive me, Mrs. Cole, I have—"

"Your wife used to visit me every week, God rest her," Mrs. Cole went on, eyeing him with displeasure.

Madeline glanced at Arthur's face, curious to see how he would respond to the mention of his late wife. But aside from a slight tightening in his jaw, she saw no other reaction from him.

"My apologies, Mrs. Cole," he said. "I have been remiss in my duties."

Mrs. Cole led them to her pew and sat down. Arthur bowed cordially, but before he stepped away the old woman grabbed his arm. "I hope you are back to stay, Mr. Vanguard. The parish needs you." She gave him a solemn nod, and Arthur excused himself to take his own seat.

Madeline was already in their usual pew with the boys, and she groaned inwardly when Arthur sat down beside her. He sat so near that his coat sleeve brushed against her arm, making her electrically aware of his presence.

There was normally a bit of conversation before the service began, but today there seemed to be more than usual. Voices rose and fell around them, buzzing in the air and echoing off the old stone walls so that it felt as if she were in a cavernous beehive. Madeline was too well-bred to turn and look behind her at those who gossiped, but every so often she caught a few words —"Vanguard" and "tutor" were ones she was accustomed to hearing, but she also caught "ward," "welfare," and "mistress." At that last whispered word Madeline felt herself flush, and she was grateful the bonnet hid her face.

"It appears my presence has made a bit of a stir," Arthur murmured, leaning his head towards her.

"Quiet, the sermon is about to start," she chided. She did not look at him, but she thought she heard his low chuckle. The sound raised the hair on her arms and produced a faint swirl in her belly, as if she had missed a stair.

"The vicar is not even in the room yet," she heard him say, though he did not lean in as before. "And as I understand it, he may be some time yet. I believe he is rather old."

"He is *very* old," Madeline said, turning to look at him. "It is high time the man retired."

"He did retire," Arthur said. "But when they closed the minster his services were again required."

Madeline turned to stare at him. "He is the vicar who retired all those years ago? When you closed the church and began attending services in York?"

Arthur nodded.

"The man is ancient!" Madeline said, striving to keep her voice down. "Why did you not find someone else to fill his position?"

Arthur shrugged. "There was not time."

"That was two years ago," she said, pinching her lips together. "Surely there has been time since then."

"I had forgotten," Arthur said dismissively, "I hardly concern myself with the affairs of the parish."

"That is certainly true," Madeline muttered, turning back to face the front of the chapel.

"What do you mean by that, precisely?" he asked, an edge to his voice.

"Look around," she said in exasperation. "You said yourself the church had not been in use for a decade or more when it reopened for services—did you even inspect it before doing so? How long has it been since repairs where made to the building?" She turned away from him, her tone now one of displeasure. "Even if you have no wish to attend services yourself, plenty of those in the village would like to worship in a church without fear of the roof falling in upon their heads."

Arthur looked up, frowning. From the corner of her eye, Madeline watched him as his eyes traveled around the room—from the sagging roof to the cracked window and over all the worn benches. His frown deepened.

Everyone rose as the ancient vicar shuffled to the front of the chapel. Madeline hushed the boys, whose whispers had not ceased upon their standing. Thomas looked up at her apologetically, and she nodded towards the front. He obediently turned his head and Madeline did the same.

"I remember him from when I was a boy," Arthur said, his voice bemused. Madeline shot him a look as they all took their seats again, but he did not seem to notice.

"Today's sermon," the elderly vicar said in a shaky voice, "is taken from the fifth chapter of the book of Ephesians. It is an exhortation to avoid the vices and unclean things of the world."

"Oh, this ought to be good," Arthur said, folding his arms across his chest and grinning.

"Be quiet," Madeline whispered, trying not to admire how handsome he looked in profile.

"If you were privy to his past, you would be as amused as I, Miss Crawford."

Madeline turned to glare at him, which Arthur took as an invitation to share. "When I was a lad," he said, leaning in and keeping his voice low. Madeline turned her face back to the front, not wanting to encourage him, but he continued. "Father Morgan was known to enjoy his drink, and apparently he took the liberty of 'tasting' the wine for the Eucharist before the Holy Communion one Sunday. He entered the chapel looking like a cherry, and slurred all the way through the service."

Madeline looked over at him in horror, but Arthur was grinning gleefully. "And when the time came to offer the prayer over the bread and wine, he added 'And send better wine, that it will be easier to get drunk on.'"

Madeline could not stop the laugh that burst out of her, which unfortunately coincided with the end of the reading. It echoed in the silence following the congregation's "amen," and everyone turned to stare at her. Horrified, Madeline bent her head, wishing she could disappear. To make matters worse, trying to swallow back the laugh resulted in giving herself a bad case of the hiccups. Arthur shook beside her with silent laughter, and Thomas tugged on her arm.

"What is so funny?" he asked, wanting in on the joke.

Madeline shook her head, her face aflame, her body twitching every few seconds with another spasm. She peeked at Arthur, who was still trembling with silent mirth.

She would never forgive him for this.

The rest of the service passed in a mortified blur. Madeline went through the motions of praying and singing and participating in the worship, but every time she glanced at the man beside her, another bubble of laughter threatened to erupt and she had to quickly look away. To make matters worse, she could not so much as glance at the good Father without imagining him red-faced and slurring, which brought on the same trouble as looking at Arthur did.

It was a very long service.

When at last the final hymn was sung and the benediction uttered, she turned to Arthur with a stern look, striving to keep her composure.

"You, sir, are never allowed to attend us to church again."

To her surprise, he burst out laughing, and everyone in the congregation turned to look at them again. Madeline wished to sink into the floor.

"Mr. Vanguard!" she hissed through her teeth. "Compose yourself!"

"Arthur," he said with feeling. "And no, I will not. I have not been so amused in years." He chuckled again, shaking his head.

They rose from the pew and Madeline swept past him, not knowing or caring if he or the children followed her. She did not stop until she reached the carriage, and then only long enough for the footman to open the door for her. Arthur and the boys arrived a short time later, but that horrid man had the audacity to still look amused.

152

"That," he said as the carriage started on its way, "was the most delightful hour I have ever spent in church."

"You are impossible, Mr. Vanguard," Madeline said stiffly, looking out the window.

"Arthur," he said, as if egging her on.

She turned her head slowly, until she met his eyes. "You are impossible, Arthur," she said sweetly, giving him an acidic smile.

Arthur chuckled, but Thomas cried out, "You called him by his Christian name! Does that mean you are friends now?"

Madeline closed her eyes, pressing a gloved hand to her forehead. Arthur answered for her.

"No, Thomas, it does not," he said, his voice light with amusement. "It only means that *I* want to be friends. Not until your sister returns the courtesy will we be truly on friendly terms."

He raised his brow at her, and she threw her hands in the air. "I'll say it again, Mr. Vanguard—you are absolutely, completely, utterly impossible."

Chapter 18

The days that followed were some of the strangest of Madeline's life. She had never been so irritated by something—or in this case, some*one*—she found so amusing. To make matters worse, Arthur himself was suddenly always underfoot. Arthur at breakfast. Arthur stopping by the schoolroom. Arthur in the gardens. Arthur at dinner. But instead of being able to ignore him in stiff, disapproving silence, the sight of him never failed to remind Madeline of the story he told and the sight of his face at church, which always brought a bubble of laughter to her lips.

Insufferable, irritating man!

"Has your father nothing better to do with his time today?" Madeline grumbled, after yet another visit to the schoolroom by Arthur. Gus looked up from his primer and frowned.

"Do you not like it when he stops by?"

"No, I do not," Madeline snapped, stuffing a book back on the shelf with more force than necessary. "His presence disrupts our lessons, and I would much rather he stay away."

The boys exchanged looks, but Thomas lifted a shoulder and they both resumed their lessons.

Madeline continued to grumble throughout the morning, and nothing they did seemed to be good enough. Gus's handwriting was sloppy. Thomas's sums were crooked. Every little thing seemed to aggravate her, and everyone was relieved when she called an end to lessons and dismissed them for the day.

The following day was more of the same. After the third time she snapped at Gus, Thomas laid a hand on her arm.

"Maddie?"

"What is it, Thomas?"

"I think I know what the problem is."

Madeline blinked. "Problem? What do you mean?"

"You keep getting vexed with me and Gus," he said, with a nod at his friend. Madeline glanced between them as Gus nodded glumly. "And I think I know why."

"Oh." She frowned. "I am sorry. I did not realize that I was—" Madeline took a deep breath, placing her hands in her lap. "What do you think the reason is?"

"I think you like Mr. Vanguard," Thomas said, looking back down at his slate and picking up his chalk. "You were quite vexed with me and our cousins when you were sweet on Charles Warren a few years ago, too. I think that is the problem."

Madeline was so dumbfounded she could only sputter at him. Gus giggled and Thomas grinned, until at last Madeline found her voice.

"Of all the ridiculous ideas! Thomas, do not ever let me hear you make such an absurd suggestion again."

Thomas shrugged, and both boys resumed their work. Madeline pressed her lips into a thin line, refusing to entertain the idea that Thomas might be right. What on earth put such a notion into his head? Mr. Vanguard certainly seemed to be more at ease in her presence than he once was, and while she had to admit that he was quite handsome, Madeline found him just as infuriating and confusing as ever.

"Mr. Vanguard is gone?"

Madeline had gone searching for her employer the following morning. When she could not find him, she inquired of Mrs. MacLeod where he might found.

"Aye miss, he left for Leeds before the sun was up. I expect he'll be gone a fair while," the housekeeper said. "His visits there are usually a fortnight or more."

Did the man *never* take his leave? Madeline tried to ignore the disappointment she felt at hearing the words, refusing to admit that she might miss someone who exasperated her more than any other person. "Very well, I shall proceed with Gus's lessons in the way I best see fit until he returns. Thank you, Mrs. MacLeod."

She returned to the schoolroom, where Thomas and Gus were bent over their books.

"What did my father say?" Gus asked, looking up at her.

"It seems he has left again without taking his leave," she said, returning to her place at the table between them. "But I'm sure he will be back soon, and we can speak to him about beginning your German lessons then."

"I bet he went to Leeds," Gus said gloomily. "Sometimes I think he loves those horses more than me."

"That cannot possibly be true," Madeline said, wrapping an arm around his shoulders. "Your father loves you very much. But yes, he did go to Leeds."

"Why does he not take me with him, then? Why does he go away and leave me?"

Madeline sighed. "Well, you *are* quite young. Most children do not go anywhere with their parents until they leave the schoolroom."

"But why?"

"Because you have lessons to attend to, and a very strict tutor who will switch you if you do not complete them on time," she said, glaring at him with mock severity. It worked—Gus's forlorn face split into a grin, and Thomas giggled.

"You have never switched anyone in your life, Maddie," he said. "Not even when Cousin Maria put pepper in your tea for making her repeat her French lessons."

The boys dissolved into fits of laughter while Madeline placed her hands on her hips, looking stern. "That may be the case, but I could certainly start with the two of you." She reached out and grabbed her brother around the middle, tickling his sides and grinning at his shrieks of laughter. She tickled Gus as well, until tears of mirth ran down his face.

"Oh Maddie," Thomas said, laying his head on the table and trying to catch his breath, "you tickle just as well as Father used to."

"You remember your father tickling you?" Gus asked.

Thomas nodded. "Barely. It is one of my earliest memories. I remember him chasing me across the room, and tickling me when he caught me." The smile on his face faded a bit. "I only wish I could remember Mother better than I do."

"I wish I had a father who tickled me," Gus said wistfully. "And I wish I could remember more about my mother, too. My memories of her are fading."

"That reminds me," Madeline said, sitting up. "I learned a few things about your mother last week."

"You did?"

"Yes. Would you like to hear them?"

Gus nearly bounced out of his chair. "Would I ever!"

Madeline laughed. "Very well, but then you need to settle down and finish your lessons, agreed?"

His little head bobbed vigorously, and Madeline felt a surge of affection for him. How she wished his mother could see him now!

"Your father told me she was a great beauty," Madeline began. Gus propped his chin in his hands, his elbows resting on the table as he listened with eager anticipation. "And that you look just like her."

Gus grinned. "I remember what she looked like. She used to wear a pink gown, and she always had flowers in her hair." He paused. "I wonder why they did not paint her portrait that way?" he mused.

"There is a portrait of your mother?"

"Yes. It used to hang in the drawing room, but father took it down after she died. It is tucked away in her art studio along with her other paintings."

Madeline nodded, intrigued. It seemed that Arthur felt such grief at her passing that he removed any and all trace of her existence after she died. What depth of feeling, how strong an attachment he must have had! She wondered what it would feel like to love someone as passionately and completely as that.

"What else did my father tell you about my mother?"

Gus's question brought Madeline out of her reverie. She smiled, and related to Gus all that Arthur had told her about Lily—how she had loved to host balls and parties, how she made everything come to life. She wished she had more to tell him, but even the few words she shared were enough to lift his spirits. He hugged her around the middle, squeezing her tightly.

"Thank you, Miss Crawford," he said, sniffling. "You make her feel real again."

Madeline hugged him back. "She was very real, and very loved. Just like you." She pressed a kiss to his head. "And if I find out anything else about your mother, I shall let you know immediately."

Gus looked up at her, his eyes bright with unshed tears. "I would like that very much."

Madeline squeezed him again. "Of course you would. Now, let us get back to our lessons, shall we?"

That night, Madeline had an idea.

It began as just a passing thought. But as she turned it over in her mind, the idea took hold of her with such vigor she could hardly sleep. Nervous and excited, she planned it out in her mind, hoping she would be able to make it come to fruition.

The first obstacle in her plan seemed the most daunting, and it took Madeline two days to gather the courage to approach Mrs. MacLeod about it.

"I'm sorry, Miss Crawford, but the household is forbidden from entering Mrs. Vanguard's studio without Mr. Vanguard's permission," the housekeeper said.

"I understand," Madeline said. "But can you not make an exception, just this once?"

"No."

"Mrs. MacLeod," Madeline said, keeping her voice even, "Mrs. Vanguard was a wife *and* a mother. Do you think it fair that all trace of her life and memory has been kept locked away from her only child, simply because of the wishes of her husband?" The housekeeper frowned, and Madeline continued, more gently this time. "I do not ask to see it out of curiosity, Mrs. MacLeod. Gus wants to remember his mother, but he is afraid of forgetting her. There is nothing in this house to remind him of her—no paintings, no mementos—it is as if she never existed."

Mrs. MacLeod sat down, looking off into the distance.

"When I told Gus what little information I had learned of her from Mr. Vanguard," Madeline said softly, sitting beside her, "he told me about his mother's portrait, and I simply cannot get the idea out of my mind. Please, Mrs. MacLeod. Lily would not have wanted her little boy to forget her."

The housekeeper was silent for a long time. At last she sniffed, withdrawing a handkerchief from her pocket. "Lily didnae want to sit for the portrait," she said. "But Mr. Vanguard insisted." She swallowed, striving to compose herself. "He said if anything ever happened to her, he wanted to still be able to see her face. But he took it down the day she died, said he couldnae bear it." She dabbed at her eyes, and Madeline squeezed her hand.

"Very well," the old Scotswoman said abruptly, "I'll let ye in to see the portrait. And young Master Gus, too. But not a word of this to anyone. Mr. Vanguard will have me head if he hears about it."

"Thank you, Mrs. MacLeod!" Madeline said, throwing her arms around her. "You won't regret it."

Startled, but pleased, the housekeeper chuckled. "I'm already regrettin' it. Och, away with ye now—I'll meet ye after lessons tomorrow to let ye in."

Madeline could hardly contain her excitement the next morning. She was just as inattentive as her pupils and ended up dismissing them early for the day. "Gus, might I have a word?" she said, as the boys stood to put away their things.

"Of course," he said.

Thomas watched them until Madeline nodded towards the door. "Run along and play, Thomas. Gus will be along a little later."

Her brother frowned, but finally shrugged and scampered off. Gus cocked his head, looking at her curiously.

"I have a surprise for you, Gus," she said, unable to keep the smile from her voice.

"A surprise? For me?"

"Yes. But you mustn't tell anyone else about it."

Gus frowned. "Not even Thomas?"

Madeline thought for a moment. "You may tell Thomas. But neither of you are to speak of it to anyone else, understand? Only to each other or to me."

Gus nodded vigorously, grinning from ear to ear.

"Come along, then."

Madeline picked up her sketchbook and led the way out of the school room. They went downstairs in search of Mrs. MacLeod, whom they found in one of the smaller drawing rooms, speaking with a maid. When she saw Madeline and Gus enter, she dismissed the servant and turned to greet them. "Are ye ready, then?" she asked.

"Yes, if you please," Madeline said.

"Mrs. MacLeod, what is the surprise?" Gus asked, bouncing on the balls of his feet. The housekeeper chuckled.

"Och, laddie, if we told ye, then it wouldnae be a surprise now, eh? Come along, then."

They followed her out of the room and down a short hallway, to the servant's stair. When they arrived on the second floor, Gus clapped his hands together. "Are we going to see my mother?" he cried in excitement.

"Shh, Gus, remember what I said," Madeline said, squeezing his shoulders. She could feel him trembling as Mrs. MacLeod unlocked the door to Mrs. Vanguard's studio and stepped aside.

"Ten minutes, Miss Crawford," she said. "I'll rap on the door when 'tis time."

"Thank you," Madeline said with feeling. Gus reached out and put his hand on the brass, pausing for a moment. Then, with a deep breath, he turned the knob and opened the door.

The room was smaller than Madeline had envisioned, but it was filled with light due to the enormous window on the opposite wall. An artist's easel stood directly in the center of the room, an unfinished painting still upon it. Madeline's throat constricted at the sight.

Gus moved slowly into the space, looking around. A large canvas drop cloth covered most of the floor, and rows of paints lined the shelves along one wall. Brushes stood on their ends in a jar like a bouquet of thistles. A stack of paintings, most of them in frames, stood along one wall, and it was to these that Gus made his way. Madeline followed slowly behind him.

The first painting in the pile was a landscape. Gus hardly looked at it as he moved it aside. The painting underneath was a still life, and then another landscape. Finally, Gus unearthed a large painting of a beautiful, fair-haired woman.

"Here," he said reverently. He stared at her face for a long time. "Hello, Mother," he said quietly.

Madeline sat beside him on the floor and put her arm around him. She glanced between the painting and the boy beside her a few times. "You do look remarkably like her," she said, and Gus's face split into a grin. "Although you have your father's chin."

Gus would not look away from the portrait. His mother's rich brown eyes stared calmly back at him, her face serene. And yet, the artist had captured his subject in an attitude of anticipation—as if she were on the verge of laughing. Gus tipped his head, studying her, trying to arrange his face into the same expression. Madeline put a hand gently on his shoulder.

"Would you mind if I look around the room a bit?" she asked. She knew she did not really need his permission, but his grateful smile and quick nod told her what she had expected: he wanted some privacy.

She got to her feet and shook out her skirts, moving quietly towards the window. Dozens of canvases leaned against the walls, and she made her way to another stack in the far corner. Gus's voice murmured quietly behind her as she crouched down, looking at the paintings.

The first few were complete and framed, but several near the back of the pile were only partially finished. She slid one out that had only a few strokes of color on the canvas, though the faint charcoal lines sketched across the surface indicated it was meant to eventually be a portrait. Madeline pulled out another unfinished painting, this one a landscape. She held it up, realizing the building off in the distance was the manor.

Madeline knew her time was short, so she quietly made her way back to where Gus was sitting cross-legged on the floor. She found a vantage point behind him where she could see over his shoulder to Lily's face, but still allow him a bit of privacy. Pulling out her notebook, she began to draw.

A few minutes later there was a soft knock on the door. Madeline sighed. Ten minutes was not enough time to do much more than sketch the general shape of Lily's head, but she was grateful Mrs. MacLeod had been willing to give them even that. She went to stand beside Gus, who hastily wiped his face with his sleeve when he saw her approaching.

"Gus dear, it is time to go," she said gently.

"May I stay a little longer?"

"I'm afraid not."

He sighed but nodded. Carefully he picked up the portrait, then turned to Madeline. "Can we put the other paintings back first, so she can be on the outside?"

"Of course."

Madeline arranged the pictures Gus had removed earlier into a neat stack. Carefully, as if holding a sparrow's egg, Gus placed his mother's portrait on the floor and leaned it gently back against the others. Lily's smiling face looked demurely out at them, and they stood together, admiring her.

Another knock sounded, this one sharper and more insistent. The door opened a crack, and the housekeeper's face appeared, looking displeased.

"We are coming, Mrs. MacLeod," Madeline said, placing a hand on Gus's shoulder and turning him gently towards the door.

In a few steps they were back in the quiet hallway. Mrs. MacLeod relocked the door and then tried the handle, ensuring it was secure. Gus watched her sadly, and when she turned back around he looked up into her face.

"When can I come back?" he asked.

The housekeeper looked at Madeline, but Madeline could not bear to tell him that Mrs. MacLeod had only promised this one visit. "We can discuss that later," she said instead. "For now, Mrs. MacLeod needs to get back to her duties."

He nodded. "Thank you for letting me spend time with my mother," he said. "She is even more lovely than I remembered."

He smiled up at the housekeeper, gave Madeline a quick hug, then turned and hurried off.

"Were you able to finish your sketch?" the housekeeper asked when he was gone.

Madeline shook her head. "I was barely able to begin. May I come again, and stay a bit longer?"

Mrs. MacLeod frowned. "It goes against me better judgment, but aye. 'Tis harder to get away in the daytime, so perhaps in the evening sometime."

"That would be wonderful. Thank you, Mrs. MacLeod," Madeline said with feeling.

The older woman nodded. "Ye are right about the lad," she said. "He deserves to remember his mother."

Chapter 19

Madeline did not know that Arthur had returned until she was summoned to change for dinner the next day.

"It is just me and the children," she told the maid, confused. "We can eat in the kitchen, as usual."

"Mr. Vanguard has returned, miss," the young lady said. "And he has requested that everyone dress for the evening."

Madeline felt a rush of feeling course through her, finally settling into a flutter of nerves in the pit of her stomach. "Of course. I shall meet you in my room shortly."

She walked slowly towards her bedchamber, examining the unexpected feelings that arose upon hearing that Arthur had returned. Surprise, of course—she had not expected him to return so soon from his trip to Leeds. But she felt anxious and nervous as well. Was it because she worried he would discover that Mrs. MacLeod had let her and Gus into Lily's art studio? Perhaps. But Madeline was beginning to think that some of her discomfort was due to more tender feelings that were beginning to grow—feelings that Thomas may have discovered even earlier than she herself.

Arthur had admired her blue dress once before, so Madeline decided to wear it again. After the maid helped her dress and do her hair, Madeline went down to the drawing room. Feeling at once both excited and nervous, she paused before the doors to take a breath and compose herself. *It is only Mr. Vanguard,* she told herself. *He is the father of your pupil and your employer, nothing more.*

But when Madeline entered the room and her eyes collided with his, her heart gave an erratic thump and she knew she was lying to herself.

She was falling in love with him. And she knew not what to do about it.

"Miss Crawford, look! Father is home!" Gus's eager cry met her ears and she smiled.

"I see that. Welcome home, Mr. Vanguard," she said, crossing the room to join them.

He inclined his head. "Thank you, Miss Crawford."

"We did not expect you back so soon."

Arthur lifted one eyebrow, the corner of his mouth drawing up. "You sound disappointed."

"Oh, no, of course not." She flushed. "I was surprised, that is all."

"I see." Arthur studied her face for a long time, then glanced at her dress. "That color is lovely on you," he said. "Is that the same dress you wore before?"

He remembers, Madeline thought, her cheeks warming once more. She inclined her head. "It is."

167

He smiled, then turned to face her brother, who was reading on the nearby sofa. "And how is young Mr. Crawford this evening? I trust you are well?"

Thomas grinned at being addressed like a gentleman. "Yes, sir."

"I am glad to hear it."

The butler entered the room just then and announced that dinner was ready. "Miss Crawford?" Arthur asked, offering his arm.

Surprised, but pleased, Madeline took it. "What is the occasion, sir?"

"Arthur," he said. "And must there be an occasion to escort a lady in to dinner?"

She raised an eyebrow at him. "Around here? Yes."

He chuckled. "Then consider this a belated birthday escort, since I was not dressed properly on the day we celebrated."

They arrived in the dining room, and Arthur helped Madeline to her seat. "Thank you, *Mr. Vanguard*," she said pointedly, giving him a playful look. He chuckled.

"Always my pleasure, Miss Crawford."

Dinner progressed as usual. The undercurrent of tension and anxiety Madeline had felt when at first entering the drawing room melted away, and the meal was a pleasant one. As they neared the end of the last course, she wondered what would come after. He had set the standard for a more formal evening by escorting her to the table—would he send the boys off to bed and request her presence in the drawing room afterwards as well? The thought made her blush, and unfortunately Arthur caught the change in her coloring.

"Is something wrong, Miss Crawford?" he asked.

Madeline forced herself to smile as she answered. "No, I am merely a bit warm, thank you."

"In that case," Arthur said, "would you care to join me for a stroll outside after dinner? There is something I would like to show you."

There was an edge of excitement in his voice, though he made an admirable effort to conceal it. Madeline took a sip from her glass while she considered her response, trying to temper her own excitement.

"Some fresh air would be most welcome, thank you."

When the meal was finished, the boys were dismissed and Madeline went to collect a shawl from her room. The day had been quite warm, but the spring evenings were still a bit chilly. She went back to the drawing room, and found Arthur waiting for her.

"Miss Crawford," he said, giving her a slight bow. "Shall we?"

Madeline nodded and took his arm, feeling a jolt of excitement. This evening felt so different from every evening before. There had been no arguments between them, no irritable glares or disapproving silence. Instead, she had enjoyed pleasant conversation and—dare she hope?—even admiration from him. What else would the evening hold?

Arthur led them through the back garden and out towards the stables. When Madeline realized their destination *was* the stables, she stopped.

"Mr. Vanguard?"

"Yes?"

She glanced up at his face, then towards the building they were approaching. "Is there a reason you are leading me to the stables?"

"Yes."

A burst of anxiety flooded her middle, and she narrowed her eyes at him. "You know how I feel about horses."

"I do."

"Then why are you taking me there?"

Arthur's voice was mild. "I told you before—there is something I would like to show you." He smiled, no doubt hoping to set her at ease, but Madeline was having none of it.

"If it is a horse, I am not interested." She dropped his arm and took a step back, but Arthur reached out and caught her hand in his.

She froze, staring at their hands, her heart beating frantically in her chest. "Miss Crawford," she heard him say. She did not respond. "Miss Crawford?" he said again, and he squeezed her fingers lightly.

"Y-yes?" she said, looking up at him.

"I promise you—it is not a horse I want to show you."

His words sank in slowly. "Not... a horse?" she repeated.

"No." He smiled, but there was a mischievous gleam in his eye. "Please, let me show you."

Madeline was torn between curiosity and fear. What could he possibly have to show her if not a horse? And if not a horse, then why the stables? Could he not bring whatever it was he wished her to see up to the house? He knew her past. He knew her fears—why did he insist on leading her straight into the midst of them?

Arthur waited patiently, and at last she nodded, letting him lead her on again. When they entered the stables, Madeline was trembling, but she still placed one foot in front of the other. Arthur led her slowly, watching her face and letting her take her time. Somewhere a horse snorted and she jumped, turning and attempting to run. But Arthur was there, his hands on her shoulders, holding her gently but firmly in place. "Miss Crawford," he said. "Miss Crawford, look at me."

Trembling, Madeline lifted her face to his. His look was gentle but his eyes were determined. "I promise, you will be safe. Just a little farther. We are almost there."

She nodded numbly, letting him turn her around. In a few steps they came to a row of stalls, tucked in a far corner of the stables, away from the pawing, snorting stallions. They appeared empty, but Arthur led them to the very last one. Madeline peeked inside.

A beautiful cream pony with a light mane and startling blue eyes looked back at her. Its ears stood no higher than her own, which left Madeline to look *down* at it, something she was not accustomed to doing and which she was not expecting. Her fear ebbed as the smart little pony stepped forward, lifting up its nose to be pet. Madeline reached out and tentatively rubbed the soft velvet. Arthur watched her carefully.

"You said you were not going to show me a horse," she murmured.

"He is not a horse," Arthur said, reaching a hand out to caress the shaggy mane. "He is a four-year-old sweetheart, and the gentlest pony I could find in my stables."

"A pony? Is that not the same thing as a horse?"

Arthur chuckled. "No, they are actually quite different. Can you not tell how much smaller he is?"

Madeline nodded.

"You said horses frightened you because they were so large and strong," Arthur said. "Winston is certainly strong, but he is not very large. I thought he might be a good specimen for your first mount."

Madeline's eyes widened. "My what?"

Arthur shrugged. "In time, your mount. But that will come later. For now, just grow accustomed to being near him."

Madeline looked back at the pony, a whirlwind of emotions swirling inside her. "I am not sure I understand."

"He is a gift, Miss Crawford."

The way he said her name caused Madeline to turn, and her heart somersaulted at the look on his face. "A gift? You mean... he belongs to me?"

"Yes." Arthur turned his attention back to the pony, stroking down his neck. "You may even change his name, if you would like."

"I like Winston," Madeline said, likewise turning her attention back to the animal in the stall. It was strange to consider that it belonged to her—it was such an unexpected, thoughtful gesture.

"Thank you," she said quietly. Arthur merely nodded, saying nothing.

They stood together next to the stall for a long time. Gradually the tension in Madeline's shoulders eased, and after a while she began talking quietly to the pony. Sometimes she reached out and stroked his nose, but for the most part she just watched him, while Arthur watched her. After thirty minutes, he cleared his throat.

"It is getting late, Miss Crawford. Would you like to return to the house?"

Madeline sighed softly. "I suppose so."

Arthur chuckled. "You sound as if you are trying to convince yourself."

"Maybe I am." She brushed off her hands and turned around, looking up at him with a smile. "Shall we?"

For a moment, Arthur did not move. Then, shaking himself, he stepped back and offered her his arm. "Miss Crawford?"

She took it and they turned, retracing their steps. She tensed as they made their way back through the stables, but the fear that had gripped her heart for so many years felt looser. Once outside she took a breath, letting it out with a sigh. Arthur glanced down at her, but before he could say anything, she spoke.

"That is why you went to Leeds," she said.

He nodded.

"Just to collect Winston?"

He shrugged. "I saw to some other business while I was there, but as my last visit was only a short time ago it was not necessary for me to stay longer. And if I am being honest," he said, clearing his throat. "I wanted to come home."

Madeline's heart beat faster. Was *she* the reason he wanted to come home?

The night air was cool, and Madeline tipped her head back to look at the sky. Wispy clouds, gray against the inky sky, hid most of the stars from view. But a few shone bravely through the darkness, winking at her as if they could read her thoughts. She was grateful that the man beside her could not.

They did not speak again until they reached the house. Madeline paused on the step, and Arthur reached out to open the door for her. "Thank you," she said, looking up at him. "For Winston. For letting my brother and I stay here. For giving me employment. For… all of it."

"You are most welcome, Miss Crawford."

"Madeline," she blurted, and immediately flushed. "You… you may call me Madeline."

Arthur frowned. "You don't need to give your permission out of a sense of obligation, Miss Crawford."

"I know. And I'm not." She looked down. "I was thinking about what you said in the carriage last week, to the boys. About wanting to be friends." Her chin lifted and she met his gaze. "And I think I would like that."

A slow smile crept across Arthur's face. "Does this mean you will be calling me Arthur, then?"

Madeline laughed lightly. "I suppose it does, if we are to be friends."

"Friends." Arthur's look softened. The longer he held her gaze, the faster Madeline's heart beat in her chest. His eyes darted down to her lips, and she heard him suck in a breath before looking away.

"I..." he said, then cleared his throat. "It has been a long time since I made a new friend. I'm not quite sure I remember how to go about it."

Madeline stepped past him into the house, breaking the tension that hung in the air. "Well, giving someone a pony is not exactly customary," she said with a wry grin.

Arthur chuckled, following her inside. They walked through the house to the main staircase, where Arthur bowed. "I have a few matters of business to see to before I retire, so I will leave you now."

"Of course. Thank you again, Mr. Vanguard."

"Arthur."

Madeline laughed lightly. "Yes. Arthur. Thank you."

He bowed again, but not before Madeline caught a glimpse of the grin stretched across his face. "Good evening," he paused, "Madeline."

Madeline's stomach flipped at the sound of her name on his lips. It was strange, but pleasant—much like the feeling swirling inside of her. She turned and started up the stairs, lifting her skirts to keep the fabric out from underfoot. When she reached the second floor landing, she looked back down, expecting the entryway to be empty. But Arthur still stood at the bottom of the stairs, looking up at her.

Chapter 20

Arthur paced in front of the fireplace in his study, his agitation growing with each step. Was he mad? What was he thinking? He had no business giving Miss Crawford—Madeline—a pony. And no business wanting to become friends. And *certainly* no business at all thinking about kissing her, as he had that evening. He did not love her, he barely even *liked* her. He loved Lily, and Madeline was so different from his late wife that the idea of kissing her was laughable.

He sat down at his desk with a groan, dropping his face into his hands. What was happening to him? The entire time he was in Leeds, he had been distracted thinking of Madeline. William had noticed that something was troubling him, but thankfully had not guessed at the reason behind Arthur's preoccupation. He had assumed the pony was for Gus, and Arthur let him assume—he was in no hurry to hear his friend crow over him.

Arthur sighed. It was difficult for him to admit that his son's tutor was the reason for his distraction, but he could not lie to himself any longer. More often than not, he found himself thinking of Madeline when before he used to think of Lily—an occurrence that left him feeling confused and, at times, guilty.

There are different kinds of love, Arthur.

Arthur could hear his late wife's voice in his mind, and could picture her face as she said it. "I do not love her," he said aloud, the words coming out rough and hard.

But you could.

He huffed and stood from his place. "Preposterous," he muttered, beginning his pacing again. But even as he said it, he knew it was not true. He *could* love Madeline. Lily had always said that love and loathing were both the same feeling, only the latter was misunderstood. And while Arthur did not loathe Madeline, she certainly got under his skin. She was so stubborn, so reckless, so passionate.

He paused.

Lily had been passionate, too, but about different things. Perhaps that is what he found so intriguing about Madeline. She had the same enthusiastic spirit that he had loved about his late wife—the same thirst for knowledge, the same exuberance for life.

And the same love for Gus.

There are different kinds of love, Arthur.

He thought the words again, but instead of dismissing them, he sighed. Perhaps it was time he opened his heart again—to his son, certainly. But perhaps to Miss Crawford as well. Did he dare take the risk? He had once allowed himself to love with unashamed fervor, and it had nearly destroyed him.

He dropped into his chair once more. *Love.* So often it was described as a breathtaking, beautiful thing—the most intoxicating feeling on earth. And it was. The years Arthur had had with Lily were the most wonderful of his life. He had never known that love could be so magical, and every day it had grown sweeter. But love was also responsible for his heartache, grief, and despair. Was the pleasure worth the pain? Was he willing to taste the bitter in order to savor the sweet once more?

Arthur was not sure, and long after he should have been in bed, he continued to pace in his study, fighting to know whether his heart or his head had the stronger argument.

Madeline was in the middle of a science lesson when Arthur popped his head into the schoolroom the next day. "Forgive the interruption, Miss Crawford, but might I have a word?"

Madeline ignored the flutter in her stomach as she answered. "Of course." She set the boys to reading a portion of the lesson and followed Arthur into the hallway.

"I wondered if you had plans this afternoon," Arthur said without preamble.

"Not particularly. I take Thomas and Gus outside after luncheon for some exercise, but they are well enough on their own for a while."

"Would you like to spend some time getting to know Winston?"

The thought of entering the stable again made Madeline feel weak, and she paled.

"We could meet in the pasture this time, away from the other horses," Arthur hastened to add.

Relief coursed through her. "That sounds lovely."

"Good. Shall we say two o'clock?"

Madeline nodded, and Arthur gave her a bow before striding off down the hall. Madeline went back into the schoolroom, where Thomas and Gus were whispering together.

"Now then, back to our lesson," she said. "Thomas, can you tell me what the three properties of matter are?"

"Did Mr. Vanguard give you a horse?" he asked, ignoring her question.

"Wherever did you hear that?"

He nodded at his friend. "Gus told me."

Madeline put her hands on her hips, lifting an eyebrow at her young pupil. He ducked his head, grinning.

"I overheard the servants talking about it," he said. "Father rarely transports his horses himself, so there was quite a stir when he brought one back with him this time."

"Well, you should not give heed to idle gossip," she said, taking her seat at the table again and opening up the book they had been reading.

"But *did* he give you a horse, Maddie?" Thomas asked.

Madeline pressed her lips into a thin line. "No, he did not." Both boys slumped in their seats, but then she grinned. "He gave me a *pony.*"

Gus whooped. "I knew it!"

"Why did he give you a pony?" Thomas asked, at the same time Gus said, "He must really like you!"

Madeline flushed. "I answered your question, but the others will have to wait. Right now we are discussing the properties of matter," she said.

"But—"

"No, Thomas. Besides, business between grown-ups should not concern little boys."

"But you are afraid of horses!" Thomas blurted. Madeline gave him a stern look, and he ducked his head. "Well, you are," he said.

They resumed their lesson, and nothing else was said about it until after lunch.

"You will need to entertain yourselves this afternoon," Madeline told them as they finished their meal. "I have an appointment with Mr. Vanguard."

"What sort of appointment?" Gus asked.

"Are you going to see your pony?" Thomas said.

"Yes, I am," Madeline said. "Mr. Vanguard hopes it will help me overcome my fear of horses."

"How will it do that?"

"I am not sure, but he seems to think it can, so I may as well try."

Gus cocked his head to the side, studying her. "Do you like my father, Miss Crawford?" he asked.

Madeline cursed the heat she felt rushing to her face. "Of course I do. I like both you and your father."

"No, I meant—"

Madeline was saved from her embarrassment by the arrival of the man himself. "Miss Crawford?" Arthur said. "Are you ready?"

"Yes, thank you," Madeline replied getting to her feet. "I need only fetch my bonnet."

"Excellent. I'll meet you in the kitchen garden." He strode off, and Madeline went up to her room to fetch her hat.

They met just outside the kitchen door, which had been thrown open to enjoy the spring air. Arthur had a small bucket filled with apples and carrots and his head was bare. Madeline walked beside him as they made their way across the lawns, drinking in the clear air and trying not to think too much about where they were headed.

"I have him separated into a smaller paddock," Arthur said. "Otherwise the other horses would be crowding around as well."

"Does he come when you call?"

"No, but he'll come over to investigate, and stay for the treats. We should have plenty of time to spend with him."

The sunshine was warm on her back as they walked, and Madeline stole glances at Arthur as they went along. He seemed much more relaxed than he used to be—he did not hold himself as stiffly nor speak as sharply as he once had. He was just as handsome as ever, but when he smiled now it was genuine—it was no longer the mocking, cynical twist of his mouth he used to employ. Madeline liked this other version of him much better.

They came to the pasture and stopped by the fence. Several horses were grazing in the field beyond, and Madeline was grateful for the distance between them.

Winston saw them and came trotting over. "Hello, boy," Madeline called as he came up to them. Her heart beat a little faster, but she did not feel the same paralyzing fear she had come to expect when she was around horses.

"Give him an apple," Arthur said, handing one to her.

"How? Won't he bite me?"

"Not if you do it properly." Arthur snapped a carrot in half and placed it on his open palm. "Hold your hand flat, with the fingers together, like so. His lips will rub against your hand but not his teeth." He held the hand balancing the carrot out to Winston, who promptly ate it. Arthur looked at her. "Now you try."

Hesitantly, Madeline placed the apple on her palm. She reached her arm out, but just as Winston mouthed the apple, she snatched back her hand with a yelp. The apple fell to the ground, and Winston dropped his head to pick it up.

"Sorry," Madeline said, looking sheepish. "I got scared."

"No matter," Arthur said. "Here, let me help." He selected another apple and handed it to her, stepping closer. Madeline's heart began to pound, but whether from the thought of feeding Winston or the nearness of Arthur she was not sure.

"Open your hand and hold your palm flat," Arthur said, and as she did so, he pressed his own palm up against the back of her hand. He stepped even closer, placing his left hand at the small of her back so that she was practically cradled between his arms.

Madeline did not dare look up at him, so instead she focused on the apple. Winston had finished the last one and was looking at them with interest.

"Are you ready?" Arthur asked, his voice soft in her ear. Madeline shivered involuntarily, but nodded.

Arthur stretched out their arms, guiding their hands towards Winston's head. Madeline's heart was pounding so hard, she felt sure that Arthur could hear it. With their arms outstretched together, Madeline was tucked right up against Arthur's chest, so close she could smell the faint scent of his soap. She breathed it in, hints of cedar and sunshine filling her head.

Winston was ready and waiting for the treat, and as soon as they were near enough, the pony's velvet lips kissed her palm, snatching up the apple. Madeline barely had time to gasp before he pulled away, munching happily.

Arthur let their arms drop, and after a moment he stepped back.

The sudden distance between them made Madeline realize how much she had enjoyed their closeness. Slowly her heart rate and breathing returned to normal.

"Well done," Arthur said. "How did that feel?"

"Scary, at first," Madeline confessed. "But then it felt… I had no idea their lips were so soft."

Arthur smiled. "Yes, they are very soft. And warm."

The way he looked at her when he said it made Madeline blush. She stepped towards the fence, afraid that if she did not move away from him she might find herself doing something foolish—like kissing him.

Arthur walked up beside her, leaning his forearms on the top rail of the fence. Madeline reached her arm over to give Winston a gentle pat. The pony's ears flicked back and forth, his tail swishing occasionally.

"Better than the stables?" Arthur asked, glancing at her. She nodded.

"Much."

"Good. Perhaps tomorrow we can get in the paddock with him."

Madeline's eyes widened. "I don't think so. I'm not quite that comfortable yet."

Arthur chuckled. "No matter. We can take as much time as you need."

They stood there at the fence, their shoulders nearly touching, for a long time. At last Arthur cleared his throat, though he kept his gaze on the pony grazing nearby.

"I have spoken with the vicar," he said.

Madeline's heart lurched. What did he mean, he had spoken with the vicar? Was he declaring himself?

"About repairs to the church," Arthur continued.

"Oh!" Heat flooded Madeline's face. She was grateful he was not looking at her—what an embarrassing misjudgment! She took a slow, deep breath, willing herself to be calm.

Arthur turned around, leaning his back against the fence so he could see her. She hoped she was not still red in the face. "You were right," he said. "I have neglected my duties to the parish."

"I never said—"

"Not in so many words," he broke in, with half a smile, "but it is what you meant, all the same."

Madeline looked away, and Arthur continued. "We are going to start with the roof," he said. "And the windows and doors. Then we shall see about ordering new benches and hymnals."

"That sounds like a marvelous plan," Madeline said, turning back to face him. "Is there a local carpenter whom you could hire to make the pews? Keeping the money within the community would be more beneficial than lining the pockets of a tradesman elsewhere."

He nodded. "An excellent idea. I shall ask my steward to make inquiries in town."

"And will you allow the poor vicar to retire again and find someone else to fill his position?"

Arthur chuckled. "I have already begun the process."

"I am glad to hear it," Madeline said with a smile. "It is nice to see you taking an interest in the community."

"It is an interest that is long overdue," he said. "Thank you for bringing it to my attention."

Madeline laughed lightly. "You are thanking me for the rebuke I gave you at church?"

He chuckled. "I suppose I am."

"Then you are very welcome," she said, throwing him a saucy smile.

Arthur reached down and picked up the bucket. Winston's ears perked up and he stepped closer. "You have had enough for today," Arthur said, giving him a pat. He turned to Madeline. "I'm going to take some treats to the other horses—would you like to accompany me?"

Madeline was torn between wanting to spend more time with Arthur, and not wanting to push herself too far, too soon with regards to the horses. "I think I had better see what sort of mischief the boys have got into while I've been out," she said.

"Very well, I shall see you at dinner."

With a nod and a smile, Arthur strode off.

Chapter 21

A fortnight had passed since Arthur first accompanied them to Sunday services, and as they pulled up in front of the church, Madeline gave him a dark look.

"Step one toe out of line, sir, and there will be severe consequences."

Arthur grinned. "What sort of consequences?"

She narrowed her eyes at him. "You do not want to know."

"She is fibbing," Thomas said. "There is nothing she can do to you."

"Thomas!"

Arthur laughed. "That may be true, young man, but I'd rather avoid a verbal lashing if I can help it. Your sister has a sharp tongue."

Arthur climbed down from the carriage, then reached up to help Madeline out. As he took her hand a jolt coursed through him. "Thank you," she said, smiling down at him, and the electricity he felt at her touch spread to every inch of his body.

They entered the church and made their way to the pew. Repairs to the building had not yet begun, but Arthur's eyes swept the room, making note of anything else that needed to be addressed. A wave of guilt washed over him as he did so. Why had he let it fall into such disrepair? He never should have neglected it as he had.

He sat beside Madeline on the bench as before, the nearness of her person distracting him from his thoughts. He stole a glance at her face, but she was calmly looking towards the front, waiting for the service to begin. Was she affected by his presence at all? Did she constantly find her thoughts drifting to him, as his did to her?

There was not as much chatter from the other parishioners this week, and as the vicar stood to begin the service, Arthur leaned over.

"How am I doing, Miss Crawford?" he asked in a low voice.

"Well enough at present," she said, trying not to smile. "But let us see how you behave during the sermon."

He chuckled, sitting up straight again and turning his attention to the pulpit.

"Today's reading," the old vicar said in a quavering voice, "is taken from the fifth chapter of second Corinthians."

He began reading the passage of scripture, and Arthur let his mind wander back to his late wife. The guilt he felt at seeing the church in such a state of ruin grew to encompass the shame he carried for the other things he had neglected since Lily's passing. His son. His spirituality. His estate. His community. He closed his eyes, resolving to do better.

Something the vicar said suddenly caught his ear, and he looked up, listening.

"'…he is a new creature,'" the vicar read, "'old things are passed away; and all things are become new.'"

All things are become new. An image of Lily on their wedding day came to his mind, and he smiled sadly to himself. It had been a new beginning, a new adventure for both of them. They had been so full of hope, so excited for their future… but their future had been cut short. Arthur had never imagined a life alone after he met Lily. He had assumed they would grow old together, comfortable and happy, and he would never love another woman again.

But Lily was gone, and with her Arthur's heart. At least, he thought he had lost it along with Lily. But then Madeline Crawford came into his life like a hurricane, uprooting his grief and tearing open his heart. *Old things are passed away, and all things are become new.* The words the vicar read came back to him, and he glanced at the woman by his side. Her face was upturned, her eyes fixed on the pulpit, a soft smile resting on her lips. Was it time to let his love for Lily rest in the past, and imagine a new future with another?

"You have been very quiet this afternoon, Arthur," Madeline said at dinner. "Is something wrong?" she asked gently.

They had just dismissed the boys from the table, and it was only the two of them. Arthur swirled the wine in his glass before taking a sip. "I have been thinking a great deal about the vicar's sermon today."

Madeline's eyebrows shot up. "That is not at all what I was expecting you to say."

Arthur chuckled. "I should think not. A heathen like me, revisiting a sermon?"

"I do not think you are a heathen, Arthur," she said. He raised an eyebrow at her, and she grinned. "Anymore, at least."

He chuckled again, but in the quiet that followed he grew more sober. Madeline sat calmly watching him, her hands folded in her lap, an expectant look upon her face. Arthur finished the last of his wine and set the empty glass back on the table before he spoke.

"The vicar spoke of letting go of old things to make way for what is new."

Madeline frowned. "Did he? I don't recall his sermon touching on that. I thought he spoke about the immortal glory we shall obtain after this life, if we follow the Lord here on Earth."

"It was something in the reading—it must have been a passing phrase—but it has not left my mind since," Arthur said.

She watched him in silence for a time, but at last he shook his head. "It does not matter. I only meant to explain my distraction today."

Madeline nodded, then rose from the table. "I understand. But if you find yourself in need of a friend to talk to," she smiled at him, "you know where to find me."

Chapter 22

Arthur and Madeline spent every afternoon of the following week together with Winston. Soon Madeline was comfortable enough to stand in the paddock with the pony, and she could feed him treats on her own. Her heart still raced around the other horses, but the time spent with Winston was certainly helping.

Arthur taught her the names and function of each piece of tack. She learned how to saddle Winston, but was too afraid to fit the bridle and halter over his head. "What if he bites me while I'm trying to get the bit in his mouth?" she said one afternoon.

"He won't bite," Arthur replied.

"I am not even going to ride him," Madeline said dismissively, "so I do not see the point of all this."

"You *will* ride him, some day," Arthur insisted. "And the more comfortable you get touching and handling him now, the easier it will be to learn to ride later."

After an hour's worth of lessons, they decided to call it a day and started back towards the house. The butler was waiting for them at the door. "There are a gentleman and lady waiting for you in the drawing room, miss," he said with a bow.

"For me?" Madeline said, surprised. "I was not expecting any visitors. Did they give you their names?"

"Mr. and Mrs. Richard Dennison, miss."

The color drained from Madeline's face. "Oh," she said weakly.

Arthur frowned. "That name is familiar. Who are they?"

Madeline swallowed, her mouth full of cotton. "My aunt and uncle."

Arthur turned to the servant. "Please inform the Dennisons that we will be with them shortly," he said. The butler bowed and retreated as Arthur turned back to Madeline. "You need to sit," he said gently, taking her by the elbow. "You look as though you might faint."

But Madeline shook her head. "No, I am well. Let us get this over with."

Arthur raised an eyebrow. "Over with? You think it will end that quickly?"

Madeline managed a weak smile. "Perhaps that is wishful thinking."

"It is certainly wishful thinking," Arthur said, taking her hand and placing it in the crook of his arm. "Come—we shall face the dragon together."

The walk to the drawing room was one of the longest of Madeline's life. They paused before the doors, and she drew a breath, looking up at Arthur. He smiled at her and squeezed her hand, then opened the door for them to enter.

A petite woman with more silver than brown in her hair sat on the sofa, looking up at the man who stood beside her. He, too, had silver at his temples and streaked through his dark hair, but he was taller and of larger build than his wife. Both of them looked over at the door as it opened, and the woman stood.

Madeline managed a smile. "Good day, Aunt Ellen." She turned to Arthur. "Mr. Vanguard, may I present my aunt and uncle, Mr. and Mrs. Dennison," Madeline said.

"How do you do," Arthur said with a slight bow.

Madeline's aunt nodded, but her uncle made no indication that he heard or even acknowledged Arthur's presence.

"Madeline," he said, his brow furrowed, "have you any idea the trouble and anxiety you have caused?"

Madeline looked down. "Forgive me, Uncle. I had hoped that my letter to Aunt upon our arrival would set you both at ease."

He snorted. "At ease? It only served to fan the flames! What possessed you to leave the safety of our home and take your brother away from our protection?"

"Please, Uncle, will you not be seated? I am sure we can—"

"I will not," he thundered. His wife reached out a hand and touched his arm, but he ignored her.

Arthur narrowed his eyes. "Sir, you will please control your voice when speaking to a lady."

Mr. Dennison glared at him. "I would like to speak with my niece alone, if you don't mind."

"Unfortunately I do mind," Arthur said coolly. "Seeing as this is my house, and she is my employee."

Mr. Dennison scoffed. "Employee? Come now, sir, do not make me discuss such indelicate matters in front of my wife."

Mrs. Dennison gasped, and Madeline turned bright red. Arthur took a step forward, his eyes flashing. "One more insult, sir, and I will have you bodily removed from the premises, is that understood?"

The two men glared at each other, but at last Madeline's uncle folded his arms and looked away. The tension in the air was thick, and Madeline felt sick to her stomach. She was grateful that Arthur stood beside her.

At last Mrs. Dennison cleared her throat. "Madeline, I should like some tea, if you please."

"Of course." Madeline went to the bell pull and rang for a servant, then once again invited her aunt and uncle to be seated. Madeline and her aunt took their seats, but the gentlemen remained standing. Soon a maid came in bearing a tea tray, and after thanking her, Madeline began pouring out.

"Your tea, aunt," she said, handing a cup and saucer to the older woman. "Cream but no sugar."

The lines around Mrs. Dennison's mouth softened almost imperceptibly. "You remember how I take my tea."

"Of course." Madeline poured some tea for Arthur and her uncle, though the latter refused his, before pouring a cup for herself. She added some sugar and cream and stirred it quietly.

"So," Arthur said, moving to stand closer to Madeline's chair, "was there a particular reason for your visit, Mrs. Dennison? Or did you merely wish to drop in on your niece and have tea?"

Mrs. Dennison blinked. "We have come to take her home, of course."

Arthur raised his brow in polite surprise. "I was not aware that Miss Crawford wished to leave. She seems to be quite settled here."

Madeline took a sip from her tea to hide a smile. She knew he was playing the farce for her benefit, but she also knew her aunt and uncle would be less amused.

Arthur turned to Madeline. "Miss Crawford? Are you displeased with your position? Would you like to return to London with your aunt and uncle?"

"No, thank you," she said politely, giving him a small smile. "As you said, I am quite settled here."

"Well then," Arthur said, turning to face her aunt once more, "if that was your sole reason in coming, I suppose there is nothing more to discuss."

"Of course there is!" Mrs. Dennison cried. She pressed her lips together in a look with which Madeline was very familiar. "Madeline. Surely you can see the impropriety of this arrangement. You belong at home—with us—in London." Her forehead pinched together. "I am sure you are aware of the damage to your reputation your actions have already caused, but I will do what I can to smooth things over. We may yet be able to find a position for you."

Madeline took another sip of her tea, the familiar warmth bringing her comfort and courage. "Thank you, Aunt, for your concern. But I assure you, I am in no danger here, and I am quite happy with my situation at present. Please do not concern yourself any longer with my welfare—Mr. Vanguard is an excellent man and a fair employer. I am quite content."

"This is nonsense," Mr. Dennison said, breaking his silence, "and I've had enough of it. Madeline, collect your things at once, and Thomas, too. We are leaving."

Madeline set her teacup on the table, steeling herself for what was coming. "No," she said.

The veins on her uncle's neck stood out as his face turned red.

"No? Good heavens child, I am not asking you, I am telling you! Go at once."

Madeline felt her temper rising, but she kept her voice calm as she answered. "I am not a child, Uncle. I am now of age and am thus beyond your control. Nothing you say will change my mind, so I must ask you not to press me any further on this subject." She clasped her hands together in her lap to keep them from trembling.

"Madeline, I don't think—"

"Quiet, Ellen," Mr. Dennison said, cutting off his wife. "If she will not accept the kindness and generosity of her only kin, let it be upon her own head." He narrowed his eyes at Madeline. "But I am still your brother's guardian, and he *will* be going back with us. Go fetch him. Now."

The color drained from Madeline's face. "You cannot take Thomas," she said, her voice barely a whisper.

Her uncle's face twisted into a sneer. "I can, and I will."

Madeline turned pleading eyes on her aunt, but the older woman would not meet her gaze. Desperate, Madeline turned to Arthur, who was standing with his arms folded across his chest, watching Mr. Dennison.

"Mr. Crawford is as settled here as his sister," he said carefully. "He is a great friend to my son, and I'd rather not disrupt my household at present by sending him away."

"I don't care whether your household is disrupted or not, sir," Mr. Dennison said. "I know my rights, and as his guardian I demand that he be brought to me."

Madeline jumped to her feet. "You cannot take Thomas!" she cried again. Arthur took a step towards her and she whirled to face him, turning her back on her aunt and uncle. "He cannot take

Thomas," she whispered, her voice cracking. "Please."

"Let me handle this, Madeline," he murmured, just loud enough for her to hear. Stepping around her to face the Dennisons, Arthur cleared his throat. "In spite of my hospitality, you continue to upset Miss Crawford and make demands upon my household with which I am not willing to comply. I must, therefore, ask you kindly to take your leave."

His words were polite, but his face was stone. Madeline, her eyes wide, looked from Arthur to her uncle, wondering how he would take the barely-concealed threat.

"I will not be dictated to, Vanguard," he growled.

"And yet, you dictate to others with practiced ease," Arthur said coolly.

Mr. Dennison curled his lip disdainfully. "I am the legal guardian of Thomas Crawford and I will not leave without my charge."

Arthur placed his hands behind his back. "I see. Then you were not made aware of recent events by Mr. Gillingham?"

"Of course I was. That is why we are here."

"I do not mean regarding Miss Crawford's whereabouts, nor her inheritance—which I'm sure you had simply forgotten to tell her about?" He lifted an eyebrow at the other gentleman, whose neck turned red but who made no reply. Arthur nodded knowingly. "I meant the recent business he conducted with my solicitor."

Three pairs of eyes stared at him, but it was Madeline's gaze he returned. "Since young Thomas Crawford is now residing in my home and under my protection, I felt it best to take certain actions in order to make his residence more permanent." He turned to watch the Dennison's reaction as he continued. "My solicitor drew up the papers, and the petition to become his legal guardian has already been presented to the court. You have no further claim on either of my guests, so I ask you once again to please take your leave."

It was silent for the length of time it took Madeline to draw a single shocked breath before the room erupted. Her uncle swore, her aunt shrieked, and Madeline could not help but laugh. Her eyes, shining with tears, never left Arthur's. He met her gaze with a soft smile, and Madeline was flooded with warmth.

"Outrageous!" her uncle shouted. "Arrogant, presumptuous—"

"That is quite enough, sir," Arthur said, raising his voice to match Mr. Dennison's.

"You put him up to this, you little chit," Madeline's uncle said, rounding on her with a snarl.

Arthur's fist flashed out, colliding with Mr. Dennison's nose with a sickening crunch. He stumbled backwards as both women screamed.

"Out!" Arthur shouted. "Get out, Dennison!" He grasped Madeline's elbow and pulled her behind him, placing himself between her and her uncle. Mr. Dennison glared at them, blood dripping from his nose.

"This is not finished, Vanguard," he said.

"It is for now," Arthur said, his voice dangerously low. "Now get out."

Madeline's uncle pressed a handkerchief to his face as he shoved past them, his sobbing wife trailing along behind him.

Trembling, Madeline reached out and touched Arthur's arm. He did not turn, but instead kept his eyes fixed on the open door and the sounds of yelling and crying coming from down the hallway. She heard the front door open and slam, then all was quiet.

Arthur relaxed and turned to face her, but before he could speak Madeline threw her arms around his neck.

"You were wonderful!" she cried. "Thank you. Thank you so much."

Madeline felt his arms reach slowly around her, and her stomach flipped. "For hitting your uncle?" he said, a smile in his voice.

She laughed, leaning her forehead against his shoulder. "For what you did for Thomas. For what you did for *me.*"

She tipped her head back to look up at him and found his face mere inches from her own. She drew a startled breath and froze, her eyes locked on his.

Arthur stared at her intently, his eyes darting to her lips and back again. Blood rushed to Madeline's face and she felt her cheeks grow hot.

"Would you care to tell me why you are blushing, Miss Crawford?" he murmured.

Madeline let out a breathless laugh. "I... I thought you were about to kiss me," she said.

"Would you like me to kiss you?"

Yes, yes! Madeline's heart cried. But she hesitated. Kissing Arthur would change everything between them, and she did not know if she was ready for that. So many things had already happened, so many things had already changed, and what if—

But she did not get to finish her thought. Arthur's mouth pressed against hers, firm and sure. She gasped, but the sound was cut off as he kissed her again. Madeline's heart pounded in her chest, her lips tingling where they were pressed against his. As suddenly as he started, Arthur drew back, but his arms did not release her.

"My apologies," he said, though he did not look the least bit sorry. "I should have waited for you to answer."

"Yes," Madeline said, the heady feeling from her first kiss making her slightly dizzy.

A smile tugged at Arthur's mouth. "Yes I should have waited, or yes you wanted me to kiss you?"

Madeline pressed her hands gently against Arthur's chest, pushing away from him. He released her immediately, and she took a step back, drawing a shaky breath. "I'll let you know when I sort that out myself," she said, and he chuckled. "For now, I... I think I'd like to go lie down."

Arthur nodded. "Of course."

Madeline walked towards the open door. "Thank you, Arthur," she said, turning back at the threshold.

His eyes were warm when they met her gaze, and her stomach flipped again. "My pleasure, Madeline," he replied.

Chapter 23

Madeline awoke to a darkened room. She sat up, disoriented, until the events of the afternoon came rushing back to her. She had gone upstairs with the intention of resting a half-hour, but judging from the faded light in the room, she had slept much longer.

She rose from her bed and went to the window. Drawing back the curtains, she looked out at the dimming light. The sky was purple, with only a faint line of lighter blue along the horizon. Turning to the washbasin, she splashed her face with water and checked her appearance in the mirror.

The house was quiet when she emerged from her room. Making her way downstairs, Madeline entered the drawing room to find Thomas and Gus bent over a puzzle. They looked up at her entrance.

"Maddie!" Thomas cried. "There you are."

"Hello, Thomas. Gus. Why did no one wake me?"

Her brother shrugged, turning back to the puzzle. "Mr. Vanguard said we should let you rest. Are you feeling better?"

"Yes, I was only tired. Did I miss dinner?"

"Not yet," Gus said, placing a piece in line with the larger image.

"Maddie," Thomas said, his look growing sober, "did you know that Aunt and Uncle Dennison were here?"

Madeline nodded. "I did. How did you hear of their visit?"

"Gus told me."

She turned to the other boy, who shrugged. "One of the maids said they came."

Madeline shook her head. "Gus, you must teach me the secret to gleaning information from the servants. It is a skill that would serve me well."

"What did they want?" Thomas asked, his voice heavy with concern. Madeline opened her arms, and Thomas went to her.

"They wanted us to return to London," Madeline said, embracing her brother.

"We don't have to go, do we?"

"Of course not. I am quite happy here in Yorkshire, aren't you?"

"Very happy," Thomas said, squeezing her tightly.

Madeline leaned down and kissed the top of his head. "Then there is no cause for concern."

Thomas looked up at her and smiled, then released her to return to the puzzle. Madeline turned to Gus. "Is your father around?" she asked.

Gus nodded. "He is in his study."

Madeline thanked him and made her way down the hall.

"Come," Arthur called in response to her knock.

She opened the door and stuck her head inside. "May I come in?"

Arthur stood from his place behind the desk. "Of course. How are you feeling?"

"Better, thank you."

She noticed that his right hand was bandaged and she frowned. "What happened to your hand?"

He chuckled. "Do you not remember? I hit a scoundrel in the face with it."

"Oh!" Her hands flew to her mouth. "I did not realize—of course you would have injured yourself. I am so sorry! Does it hurt a great deal?"

Arthur shrugged, but she saw him wince as he tried to stretch out his fingers. "It is quite swollen and tender, but it will heal."

He came around the desk as she stepped closer. "Was there something you needed?" he asked.

Madeline looked down. "No, I just…" *I just wanted to see you.* "I just wanted to thank you again for becoming Thomas's guardian," she said.

"It is not a settled thing," Arthur said. "I wanted your uncle to think it was, but the courts have yet to grant me official guardianship. I must travel to London in a few weeks' time for the hearing."

Madeline bit her lip. "Do you think it will be granted?"

"I do. Your uncle and I are of equal station and fortune—if anything, I may have the upper hand in that regard. That is all the courts are concerned about when assigning guardianship. And since Thomas lives here now, it is likely they will grant the petition."

"I hope so," Madeline said.

"Would you like to tell your brother about it?" Arthur asked. "There is still time to withdraw the petition if he is averse to the idea."

Madeline smiled. "Nothing will delight him more, I am sure. Come," she said, holding out her hand to him, "let us tell him together."

Arthur took her hand, rubbing his thumb gently across her knuckles. Her heart skittered, and she glanced up at him. His look was intense, and she wondered if he, like she, was thinking of their kiss earlier.

But Madeline was not yet ready to explore those feelings. She tugged gently on his arm, leading him back to the drawing room.

Thomas and Gus had just completed the puzzle when Arthur and Madeline arrived. Gus looked up at their entrance, then frowned as he noticed the bandage.

"What happened to your hand, Father?"

Arthur and Madeline exchanged glances. "My fist collided with a hard object," he said wryly. "But it will heal, soon enough."

Thomas went to his sister, who asked him to sit beside her on the settee. Gus sat on the other side of him, and they all looked up at Arthur, who cleared his throat.

"Thomas," he said, "there is a question I would like to ask you."

Thomas glanced at his sister, who gave him a quick smile and nodded. He turned back to Arthur. "Yes, Mr. Vanguard?"

"How would you like to make Milford Manor your permanent home?"

Thomas frowned. "I thought it already was."

"What Mr. Vanguard means to say," Madeline said, "is that he would like your permission to become your guardian."

"Your sister is correct," Arthur said. "According to your father's solicitor, you are the heir to an inheritance, and as such, you are required by law to have a guardian to manage such property for you until you come of age. Currently, your guardian is your Uncle Dennison, but if you do not mind, I would like to request a transfer of guardianship to myself."

"I have an inheritance?" Thomas turned to his sister. "Do you?"

Madeline smiled, her throat growing tight. "I do. It seems Papa was looking out for our futures without us even knowing."

"Is it a large sum?"

"I am not sure of the particular amount," Arthur said.

"Nor does it matter," Madeline added, lifting an eyebrow at her brother, who ducked his head.

"What matters is whether or not you would like me to become your guardian, and to make York your permanent home," Arthur said.

Thomas looked to Gus, who grinned at him and nodded. Thomas smiled. "I would like that very much, sir."

Madeline insisted that they put their afternoon lessons on hold until Arthur recovered, but Arthur argued that all their hard work would be for naught if they took a week or two off. Madeline suspected that he was only trying to find an excuse to continue spending time with her each day, but since she wanted the same thing, she allowed herself to be persuaded.

Each day Madeline grew a little more comfortable, a bit more confident in her movements around the little pony, and just as Arthur had predicted, it helped her overcome her fear of horses. She could climb into and out of the carriage now with ease, and walking through the stables no longer caused her anxiety. She still did not wish to feed or handle the other horses, but as her relationship with Winston grew, her fear for the others subsided.

For several days following the visit from her aunt and uncle, there was little Arthur could do with his hand, which gave Madeline ample opportunity to practice what she had learned. She fed Winston treats and brushed his coat. She practiced putting on and taking off his saddle and harness—including the bit and bridle. She fed him, walked him, and learned commands, but still she would not ride him.

"I am not ready," she said one afternoon, when Arthur mentioned it again.

"You have been saying that for weeks," he replied.

They had finished in the pasture for the day, and Madeline was leading Winston back to the stables while Arthur walked beside her.

"You have learned all there is to know that I can teach you whilst unmounted, but now we must get you in the saddle."

"Not yet," Madeline said, leading Winston into the stall and turning him around. Arthur shut the door, remaining on the outside, while Madeline stood inside and undid the buckles of the harness. "Besides, I cannot possibly ride him while you remain on the ground. I would want you on a mount beside me. And you cannot yet ride with your injured hand."

Arthur rested his forearms on the edge of the door. "Then when my hand is healed, may we begin mounted lessons?"

Madeline hung the harness on a nail and picked up the brush. Slowly she began stroking it along the length of Winston's body. "Perhaps," she said, not looking at Arthur.

He sighed, shaking his head. "Madeline, you are the most stubborn woman I have ever met."

She narrowed her eyes at him. "I could say the same thing about you, you know."

He chuckled, and she finished brushing Winston in silence. Giving him a final pat, she let herself out of the stall and looked up into Arthur's face. His smile was gentle as he lifted her hand and pressed a kiss upon her knuckles. Her heart stuttered, and she let out a breathless laugh.

"What was that for?" she asked.

Arthur released her hand, giving her a soft smile. "Have you given any thought to what I asked you in the drawing room after your aunt and uncle came to call?"

Madeline flushed. "I have."

Arthur stepped towards her, closing the distance between them. Madeline's pulse shot up, her skin tingling in anticipation of his touch.

"And?"

They were so close Madeline felt sure Arthur could hear her heart pounding. He reached up with his uninjured hand to touch her cheek. Madeline swallowed.

"And... I do not mind that you kissed me," she said.

Arthur let out a low chuckle. "That is not the same thing as *wanting* me to kiss you, Madeline." When she made no reply, he tipped her chin up. "Shall I ask you again?" He traced his thumb along her jaw. "Madeline Crawford," he murmured, "would you like me to kiss you?"

Madeline closed her eyes. "Yes," she breathed.

She waited, trembling... but nothing happened. Her eyes fluttered open, and to her surprise, he was no longer smiling.

"I'm sorry, Madeline. I... I don't know how to be with you," he said, his brow furrowing. "It is one thing to train a horse, but quite another to train a heart. I'm not sure how to go about it."

Madeline reached up and placed her hand over his. "Then it is a good thing I am an excellent teacher," she said.

Stretching up on her toes, she brushed a kiss, soft and sweet, against his lips. When she dropped back onto her heels, Arthur placed his other hand gently on her cheek, cupping her face. Slowly he bent his head to meet hers.

Madeline had been so surprised at Arthur's kiss the week before that she had not had much opportunity to enjoy it. But this! This was everything she ever imagined a kiss to be. His lips pressed against hers, gentle but sure. He drew back for a moment, only to kiss her again, and again. His lips traveled up her jawline and back, brushing along her neck, and Madeline felt her stomach quiver. His kisses grew more soft, and his good hand moved to press against the small of her back, holding her close. Madeline wrapped her arms around his neck, twining her fingers in his hair. All she could think about was how perfect this moment was, and how desperately she wanted to keep kissing him.

"Madeline," Arthur murmured, breaking away from her for a moment. "I don't know how… I cannot…"

She pulled his face down to meet hers again, her mouth exploring his lips, her heart beating erratically in her chest. He moaned, and Madeline cupped his face, pressing one last kiss, long and lingering, to his lips.

Slowly Madeline opened her eyes, and was shocked to see that the look on Arthur's face did not reflect the joy and excitement she felt herself. It was wary, nervous, even a little ashamed.

"I…" He swallowed. "I should not have kissed you."

The elation Madeline had felt came crashing down, landing in a leaden heap in her gut. Arthur stepped back, taking a deep breath and turning away from her.

"Oh," she whispered, unable to meet his eyes.

"I am sorry, Madeline. So sorry," he said. She looked up at him, and his eyes were earnest. Sincere. She could see that he cared for her, and yet, something was clearly troubling him.

He shook his head angrily. "I should not have—" He broke off, running his good hand up through his hair. "I'm so confused," he murmured, closing his eyes.

"Confused?"

"Yes." He opened his eyes and looked at her. "I care about you, Madeline, truly, I do. But my heart..." He sighed, his shoulders slumping. "I gave my heart to Lily. I don't know that I ever got it back."

Madeline was quiet for a long time, trying to soothe the ache in her chest long enough to answer him without bursting into tears. "I am not trying to take her place, Arthur," she said quietly.

"I know that," he said. "But..." He reached out and gently pulled her chin up, forcing her to look at him. "But I don't know if there is room enough for both of you in my heart."

Madeline nodded, wrapping her arms around her torso, desperate to hold herself together. "I understand," she said quietly. "And I don't want to make you choose."

They were silent for several minutes, each lost in their own thoughts, until Madeline cleared her throat.

"Why don't you take some time, Arthur," she said, "to examine your heart and your feelings. There is no rush, and no need to move forward unless that is what you want."

Relief washed over his face. "Yes," he said. "Yes—I need some time."

She smiled sadly at him. "Take all the time you need. I shall be here waiting when you have made a decision."

She stepped forward and brushed a kiss on his cheek, then turned and left the stables.

Chapter 24

Madeline cried herself to sleep that night. She did not realize she had already lost her heart to Arthur until he confessed that he could not give her his own. But she awoke in the morning resolved to cherish the friendship they had formed, whether or not it led to something more.

Their days followed the same routine as before: lessons with the boys in the morning, lessons with Arthur and Winston in the afternoon. Arthur acted as if neither kiss had happened, and Madeline found that, with only minimal embarrassment, she could as well. She was relieved to find that their friendship remained intact.

"I have received a letter from my solicitor," Arthur said one afternoon as he and Madeline walked in the gardens. "I am wanted in London on Thursday next, when my petition will be presented to the court."

Madeline nodded. "How long will you be gone?"

"No more than a few days, I would imagine," he said, placing his hands behind his back. "I am hoping it will not be a long, drawn-out process, though I imagine I will need to meet with Mr. Gillingham afterwards to go over your brother's account."

The day was warm but damp, and though it was not raining, the sky overhead was dreary and gray. Madeline turned her head to watch as Thomas and Gus raced a hoop down one of the garden paths.

"And if it becomes a long, drawn-out process?" she asked.

Arthur sighed. "Then it will be a lonely few weeks in London," he said. One corner of his mouth pulled up in a grin. "There was a time when I would have enjoyed the solitude. But it appears I have grown accustomed to certain company."

Madeline ignored the flutter in her middle at his words. "It does not have to be lonely," she said with a smile. "It is the middle of the Season, after all. I am sure that the minute your friends and acquaintances discover you are in town, you will have invitations to more balls and parties than you care to attend."

"It has been so long since I attended a supper party, and even longer since I attended a ball, I would not remember how to behave."

Madeline laughed lightly. "Then I insist that you practice while you are there. You cannot always keep the company of horses— your social manners must be kept sharp as well."

Arthur chuckled. They continued through the garden until they came to a bench in sight of the area where the boys were playing. Madeline sat down and Arthur sat beside her. He reached his right hand out in front of him, opening and closing his fist slowly. Madeline watched him.

"Is it getting any better?" she asked.

"Slowly," he said. "I still cannot fit a glove on my hand, and it is painful to make a fist or hold anything of substance. But I am not concerned. It will continue to improve."

Gus ran over to them, and they both looked up at his approach. "Father, may we have a picnic?" he asked.

"That is an excellent idea," Arthur said. "I must away to London next week, so let us plan the picnic before I leave."

Gus cheered, then ran off to tell Thomas. Madeline smiled at Arthur. "A picnic?" she said.

"Indeed," he replied, his eyes dancing. "And I know just the place."

The date for the picnic was set for the following Tuesday. Gus and Thomas put their heads together as soon as they returned to the house, making a list of the foods they wanted the cook to provide, then took it to Mrs. Whittecombe. When Madeline heard what they had done, she went down to the kitchen to apologize.

"Nonsense!" the jolly cook said when she understood Madeline's errand. "Filling bellies and filling hearts is what I like best," she said. "Besides, young Mr. Crawford put in a request for a few of your favorite treats as well." She winked at Madeline and shooed her out of the kitchen, insisting she was busy.

Madeline went in search of the housekeeper when she left the kitchen. She found her in the breakfast room going over the accounts.

"Mrs. MacLeod, might I have a word?" she asked.

"Of course," came the reply. "I was wondering when I might see ye."

"Have you been expecting me?"

"Aye, and I expect I know what ye'll be asking. Ye want to visit Mrs. Vanguard's studio again, don't ye?"

Madeline smiled. "I do. I have not had much opportunity to do so, since Arth—" she blushed, "since Mr. Vanguard has not gone away for some time. But he will be going to London shortly, and I wondered if you would let me into the studio while he is away so that I can finish the sketch I started."

The housekeeper sighed. "Och, I'm afraid I cannae do so, Miss. I'll be attendin' Mr. Vanguard to London."

Madeline's eyebrows shot up. "You are going with him?"

"Aye. Mr. Vanguard's townhouse has been shut up for so long, there's no telling what the place needs to make it livable. I'm leaving first thing tomorrow morning with a few other servants to get started on it."

"Oh. I see." Madeline bit her lip, considering. "Will there be someone else here that you would trust to let me in?" she asked.

"Not a single one 'o the servants," Mrs. MacLeod said, and Madeline's heart sank. "But... well, I trust *ye,* Miss Crawford. And if ye promise not to let young Master Augustus in with ye, and to keep the room exactly as ye find it, and to lock the door after ye... well, I suppose I can leave ye the key."

"Oh, thank you, Mrs. MacLeod!" Madeline cried, clapping her hands together. "I promise, just as you said. I cannot wait to see Gus's face when I finish the likeness."

The housekeeper removed the key to Lily's studio and handed it to Madeline. "Protect this with your life, Miss Crawford," she said.

Madeline clutched it in her hand, holding it close to her heart. "I will," she said. "I promise."

It rained the whole of Sunday, and continued into Monday. Thomas and Gus fretted over their picnic the next day, but Tuesday morning dawned bright and clear. Everyone was in the best of spirits at breakfast.

"Where shall we have our picnic?" Gus asked between bites.

"I thought we could take Miss Crawford and Thomas down to the pond," Arthur said.

"Oh yes!" Gus cried. "We have not been to the pond in ages!"

"What pond?" Thomas asked.

"There is a large pond a few miles from the house," Gus said. "All sorts of waterfowl live there, and Father took me fishing there once." He beamed up at Arthur, who smiled indulgently.

"Yes, but we won't be fishing today. We will bring the nine pins, and you and Thomas can fly your kite. We shall leave as soon as you are finished with your lessons."

The boys wolfed down the rest of their breakfast, badgering Madeline to hurry up so they could do their schoolwork. For the first time in ages, Madeline did not have to encourage the boys to finish their lessons. They paid attention and did their work without complaint, and Madeline teased that they should have a picnic every day if that is all the motivation they needed.

At last their lessons were finished, and they made their way down to the kitchen, where they were to meet Arthur. He came in from the garden just as they arrived.

"Finished already?" he asked when the boys trooped in.

"Yes! Is it time to go?" Gus asked.

Arthur laughed. "Almost. There are a few things left to pack."

They followed him out the door, where they found Winston attached to a small yellow cart, piled high with all of their picnic things. Madeline clapped her hands in delight.

"How wonderful!" she cried.

"Your pony!" Gus said.

They all walked over to the cart, and Gus gave Winston's side a pat. "We have seen him out in the pasture, but I'm not allowed in the stables. He is smaller than I realized."

Winston whinnied and she laughed. "I think he is perfect," Madeline said, rubbing his nose. Thomas's eyes grew wide.

"Maddie, look at you!"

Madeline grinned. "Is it not a miracle? And all thanks to Mr. Vanguard."

Arthur smiled. "You have done the work to overcome your fears yourself, Madeline. I only supplied the means and method."

Thomas came forward to stroke Winston's neck as Arthur went back inside to fetch a few last minute items. "He called you Madeline," Thomas said quietly. "Does that mean you are friends now?"

Madeline tousled her brother's hair. He had grown taller, and soon she would not be able to do so anymore. "Yes, Thomas. We are friends now."

"I'm glad," he said.

Arthur returned carrying a large basket covered with a blue cloth. "That is the last of it," he said. "Shall we go?"

The four of them started off, with Arthur leading the way and a footman guiding Winston behind them. The boys scampered ahead of Arthur and Madeline, stopping every now and then to pick up a treasure for their pockets. The afternoon was warm and bright, and Madeline pulled at the ribbon on her bonnet. She wished she would have brought her parasol instead.

"Have you decided how you will spend your time in London?" Madeline asked Arthur as they walked along.

"I have, in fact. And I've already accepted an invitation to dinner while I am there."

"Indeed!"

He laughed at the look Madeline gave him. "Surprised?"

"Very," she replied. "Though I am pleased, of course."

Arthur shrugged. "It will not be a major social gathering. My sister-in-law, Mrs. Weber, lives there with her husband and family. We are not very close—I was at school and she was already married when my father married her mother. But I often see her when I go to town, and she has extended an invitation to dine with them while I am there."

"I am glad of it," Madeline said, giving him a smile.

"The hearing is scheduled for Friday, and if all goes well, the authorization should be signed and I will be home again a few days later. I will send word when it is known what the courts have decided."

"Thank you," Madeline said. "I would appreciate that very much."

The walk to the pond was not overly taxing. Once beyond the manicured lawns of the house, they crossed a large meadow before coming to a small wood. This they skirted, moving further west until a larger path through the trees allowed easier passage for the pony and wagon. Birds and squirrels chattered at them from the treetops as they walked along, last year's leaves crunching underfoot.

At last they came to the pond. It was so large it might have been considered a small lake. Ducks and geese swam along its surface, the sun's light dancing in their wakes.

"What a beautiful spot," Madeline said upon seeing it.

"There is a clearing further to the north," Arthur said. "Now that we are through the thickest of the trees it will be easier to get there."

They followed him along the edge of the water until they came to a small grassy field on a higher bit of ground. It was set further back from the pond but allowed an excellent view of the water. The footman started unloading things from the wagon while Madeline and the boys went down to the shore.

"Look what I found, Maddie," Thomas said, pulling a smooth, flat stone roughly the size of a walnut from his pocket. "Mr. Vanguard said he will teach Gus and me how to skip stones across the water."

Arthur walked up in time to hear this announcement. "Indeed I will," he said. "But first, shall we eat? I'm feeling rather hungry after all that walking."

They agreed, and climbed back to where a few chairs and a small coaching table had been set up for their repast. Mrs. Whittecombe had outdone herself. There were meat pies and pastries, sausage rolls, tarts, cold cuts of ham and beef, pickled vegetables, dried fruits, and several kinds of cheeses.

"Everything tastes better when eaten out of doors, does it not?" Madeline asked, taking a bite of tart. The boys nodded, their mouths too full to reply.

"I don't believe I have had a picnic in years," Arthur said, taking a sip of cider. "We must do this more often."

After they had eaten, Arthur went down to the water with the boys to teach them how to skim a stone across the surface of the pond. Madeline observed from her chair, laughing when Thomas and Gus's stones sank on the first toss. Arthur demonstrated over and over, and she smiled as she watched them.

Suddenly a small bird with a bright red breast landed on the grass in front of her. He cocked his head at her, hopping to and fro.

"Hello there," she said. "Come to pick up the crumbs, have you?"

The robin chirped as if in reply, then began pecking at the ground. Madeline watched it quietly, until a shout from the trio at the water's edge startled it into flight. Madeline stood from her seat and went down to meet the others.

She arrived just in time to see Thomas make his stone skip on the surface.

"Maddie, Maddie! Did you see that?" he cried, jumping up and down excitedly. "I've done it twice now!"

"Wonderful job, Thomas!" she said.

Arthur stood nearby, helping Gus to position his arm properly for the toss. "Remember," he said to his son, "you want to throw the stone as horizontally as possible, so that the momentum carries the stone over the water, rather than driving it into the water."

Gus nodded, drawing back his arm and throwing the stone as hard as he could. It splashed into the water a few feet from the shore. He frowned.

"Never mind, son." Arthur said. "Just keep trying until you get the feel for it."

Leaving the boys to practice their new skill, Arthur and Madeline walked further along the shore. "This is such a beautiful spot," Madeline said.

"Lily loved it here as well," Arthur said. "Perhaps that is why I do not come very often."

Madeline studied him for a moment. "It does not seem to be as painful for you to speak of her as it once was," she said.

Arthur did not immediately reply. She watched him quietly, and eventually he nodded. "I still miss her. But yes, it is easier to speak of her. Somehow, it has helped to share pieces of her with you." He gave her a soft smile.

"Gus continues to ask me about her," Madeline said. "I told him everything you told me before, on our ride back from York."

Arthur sighed. "I wish he could have had more time with her. She was a wonderful mother."

"He wants to remember her," Madeline said. "Perhaps you can share more with him sometime."

They came to a fallen log near the shore and sat down. Madeline watched a brood of ducklings swimming haphazardly behind their mother around the edge of the pond.

"I have given some thought to the counsel you gave me last week," Arthur said, picking up a leaf from the ground.

Madeline's stomach rolled over. She was not sure she was ready to hear what he had to say, but she folded her hands in her lap, waiting for him to continue.

"I think of Lily every day," Arthur said at last. "And I miss her terribly. But the truth is, Madeline, that I cannot stop thinking about you." As he spoke, he tore up the leaf into little pieces, methodically dropping them onto the ground until nothing remained. He brushed off his hands and looked over at her. "For weeks I have not known what to do, but your advice has helped me determine a course of action." He reached over and gently picked up her hand, pressing a kiss on the back of it. A thrill coursed through her at his touch, and Madeline had to remind her heart not to get too excited.

"I am going to follow your suggestion, and take advantage of my time alone in London to examine my feelings," he said. "It would not be fair to either of us if I cannot give you my whole heart. When I am with you, as we are now, I want nothing more than to take you in my arms and never let go. But when I am alone again in my room, with only my thoughts and my memories for company..." He swallowed. "I need to know if I can let go of my love for Lily. If I can let it rest in the past instead of allowing it to dictate my future."

A cloud passed before the sun as they sat there, and the sudden chill made Madeline shiver. Arthur was watching her carefully, and Madeline was mindful to keep her expression neutral.

"That sounds like a good plan," she said.

Arthur nodded. "I hope to be able to give you an answer when I return," he said.

Madeline smiled. "Then I shall look forward to it all the more."

Chapter 25

Arthur left immediately after breakfast the next day. He bid farewell to his son, shook Thomas's hand, and pressed a kiss to Madeline's knuckles as he departed. Madeline tried to focus on the boys and their lessons after he was gone, but her mind kept wandering. She felt anxious about the hearing, worrying and wondering if the courts would accept Arthur's petition and grant him guardianship. Though his request for guardianship was separate and distinct from his feelings for her, Madeline could not help but see how closely the two decisions were connected. If he was granted guardianship, but he found he could not love her, could she stay and continue to tutor his son? Would she even wish to stay?

And though she did not like to think of it, the opposite outcome provided as difficult a conundrum as well. If he chose Madeline over the memory of his late wife, and yet his petition to the courts was not granted, could she let Thomas go back to their aunt and uncle in London while she stayed in Milford with Arthur, or would she choose her brother over the wishes of her own heart? Back and forth, her head and her heart waged a war, while she tried to keep her wits about her enough to help Thomas and Gus understand the rules of grammar involved in past participial phrases.

It was a very long day.

Thursday was no better than the day before. Incessant rain kept them all indoors, and in the evening a powerful wind sprung up. It moaned and howled, whistling across the chimneys and shrieking at the windows. Thomas was so frightened that he would not go to bed unless Madeline stayed beside him all night long. She sat in an armchair, holding his hand, until the wind finally ceased and she fell asleep.

Madeline was so exhausted and stiff from spending the night sitting up with Thomas, that she canceled their lessons the next day. She soon regretted it, however, for now she had nothing to fill the long, lonely hours, knowing that the hearing was taking place in London and wondering what the outcome would be.

On Friday evening, after tucking the boys into bed, she took her sketchbook and the key Mrs. MacLeod had given her and made her way silently to the end of the second floor corridor. Once she was sure that no one else was around, she unlocked the door to Lily's studio and slipped inside.

It was dark, and Madeline had not brought a lamp. Not only that, but it was cold. The recent rain and wind had made the temperature drop, and with no fire in the grate, the room was more chilly than Madeline had anticipated. She bit her lip, considering. Should she retrieve an oil lamp to give light to the studio, or should she take the portrait back to her room, where there was warmth and light already? Since the housekeeper had not given her permission to remove the portrait, Madeline decided on the former course of action, and went to her room to retrieve the lamp there.

With light by which to see, Madeline began again on the sketch of Lily's portrait. But it was not long before her hands grew stiff from the cold, and her pencil strokes uneven. She sighed, seeing only two alternatives. The first option would be to get one of the maids to come light a fire in the room. But Madeline knew that no one else had been given permission to enter the studio, and she knew not what effect the light and heat of the fire might have on the paintings and art supplies in the room. Which left her to follow the second option, and take Lily's portrait back to her bedchamber.

I shall return the portrait the moment I finish the likeness, she thought to herself, *and no one will be the wiser.* Gathering her supplies, she made ready to leave the studio, Lily's portrait clutched in her arms.

Arthur breathed a sigh of relief as he exited the building and placed his hat upon his head. The court had granted his petition, and he was now the legal guardian of Thomas Crawford. He smiled to himself—he could not wait to send word to Madeline letting her know.

As suddenly as his excitement flared it burned out, and he sobered. He had accomplished one task, but what of the other? Madeline would expect an answer from him regarding his affections when he returned, but he was no closer to a decision on that matter than when he had arrived in London. It was true that thus far he had been occupied with the hearing, but now his resolve to spend time considering whether or not he could allow his love for Lily to make way for Madeline loomed before him. He sighed. How was he to make a choice?

"Mr. Vanguard!"

Arthur turned to see Mr. Gillingham coming down the steps behind him. "Congratulations," the man said with a grin, extending his hand.

Arthur grasped it firmly. "Thank you," he said. "I am glad to have it settled so easily."

"Easily?" The solicitor laughed. "Easy for you. You have not had to manage Mr. Dennison's temper the last few weeks." He shook his head. "After being thrust out of the courtroom today, I hate to think of the state he will be in when he next calls upon me in my office."

"I would offer my apologies, but I have none," Arthur said with a wry grin, "so I will offer my condolences instead."

They walked along the road together for a time. "I should like to discuss the particulars of Thomas Crawford's holdings with you, before I return to York," Arthur said. "When is most convenient for you?"

Mr. Gillingham was thoughtful. "I do not usually open my office on Mondays, but perhaps that would be best," he said. "Then we can be assured that Mr. Dennison will not accost us."

Arthur nodded, looking down as he flexed his fingers. "Indeed. My hand is only just recovered from our last meeting—I would hate to injure it again."

Mr. Gillingham laughed. "Then it is settled. I shall have everything ready for you on Monday."

"Excellent, thank you."

Arthur nodded, bidding him good day as they parted.

"You were very quiet at dinner this evening, Arthur," his sister Josephine said, as Arthur took the seat beside her on the settee.

"There is much on my mind," he said.

The gentlemen had recently joined the ladies in the drawing room after supper. It was a larger party than Arthur had anticipated, but he surprised himself at how easily he was able to converse with the other guests.

"More than just the hearing?" his sister asked.

Arthur nodded. "It has been nearly three years since Lily died," he said. "And while I never intended it to happen... I have met a young lady."

"Indeed!"

"Yes. She is my son's tutor."

Josephine frowned. "His tutor? But you said you had met a young lady."

"It is a long story," Arthur said. "And before you lecture me on social spheres and pedigrees, I must assure you that I am well aware of what society deems appropriate, and I do not care at all."

His sister chuckled. "Very well, I shall spare you my opinion on the subject, then."

A few of the guests formed a table of cards across the room, and they watched them in silence for a while. Josephine studied Arthur, but when he said nothing else, she nudged him on the arm.

"For having met a young lady who captures your fancy," she said, "you do not seem very happy about it."

He sighed. "I am conflicted, that is all. I would be glad of some advice."

"What is your dilemma?"

Arthur pulled at the cuff of his jacket, not looking at her as he spoke. "Miss Crawford—that is the young lady's name—has awakened in me feelings which I never thought possible to feel again. Feelings I have only ever held for my late wife."

"I see."

"Do you?" Arthur stared at her intently, "because I do not. How can I possibly hold for someone the same tender feelings that I once vowed never to share with another? It certainly feels like infidelity, even if my wife is no longer alive."

Josephine placed a hand on his arm. "Of course you feel that way, Arthur. And it does you credit. It shows a depth of feeling few men would ever allow, let alone admit." She sighed, looking around the room at the other guests as she gathered her thoughts. "Did I ever share with you what my mother told me, when I asked her why she had agreed to marry your father?"

Arthur shook his head. "I do not believe so."

"She told me that once a heart has been touched by love, it yearns to love again." Josephine gave Arthur a gentle smile. "And when I asked if her love for your father had replaced the love she felt for my father, she said no."

"But how? How did she love them both?"

Arthur's voice was so passionate that it attracted the notice of a few nearby guests. Josephine waved them off with a polite smile, and when their attention was once again diverted, she turned and answered him, though in a quieter voice.

"She told me that their love did not compete for a place in her heart, because she had a heart for each of them."

Arthur frowned. "I do not understand."

"Think of it, Arthur," his sister said, her voice earnest, "when your son was born, how did you feel? Did you love him at once?"

"I did—more than anything."

She nodded. "And did your love for your son compete with the love you felt for your wife?"

"Of course not, it—" Revelation dawned in his eyes, and his sister smiled.

"That is how, dear Arthur," she said gently. "You love them both because you have a heart for each of them. So rather than trying to fit your love for—Miss Crawford, is it?—into the heart that belongs to Lily, you must allow space in your life for a new heart that is all her own."

Arthur nodded slowly. "I think I understand."

"Good. Then I shall leave you to contemplate my words while I see to the comfort of my other guests."

Arthur stood as his sister got to her feet. "Thank you, Josie," he said, clasping her hand. "You have been immensely helpful."

Chapter 26

"Miss Crawford! Miss Crawford!"

Madeline turned towards the house from whence the call had come, shielding her face from the sun. She saw a maid waving at her from the back steps, and Madeline raised a hand to acknowledge she had heard her.

"I'll be just a moment," she said to the boys, who were playing nine pins on the lawn. She walked back to the house, her nerves twisting in her stomach like a snake.

"An express has just come, miss," the maid said, handing her an envelope with a curtsy.

"Thank you."

Madeline saw her name written in Arthur's neat hand. With heart pounding, she broke the seal and unfolded the short note.

> *Madeline,*
> *My petition was granted—Thomas is safe. I shall*

return when my business here is settled.
  - A

A flood of relief washed over her, and she steadied herself against the balustrade to prevent herself from falling to her knees. Thomas was safe! She read the note again, hardly daring to believe it was true. But she had not imagined it—Arthur's petition had been granted, and her uncle had no further claim on her brother.

She folded the note and walked back to where the boys were playing, anxious to give them the news. When Thomas saw her coming, he dropped the ball and ran to meet her. "Is it a letter from London?" he asked.

"It is. From Mr. Vanguard."

"What does it say?"

Madeline smiled. "It says that he is your new guardian."

With a cry of delight, Thomas threw his arms in the air and hugged his sister. Madeline laughed, holding him tight.

"Now we shall never have to leave!" he said.

He grinned up at her, but when he released her to return to his game, Madeline felt the smile leave her face. One obstacle had been overcome, but the outcome of the other remained to be seen. Arthur's letter had been short and concise, conveying the message he had promised to deliver but nothing more. There was no hint regarding his other assignment in London, no line of affection or suggestion that he wanted a future with her by his side. She tried not to think of it, resolved not to worry until Arthur was home and could give her an answer himself. That is what he had promised, and until he returned, she would put it from her mind.

The rest of the day passed uneventfully. They played in the

garden, enjoying the late spring sunshine, and in the evening Madeline read to the boys before tucking them in for the night.

"I am glad that Mr. Vanguard is now my guardian," Thomas said sleepily as Madeline kissed him on the forehead. "I did not want to go back to London."

"I am glad, too," Madeline said, though she was less certain about their future than Thomas seemed to be. "Now go to sleep."

Thomas murmured goodnight and rolled over, and after kissing Gus goodnight as well, Madeline went back to her room. She was anxious to get to work on her sketch again, knowing that Mr. Vanguard would soon return.

She had spent the entire evening prior in her bedchamber, working on the image for Gus. She had not completed it, however, and rather than return the portrait to the studio only to retrieve it again the following night, Madeline had left it in her room. She wrapped it carefully in an extra blanket and tucked it underneath the bed, hoping the maids would not disturb it.

It appeared they had not, and Madeline pulled it out carefully, propping it against the wall as she sat at her desk. She studied the likeness she was creating, comparing it with the painting and noting the places where she needed to add more detail or rub out a mistake. Madeline had only moderate skills as an artist, but she was determined to go as slowly and carefully as needed to create as like a sketch as possible.

Picking up her pencil, Madeline set her hand once again to the page. With any luck, she would be finished with a few more evenings' work.

Arthur was anxious to return home and left town immediately following his meeting with Mr. Gillingham on Monday. The train to York had already left for the day, so he took a train to Manchester instead. It was a bit out of the way, but it would get him home sooner than waiting for the following day to catch the direct line.

The revelation at his sister's house did not leave him. It was so simple, and merely required a shift in his perspective to make a place for Madeline in his life—her *own* place. With her own heart. The relief at not having to choose between Lily and Madeline was nearly palpable, and with every passing hour he grew more certain. Whether the feelings he had for her now were love, or whether love would come in time he did not know, but of one thing he was absolutely certain: he wanted Madeline in his life. He needed her. Gus needed her. She belonged with them, and he could not wait to get home and tell her.

He spent the night at an inn in Manchester and caught the early train to York on Tuesday. He wanted to see Madeline straight away, but he knew there was something he needed to do first. He only hoped he would arrive before her lessons were finished so he could slip past the schoolroom undetected.

Arthur arrived at the manor shortly before the midday meal and went straight to his study. Retrieving a key from his desk, he made his way to the second floor corridor. He paused outside the schoolroom, listening, until he heard the murmur of Madeline's voice, followed by one of the boys'. An overwhelming sense of comfort settled upon him, and excitement at seeing her again made his heart beat faster. But he moved on, knowing what he must do.

Arthur made his way down the hall, stopping in front of the door he had not opened in years. Fitting the key in the lock, he turned the latch and entered.

He thought that after three years he was ready to face his past, but no amount of time could have prepared him for the onslaught of memories that hit him upon his entrance to Lily's studio. It was like stepping into the hidden recesses of his heart, demanding that he face the pain he had buried long ago.

He drew a jagged breath, forcing himself to look around the room. It was exactly as he remembered it—Lily's easel set up right where she left it, an unfinished canvas waiting upon it for the hand that would never return. The rows of paint, the bundles of brushes, the stacks of canvases—even the light filtering in through the window seemed to hold an air of anticipation, as if Lily was moments away from entering the space and bringing them all back to life.

Arthur's chest grew tight as he walked slowly through the room, his hungry eyes taking everything in. They lingered on some of the canvases stacked along the floor, remembering when she had painted them and where they had hung in the house before he ordered them all removed. "Oh, Lily," he breathed, coming to a stop in front of the window, "why did you have to go?"

He sat down in a chair and dropped his head into his hands. Suddenly what had seemed so easy in his sister's drawing room now seemed impossible. The heart belonging to Lily seemed to fill his entire chest, swelling with pain until everything else was crowded out. There was not room for anything—or anyone—else.

He stood abruptly, his eyes sweeping the room, hunting for the frame that had housed his late wife's portrait. He had to see her face. He had to look in her eyes.

Walking around the room, he tipped the canvases forward to see the paintings underneath. Landscapes, still lifes, even a small portrait of himself that Lily had done early in their marriage, but he could not find the one he was searching for.

Panic was just beginning to set in when he heard the scrape of metal in the latch, and turned to see the door open as someone stepped into the room.

"Madeline?" he said, his voice incredulous.

She froze in the doorway, the blood draining from her face. "Arthur?" She sounded as surprised to see him as he was to see her.

His eyes darted to the painting she clutched to her chest. "What are you doing here? What is that?"

Madeline's eyes were wide. "Arthur, I…" She cleared her throat. "I did not know you were back. I only came to return something."

"What do you mean?"

She turned the canvas around slowly, holding it out to him. Lily's laughing eyes gazed out at him from her portrait, and he took it automatically, trying to make sense of what it meant.

"How did you…" Arthur frowned, shaking his head. "I don't understand. What were you doing with Lily's portrait?" He looked around, his anger growing. "What were you doing in here?"

Madeline wrung her hands. "Mrs. MacLeod gave me her key so that I could come in here to work in the evenings after I put the boys to bed. I've been sketching Lily's likeness, you see. But it was so cold and dark in here, and I could not light a fire, that I decided to take the portrait to work on it in my room." Her voice grew small. "I've had it there since Friday. I completed my sketch last night, but did not return the painting since it was so late when I finished. I dismissed the boys from lessons today and went to fetch it straight away, so that I could put it back."

Arthur stared at his late wife's face, his expression dark. He reached a hand out and gently touched her painted cheek.

"You must not blame Mrs. MacLeod," Madeline said, her voice stronger. "She never wanted to let me in the room, but I convinced her, since I was working on a gift for Augustus."

Still Arthur said nothing.

"I should have asked permission before removing the portrait," Madeline said, growing agitated, "but Mrs. MacLeod was away with you in London, and I so wanted to finish the picture of Lily before you returned. I was very careful," she said, twisting her hands together.

The silence in the room was deafening, but Arthur did not trust himself to speak. A thousand emotions tore through his insides, raging against the walls of his mind and his heart like a caged beast.

"Please, Arthur—have you nothing to say? Speak to me."

"How dare you," Arthur said, his voice low, his eyes still on the painting he held. "How dare you come in here and disturb my wife's things. How dare you take her portrait. How dare you think you had any right at all to—" He looked up at her, the fierceness of his gaze causing Madeline to step back. "I was wrong to let you in. I was wrong to let you stay. I see that now."

"Arthur, I—"

"I don't want your excuses, Miss Crawford," he said, his voice a dagger. "I want you to get out."

"Please, Arthur, if you would only—"

"Out!" he shouted, making her jump. "Out of this room! Out of this house! Take your brother and take your leave—your services are no longer required."

Madeline's hands flew to her mouth. With a sob, she turned and dashed from the room, leaving Arthur staring at his wife's face, the hole in his chest ragged and bleeding once more.

Madeline ran from the room, her eyes streaming with tears. *Why, why, why…* The question pounded in her head with every heartbeat, her feet flying as she sought the solitude of her room. Why had she taken the portrait? Why had she not returned it the night before? Why had Arthur gone to the studio today, of all days? Why had he sent her away?

Why, why, why?

Madeline reached her bedchamber and burst through the door, throwing herself onto the bed. She sobbed harder than she had sobbed in years. The pain of losing her parents, the rejection of never living up to her aunt's expectations—all the hurt she held inside came rushing forth in a torrent of tears. She cried until there were no tears left to cry, until she was tired and weak, exhausted from the pain.

She lay there for hours, not knowing or caring that the time passed, but as the light in her room began to fade, there was a timid knock on her door. It brought her out of her well of misery and back into the present. She rose from her bed and went to the door, opening it only a crack.

"Maddie?" Thomas's frightened face looked up at her. "What happened? What is wrong?"

Madeline opened the door wider and let him in. He wrapped his arms around her and held her tight, and Madeline's tears started afresh.

"Mr. Vanguard is back, but he is in the worst temper I've ever seen," Thomas said. "He sent me to my room and ordered me to stay there until you came to get me, but you never came."

Madeline sniffed, stroking his head. "I am so sorry, Thomas. I did not come, because—" she swallowed, trying not to let the grief overtake her again, "because I have something difficult to tell you. And I did not have the courage yet."

Thomas pulled back, a look of determination on his face. "Tell me, Maddie, at once. What has happened?"

Madeline was not openly crying, but the tears leaked out of her eyes and streamed down her face in a constant flow. "Mr. Vanguard wishes us to leave," she said, her voice nearly a whisper. "We must go back to London."

"What! Why?" he cried.

"I wish I could give you a reason, but I am afraid I cannot," Madeline said. "I only know that he is hurting, and he is very, very angry."

"But why send us away? I thought he was my guardian now?"

Madeline hugged him tight. "I don't have any answers for you, Tom. I wish I did. All I know is that he wishes us gone, so we shall go. We will pack our things and catch the morning train."

"But I don't want to leave, I want to stay here." Thomas began to cry. "I thought this was our home now. I thought we could live here forever. I thought Gus was going to be my brother."

Madeline held him, the crack in her heart splitting open even wider at his grief. She let him cry until his sobs began to subside, then she crouched down and handed him a handkerchief.

"Come," she said gently, "we must tell Gus."

When Madeline knocked on Gus's door a few minutes later,

there was no answer. After a moment she knocked again. "Gus?" she called. "It is Miss Crawford and Thomas. Are you there?"

After a moment the door opened, and Gus stood before them with hanging head and puffy eyes.

"Oh, darling," Madeline said, opening her arms. He rushed to her, putting his arms around her and hugging her while he cried.

"Father told me you must leave," he said between sobs, "but he did not tell me why."

"I am so sorry, dear. I wish it was not so."

He pulled back to look up at her. "Did you quarrel? Can you not say you are sorry and be friends again?"

Madeline stroked his hair. "I wish it was something that could be mended so easily," Madeline said, "but I am afraid it cannot."

Suddenly Gus stomped his foot, his face twisting in anger. "I won't let him send you away, I won't!" he cried.

"Hush dearest, don't carry on so," Madeline said. She led the boys into the room and sat them on the edge of Gus's bed. Kneeling before them, she took each of them by the hand. "I am sure we shall see each other again."

Gus sniffed. "But when?"

Madeline sighed, looking at Thomas, who sat dejectedly next to his friend. "I do not know. But we shall send you word as soon as we are settled. Perhaps you can come visit us."

"When will you leave?"

"Tomorrow morning."

Gus nodded, his eyes filling with tears once more as Madeline stood. "Thomas, I am going to go pack our things. Would you like to stay here with Gus for now?" Her brother nodded. "Very well. I shall come back for you in an hour."

Chapter 27

Madeline spent the next hour packing their things, trying not to let her mind dwell on anything other than the methodical act of folding dresses, petticoats, and stockings. She filled her trunk with their clothes and packed their little travel valises, laying her reticule on top of her bureau where she would be sure to remember it. She placed Thomas's luggage near his door and placed his sleepshirt on the bed—he would dress in the same clothing tomorrow for the trip to London. When she had finished, she took her sketchbook and went back to Gus's room to collect her brother.

The boys were no longer crying. In fact, they hardly looked upset any longer. They were still sitting on the edge of the bed when she came in, but they stopped talking at her entrance.

"Thomas," Madeline said. "It is time to say goodnight. We have an early morning tomorrow."

Thomas nodded and rose from the bed. Madeline sat down beside Gus and placed her sketchbook on her lap. "I have something for you," she said. She pulled out the likeness she had drawn and handed it to him. Gus's eyes widened and a soft *oh!* escaped his lips.

"I had permission from Mrs. MacLeod to visit your mother's studio and sketch her likeness from her portrait," Madeline said. "I had planned on having it framed before giving it to you, but under the circumstances, I knew you would be happy to have it even like this."

Gus looked at the sketch of his mother's face for a long time without speaking. One large, fat tear rolled down his cheek, and Madeline reached out to wipe it away. He finally looked up at her.

"Thank you," he said. "It is the best present ever."

Madeline hugged him. "I hope it will bring you comfort when we are gone," she said.

Gus scowled. "My father will be sorry he tried to send you away," he said darkly.

Madeline was alarmed at his look. "Oh no, Gus, you mustn't do anything to upset your father! Please. It is not his fault."

"Is it your fault, then?"

"No," Madeline said slowly. "No one is to blame, dear."

"Then why is he sending you away?"

Madeline sighed. "Sometimes," she said carefully, "when people are very sad, they say and do things that they would not otherwise say or do. If someone is hurting, they often hurt others without really meaning to."

Gus made no reply, and Madeline bent down to kiss his head. "I love you, Augustus. Promise me you will be good when I am gone, please?"

He shrugged but did not say anything. With a final hug,

Madeline rose to her feet. "Come along, Thomas. It is time for bed."

Madeline was afraid she would not sleep that night, but she was so drained from crying and the emotional turmoil of the day that she fell asleep almost instantly. She awoke in the predawn light, feeling heavier and more exhausted than when she went to bed.

She dressed quickly and quietly, then crept down the hall and knocked softly on Thomas's door. When he did not answer, she opened the door and peeked inside.

The room was dark and gray, the dimness of the morning leeching all the color from the scene. But even without the light, Madeline could see that Thomas was not in bed. In fact, it did not look as if the bed had even been slept in. A shadow of worry drifted into her mind, but she shook it off. He probably snuck back into Gus's room after she bid him goodnight and spent the night with him. She went down the hall to check. After knocking on Gus's door and hearing nothing within, Madeline opened the door and looked inside.

A wave of relief washed over her when she saw the disheveled bed. It was as she suspected—the boys must have spent the night together here in Gus's bedchamber. But where were they now? Puzzled, she looked around the room, but there did not appear to be any sign of them. Perhaps they had arisen early and gone downstairs for something to eat.

It was too early for breakfast to be served, so Madeline went straight to the kitchen. She fully expected to see them sitting at the large table in the middle of the room, but neither boy was in sight.

"'Morning, Miss Crawford," the kindly cook said, coming over to her. "I was mighty sad to hear the news. You will be sorely missed."

"Thank you," Madeline said, her worry making the reply come out more clipped than she intended. "Have you seen my brother? Or Gus? They are not in their rooms. I thought they might be down here."

Mrs. Whittecombe frowned. "I've not seen either one of them since yesterday."

A stone rolled over in Madeline's stomach, and she felt she might be sick. "Thank you, Mrs. Whittecombe," she said, turning and rushing off.

Madeline heard the cook call out to her as she ran, but Madeline did not stop. She ran up the stairs two at a time, pounding down the hallway and bursting into her brother's room. She looked around frantically.

His valise was gone.

She ran to her room, throwing open the door and heading straight past the little pile of luggage at the foot of the bed to the bureau across the room. A sob ripped out of her as she realized her reticule was also missing.

Desperate to be proven wrong, she ran again down the hall, this time to Gus's bedchamber. All of the running and slamming of doors had brought several maids and footmen to the corridor, and they watched with wide eyes as she tore past them. Gus's room was already in shambles, but as Madeline searched through his wardrobe and across the little desk she found a folded piece of paper with the word *Father* written across it in Gus's untidy hand. Not caring that it was not addressed to her, she unfolded the note.

Father,

You wer very rong to send Miss Crawford and her bruther away. I dont noe what hapened, but Thomas and I are going to liv somwhere together until you can sort it owt. Dont wory abowt us, we hav lots of biskits.

Love, Gus

Madeline's hand flew to her mouth, her sobs coming one right after another. A maid edged her way into the room at the sound.

"Miss Crawford?" she said. "Can I do anything for you, miss? What's wrong?"

Madeline quickly wiped at her eyes with the back of her hand. "Where is Mr. Vanguard?" she said, trying desperately to stop her tears. "I must speak to him at once."

"Still in his room, miss."

Madeline marched past her, down the length of the corridor to Arthur's room. She had never been inside, of course, but she remembered where it was from Mrs. MacLeod's pointing it out to her on her initial tour.

Madeline pounded on the door. "Mr. Vanguard? Mr. Vanguard! Mr. Vanguard, I must speak with you. Please—"

The door swung open suddenly and Arthur stood there—his dressing gown open, his hair disheveled, a look of sleepy confusion on his face. He stared at her for a moment.

"Madeline," he said, sounding at once both relieved and displeased to see her standing there. His eyes darted to the servants gathered loosely about the hall. "What is going on?"

"The boys are gone," Madeline said without preamble. "I found this note in Gus's room."

She thrust the paper out in front of her, but Arthur merely frowned. "Gone? What do you mean, gone?"

She waved the paper at him. "See for yourself. Thomas took his valise that I packed last night, as well as my reticule." Fear and despair threatened to overtake her as Madeline heard herself say the words, but she forced herself to maintain her composure.

Arthur took the note from her and read it. He cursed, crumpling the paper in his hand and striding out into the hallway.

"You," he said, pointing to the first footman he saw, "wake my steward and get him here at once. And you," he said, pointing to another, "have the carriage readied with my fastest horses."

The servants jumped to attention and ran off. "Matthews," Arthur said, addressing one of the remaining footmen, "stay here. The rest of you," he said, looking around, "gather the household and begin a search of the grounds immediately."

The servants scattered as Arthur went back into his room. He sat down at his writing desk, pulled out a piece of paper, and began to write. Madeline stood in the doorway, watching him.

"What are you doing?" she said.

"I'm going to find my son."

"And my brother," she cried.

Arthur snorted. "Your brother is likely the reason they are missing in the first place. You Crawfords have a penchant for running away," he said, still focused on his writing.

Madeline seethed but made no reply.

Arthur finished his note, folded it, and went back into the hall. "Have this delivered to the constable at once," he said, thrusting the paper at the waiting footman. The servant took it from his hand and dashed off as Arthur turned around again. Madeline stood in the doorway, barring his entrance into his room.

"If you would excuse me, Miss Crawford," he said.

"I will not," Madeline replied, looking haughtily up at him. "What about the boys?"

"I meant, please excuse me while I get dressed. Unless you do not trust me to complete that task on my own? In which case you are welcome to observe the process."

Blood rushed to her face and she stepped aside. With a smirk, Arthur reentered his room and shut the door.

Madeline paced in the hallway, wringing her hands. Thoughtless, silly boys! Why had they run away? Where had they gone? They could get lost or injured, or be snatched up and sold as chimney sweeps. The longer she paced, the more wild her imagination ran. Oh, what was taking Arthur so long!

As if summoned by her thoughts, Arthur's door swung open again and he emerged, fully dressed. He hardly glanced at her as he strode swiftly away. She hurried to keep pace with him.

"What are we going to do?" Madeline said as they descended the stairs. Arthur gave her a dark look.

"*We* are not going to do anything. You are going to remain here while I head to town and sort out this mess."

"I am coming with you."

They had reached the main floor and were starting down the hallway when Madeline made this declaration. Arthur stopped, whirling around. Madeline nearly ran into him.

"You will do no such thing," he said. "You have caused nothing but trouble since your arrival, and even more trouble now at your departure."

Madeline narrowed her eyes at him. "My brother is missing, and if you think I am going to sit here and do nothing while you try to 'sort out this mess' by yourself, you are grossly mistaken."

"This is entirely your fault!" Arthur shouted, throwing his hands in the air.

"*My* fault?" Madeline cried, incredulous. "It was your ordering us to leave which caused them to run away!"

"If you had not been meddling in places and things that did not concern you, I would not have sent you away," Arthur growled.

"If you would not have ostracized your son and denied him from knowing his mother, I never would have interfered!"

They glared at each other for a long moment. "If we both go," Arthur said at last, through gritted teeth, "what will happen if they come back to the house and neither one of us is here to greet them?"

Madeline felt a flash of uncertainty at his words, but Arthur saw it in her eyes and pounced. "I am going to town to meet with the constable. The servants are already searching the grounds and will likely find them before long. They could not have gone far. *Stay here*," he directed.

He strode off, leaving Madeline fuming in the hallway.

Arthur left for town in the carriage a few minutes later. Madeline watched him go with mixed emotions. She felt an overwhelming anxiety for her brother and Gus, but also a grudging admiration for the speed and determination with which Arthur had taken action. She still wished she was in the carriage beside him, but she had to admit that he was right—if the boys turned up back at the manor, someone needed to be here to meet them.

The house was eerily quiet as Madeline made her way to the kitchen. She poured herself a cup of tea and sat down to wait, her nerves strung tighter than a bow. She sipped at the soothing liquid, her eyes unfocused. A robin landed on the window sill, and she watched it, remembering the bird she saw on their picnic the prior week.

Suddenly she sat bolt upright. *The pond!* Arthur had gone to town in the carriage, but what if the boys had gone to the pond and not the train station? Did not Gus say how much he loved it, and how he wished they could remain there always?

Stumbling to her feet, Madeline sprang for the door and rushed across the lawn towards the stables. She could see and hear the servants scattered all over the park, calling for Thomas and Gus, but she paid them no heed. She knew exactly what she must do.

The stables were empty of groomsmen but full of horses. Madeline strode swiftly down the main walkway, her mind focused on the task at hand and refusing to be distracted by her fears. She came around the corner of the far corridor and saw Winston sticking his nose out of the stall, as if waiting for her.

"Winston!" she cried, rushing over to him. He let out a whinny as she stroked his neck.

"I need your help, boy," she said, her heart pounding as she realized the magnitude of what she had planned. "We are going for a ride."

She went to the wall and collected his saddle and blanket before stepping into the stall with him. As she was cinching it to his back, she realized she was not exactly sure how to sit correctly in a sidesaddle.

"I suppose I will do my best," Madeline murmured, slipping the halter over Winston's head. He could feel her nervous energy and kept stomping and pacing, but Madeline was not frightened.

"I know, boy, I know. But we have to get to Thomas. We have to find them."

Winston's ears flicked back and forth, but then he stood still, letting her finish fastening all the straps and buckles.

At last he was ready. Madeline led him out of the stall and through the stable to the mounting block just outside the back entrance. He did not stand very tall, but Madeline was not sure how she was going to manage to get on him with her bulky skirts in the way.

Glancing around to ensure no one was near, Madeline hiked up her skirts and climbed onto the mounting block. Standing up there, the realization of what she was about to do suddenly hit her, and her stomach turned over.

"For Thomas," she whispered, "and Gus. I can do this for them."

It took a few tries and several awkward readjustments, but at last Madeline managed to seat herself on the saddle. Winston stepped sideways and she clutched his mane, striving for balance. Once he settled, she sat up straight, grabbing the reins.

"Come on boy," she called softly. "Let's go."

She gently kicked his flank with her heel, and he started walking. But as soon as they were moving, panic seized her breast and she pull back on the reins. He stopped.

Madeline sat there, her heart hammering in her chest, the desire to go after her brother warring with the fear that gripped her heart. She closed her eyes, murmuring a silent prayer.

After what seemed an eternity, Madeline felt her pulse return to a more normal pace. Winston stood patiently, waiting for her command, so she nudged him onward again. He started walking, and though Madeline's pulse shot up once more, she did not pull back on the reins this time.

She guided him around until they were facing the direction of the pond. Madeline could not remember all the landmarks specifically, but she hoped that as they drew closer she would recognize the route they had taken earlier.

Once they were headed in the right direction, Madeline urged her pony into a trot. He was happy to oblige, and Madeline surprised herself at how well she was able to control him. She remembered the calls and commands Arthur had taught her, and soon they had covered twice as much ground as she could have on foot.

The sun had risen some time ago, illuminating the sky and making everything appear brighter and more vibrant. The longer she sat on Winston's back, the easier she felt, and if Madeline had not been so anxious about the boys, she would have enjoyed the ride.

After what seemed an eternity, they neared the wood surrounding the pond. She remembered that they had skirted the trees, moving west before entering the wood, so she steered Winston in that direction. In due course she came to the break in the trees, and she followed it into the wood.

As soon as Madeline came in sight of the pond, she pulled Winston to a stop. "Thomas! Gus!" she called, then listened for a reply.

Nothing.

She encouraged Winston to keep going, and as they drew near the water she turned him north, hugging the edge of the pond as they had done before. Every few minutes she stopped and called, but only silence and the occasional cry of a loon was her reply.

At last she came to the little meadow where they had picnicked with Arthur. She guided Winston up the little hill and paused at the top, looking around. "Thomas! Gus!" she called.

A flash of white out of the corner of her eye caused Madeline to turn her head. There, at the edge of the field across from the pond she saw a makeshift shelter, with two little faces peeking out at her.

"Maddie?" Thomas called.

"Thomas!" Madeline cried, pulling her leg free of the pommel and dropping down the side of the pony. Her skirts became tangled as she tried to dismount, and she fell to the ground on her hands and knees, scraping her palms. But she did not care. With a sob, she got to her feet and ran towards her brother, calling his name and crying as she went.

"Thomas, Thomas!" she cried.

"Maddie!" Thomas called, running to meet her.

The siblings collided, and Madeline sank to her knees, sobbing. "Thank the Lord you are safe," she said between her tears. "I have been so worried about you!"

"I am sorry, Maddie," Thomas said. "But Gus and I could think of no other way to stay together."

Madeline hugged him tightly, not trusting herself to speak. She did not know whether to laugh or cry at his logic, so she just held him.

After a moment she looked up, and saw that Gus had walked over to join them. He looked anxious and a little sad, and she opened one arm to invite him into their embrace. He crowded in and she held him tightly, vowing within herself she would never let either of them go again.

When her tears and fears had subsided, Madeline arose. The

boys led her over to their makeshift camp, excited to show her what they had brought and how they intended to live. She let them chatter on about the biscuits and fruit they had pinched from the kitchen, and the little penknife belonging to Gus they had attached to a stick to make a spear, so they could catch fish in the pond.

"And how are you planning to cook the fish?" she asked.

"We will make a fire, of course," Thomas said matter-of-factly. Madeline smiled indulgently, shaking her head.

"This all looks like a grand adventure to you both, I'm sure," she said. "But Mr. Vanguard and I—and the rest of the household, for that matter—have been worried sick. It was very unwise to run off by yourselves, and you are far too young to manage on your own out here. Please, won't you come back to the manor with me?"

Thomas looked to Gus, who folded his arms and huffed. "We are not going back unless Father agrees that you don't have to leave."

Thomas nodded, folding his arms as well. Madeline sighed. "I do not think that very likely, I'm afraid."

"Then I'm afraid we won't be able to go back with you," Gus said. Suddenly he grinned. "But you are welcome to come visit us anytime."

Madeline could not help but laugh. "You are a cheeky rascal, Augustus Vanguard," she said, twitching his nose.

The boys laughed, and Madeline took a deep breath, considering. Should she ride back to the house and let the others know where they were? It seemed the logical course of action… but Madeline's heart had been through enough in the last twenty-four hours. What if something happened to them while she was gone? What if she lost her way? She sighed, knowing full well how angry Arthur would be when he returned to the manor and discovered her missing, but there did not seem to be any help for it.

"Well, I suppose I will just have to live with you, then," Madeline said, throwing up her hands in mock surrender. "Because I am not leaving without you."

The boys whooped in delight, and she sat down beside them on the ground, settling in.

It was going to be a long day.

Chapter 28

It was easy for Arthur to hide his fear behind a mask of anger, but the truth is, he was terrified. Ever since reading Gus's note that morning, he had been afraid. Afraid that Gus was lost or hurt. Afraid that Madeline blamed him for the boys running away. Afraid that it was all his fault. Afraid that his temper and his pain had driven away the only people alive in the world whom he truly cared about.

He rubbed a hand across his eyes, feeling as if he had aged a hundred years since he awoke that morning. The carriage bumped along the road back to the manor, Arthur's spirits sinking further with every mile. The constable had sent inquiries all over town, and Arthur himself went everywhere he could possibly think the boys might go. They had not been seen at the train station or the mercantile. They were not at the church. Arthur even stopped in Milford Village and knocked on every door, desperately hoping for news of his son or Miss Crawford's brother. But there was not a trace of them.

The carriage pulled up in front of the manor and Arthur climbed out. He hoped, rather than believed, that the boys had come home in his absence. As the hours had passed, Arthur's anger gave way to shame and remorse. He had done this. He had caused this tragedy. He was to blame.

He strode into the house, calling for Madeline as he removed his hat. "Madeline? Madeline!" A footman came down the hall, and Arthur turned to him. "Where is Miss Crawford? Have the boys been located?"

"No, sir," the footman replied. "Most of the servants have returned, after a thorough search of the garden and grounds. Several are now out on horseback, searching the park."

Arthur nodded. "Good. And Miss Crawford?"

"I cannot tell you, sir," the servant said. "She has not been seen since this morning. It appears she is gone."

"Gone!" Arthur cried. "What do you mean, gone?"

"Her things are still in her room, sir, but her person is not in the house. We have looked everywhere."

Arthur rubbed his forehead. Why had she not stayed at the manor as he instructed? Now she was missing as well.

"Very well. I shall go to the stables and speak to the groomsmen to find where the others are searching."

He strode through the house and out the back door, ignoring the hunger pangs that shot through him. It was well past teatime, but aside from a glass of brandy in town and a mouthful of bread, he had eaten nothing all day. He did not care if he ever ate again—he had to find his son. He *had* to.

There was only one groomsman in the stables when Arthur

arrived. "Where are the others searching?" he asked.

"They went mostly south and east, sir," the man replied. "That seemed the most likely, as it is easier traveling."

Arthur nodded. "Good. I will join them."

"Sir," the servant said, his voice hesitant. "It might do well to trawl the river."

Arthur blanched. "No," he said, his stomach turning over. "No, I will not even discuss such a thing."

"As you wish, sir."

"Have you seen Miss Crawford?" Arthur said, trying to rid his mind of the image of Gus's lifeless body, cold and blue.

"No sir, but her pony is missing as well."

Arthur froze, convinced he had misheard the man. "Did you say her pony is missing?"

"Yes, sir. It was not in the stables when we returned from searching the grounds, nor was it in the pasture."

Arthur did not wait for the man to finish speaking. He strode through the stables to Winston's stall. Sure enough, the pony was gone, and what was more, so was all his tack. Arthur cursed. What was she thinking, taking the pony? She did not even know how to ride! His anger suddenly vanished as an image of Madeline, broken and bleeding, lying in a field somewhere sprang unbidden to his mind. He squeezed his eyes shut, desperately trying to stop the panic that threatened to overtake him.

This was all his fault, and it might be too late to make it right.

"Saddle my horse," Arthur barked to the groomsman. "And saddle another for yourself; you are coming with me."

Madeline was achey and cold by the time the sun started to set. She and the boys had eaten all the biscuits and most of the apples, and the novelty of camping out had long been exhausted. But whenever Madeline suggested they return to the manor, the boys flatly refused, stubbornly insisting that they would not return unless Thomas and Madeline could stay.

The golden light of day had given way to the softness of dusk when Madeline heard a sound. Not the sounds of the wood they had grown accustomed to, but a voice, calling from somewhere in the trees.

"Augustus! Miss Crawford! Is anyone out there?"

Madeline scrambled to her feet, sucking in a breath as she leaned upon her hands, the palms smarting as they pressed against the ground. "Yes, yes!" she called, running to the top of the little hill. "We are here, we are over here!"

She stood in the grass, scanning the edge of the woods for signs of life. At last she saw a horse and rider emerge from the trees, far to the south along the shore. She raised her arm, waving it in the air. "Here!" she shouted. "Over here!"

The rider turned in her direction, and he kicked the horse into a trot. Another horse and rider came out of the woods behind him, following them.

Madeline looked back at the boys, who sat stubbornly in their makeshift camp, watching her. "Someone is coming," she called to them. The boys exchanged looks but did not move.

Madeline turned back to watch the approaching riders, who were nearly to the meadow. Even in the fading light she recognized Arthur, and her body tensed. *He will be angry,* she thought. But she lifted her head, determined to face him once more. As soon as his horse reached firmer ground, Arthur kicked it into a gallop, and in a moment he was sliding off his mount, running the last few steps to meet her.

"I found the boys this morning," she said, turning to point. "They are well, only—"

She was abruptly cut off as Arthur crushed her to his chest. She gasped, shocked.

"Madeline," he said, his voice husky with emotion. "I cannot tell you how sorry I am. I was so afraid that you—" His voice caught. "Don't ever frighten me like that again."

Shocked, Madeline did not know what to say. As quickly as he had embraced her, Arthur let her go. "Now, where is my son?"

Madeline pointed, still too dumbfounded to speak. Arthur headed in the direction she indicated, and she followed after him.

"Augustus!" Arthur cried, striding towards the boys. Gus and Thomas stood, giving each other one last, determined look. "I have been so worried. Are you all right?"

Gus nodded. "Yes, Father."

Arthur embraced his son the same way he had Madeline, crushing the boy to his chest. After a moment he released him, crouching down to look in his eyes.

"That was very wrong of you to run off, son. What if something had happened to you?"

"I am not sorry," Gus said, much to the surprise of Madeline and, from the looks of it, to Arthur as well. "It was the only way I would be able to stay with Thomas."

"I understand. But let us discuss this later—we need to head back to the manor, it will be full dark soon."

"No."

Arthur stood just as his son replied. He paused. "No?" he said with some surprise.

"No," Gus repeated. "Miss Crawford has been trying to get us to go home with her all day. But we are not going anywhere."

He folded his arms across his chest, and Thomas followed suit. Arthur looked at Madeline, who shrugged.

"They have refused all day, as he said. I did not want to leave them to get help, and—quite frankly—I was afraid I might get lost. So I stayed with them, trusting that eventually someone would come." She allowed herself a small smile. "How did you know where to find us, anyway?"

"When I discovered that Winston was gone," Arthur said, indicating the pony that stood quietly in the grass, "I assumed you had come here. It was the only place I could think of that you might know where to look."

He returned her smile, and Madeline felt her insides warm. Had he reconsidered his ultimatum in the studio? He certainly appeared to be in another frame of mind at present, but Madeline was almost too afraid to hope.

Arthur turned back to the boys. "And why do you still refuse to come home?" he asked.

"Because you sent Thomas and Miss Crawford away," Gus said angrily, taking a step towards his father. Arthur's eyebrows shot up but he said nothing.

"Miss Crawford's coming is the best thing to ever happen to us," Gus went on. "I gained a friend who feels like a brother, and a tutor who is more like a mother."

Tears sprang to Madeline's eyes as he looked at her. He gave her a smile, but then turned, scowling, back to his father. "I won't go home unless you promise that Thomas and Miss Crawford can stay."

No one spoke. In the growing darkness, the sounds of crickets and frogs replaced the calls of birds and squirrels. One of the horses whinnied, and Madeline looked back, noticing the groom who stood holding the reins of both his and Arthur's horses. She turned back to watch the exchange between father and son.

"Augustus," Arthur said, his voice quiet, "you have every right to be angry with me. I am angry with myself, to be honest. And I understand your feelings about Miss Crawford and her brother. But I am afraid I cannot promise that they will stay, because that is for them to decide." Arthur took a step towards Madeline, watching her carefully.

"It was very wrong of me to send you away," he said quietly, "and I have nothing but regret for what I said. If you can find it in your heart to forgive me, I would like nothing better than for you to remain at Milford Manor with Augustus and myself."

For one moment, all was silent. Then with a jubilant cry, Thomas punched the air.

"Hurrah!" he shouted. "We can stay, we can stay!"

Madeline laughed, the tension in the air having burst when her brother cried out. The boys were shouting over one another in an effort to be heard, but Madeline only had eyes for Arthur.

"Yes," she said quietly, knowing he would hear her, "yes, I can forgive you. I do. I would love to stay."

In two steps Arthur swept her into his arms in another embrace, surprising her again. He held her close, and this time Madeline wrapped her arms around him, hugging him back.

"There is more I wish to say," Arthur murmured in her ear, "but for now it will have to wait." He released her slowly, stepping back.

A small form collided with him as he did so, the fair head of his son bright in the darkness. "Thank you, Father," he said. "Thank you."

"We will discuss it further once we get home," Arthur said. "Now gather your things; it is time to go."

The boys moved off to break camp as Arthur turned to Madeline. "Do you think you can ride Winston back to the manor, if I am with you?"

Madeline started to nod, but paused, looking down at her hands. "I do, but I scraped my palms when I dismounted earlier," she said. "I bathed them in the water, but they still sting."

Gently Arthur took one of her hands in his. He turned it over, inspecting the wound. Slowly he bent down, brushing a kiss on her open palm. Madeline sucked in a breath, her heart pounding.

"Here," Arthur said, removing his gloves, "put these on. They will be too large, but they will protect your hands from the reins."

Madeline stared. "Your hand! Is it healed, then?"

He smiled softly. "Yes, it is."

Madeline pulled the gloves onto her hands and wriggled her fingers. They were indeed too large, but she smiled at him. "Thank you," she said.

"Of course."

The boys finished their packing and came to join them. "Now then," Arthur said. "Thomas, you will ride with Peter; Augustus, you will ride with me, and Madeline, you ride on Winston."

Arthur helped Madeline get situated on her pony. "You look quite comfortable up there," he remarked, handing her the reins.

Madeline gave him a nervous laugh. "I assure you I am quite the opposite," she said. "I don't know how we will find our way home in the dark."

Arthur set Gus upon the horse, then swung himself up behind him. Thomas and the groomsman were already mounted and waiting. "Remember when we rode home from York?" Arthur said. "The horses will do just fine in the dark. And they are herd animals, so they will stick together." He gave her an encouraging smile, then nudged his horse into a walk. "Come—let us go home."

Chapter 29

Madeline shut the door softly to Thomas's room. She looked up at Arthur, who stood beside her in the hallway. "He is asleep," she said.

"So is Augustus."

Madeline blew out her breath. "What a day," she said. "I feel as if I have lived a thousand years since morning."

"Would you like to turn in for the night?" Arthur asked.

Madeline looked sheepish. "Yes… and no."

Arthur chuckled. "I know precisely what you mean."

He picked up her hand, being careful of the bandage, and tucked it into the crook of his arm, leading her down the hall.

"How are your hands?" he asked.

"Much better. That balm of Mrs. Whittecombe's is wonderful. They shall be healed in a few days, I'm sure."

"I still cannot believe you rode Winston all by yourself," Arthur said, shaking his head.

"I would do anything for my brother. And for Gus," she said. "But you know it is all with thanks to you. Without your help and encouragement, and all our lessons, I never would have dared."

"Does this mean you would consider real riding lessons now?"

Madeline laughed lightly. "Perhaps. Since it appears I will not be leaving after all."

She glanced up at him, and Arthur gave her a strained smile. "Come," he said. "I have much to say on that point."

By now they had entered one of the smaller drawing rooms, and Arthur led Madeline to the settee, then sat down beside her.

"I don't know how to adequately express how sorry I am for what happened yesterday," he said.

Madeline sat quietly with her hands in her lap, knowing there was more he wanted to say.

"When I left for London," he said, choosing his words carefully, "I was so confused. How could I have a future with you unless I offered you my whole heart? And yet, how could I turn my back on the love I felt for my late wife? I did not know what to do. It seemed an impossible conundrum." Arthur picked up her hand, holding it gently between his own. "But my sister helped me see that it was never a choice at all."

Madeline frowned. "What do you mean?"

"She pointed out that my love for my son had never competed with my love for my wife. She described it as my having separate hearts for each of them." He looked down at their hands. "I realized that I was trying to fit you into the heart I grew for Lily, but there was not room for both of you since it was never meant to be yours. And I could not dispose of my love for her to make room for you there—it felt like a betrayal to give you something that had belonged to her."

He paused, looking up at her again. He wore such a tender expression on his face that it made Madeline blush. He saw her color and reached up, cupping her cheek with his hand.

"I realized," he said softly, "that you deserve your own heart. One that belongs entirely to you."

Madeline covered his hand with her own. "I never wanted you to choose between us, Arthur," she said.

"I know. But I did not know there was another way." He pulled his hand away and sighed. "And once I did, I then had a different choice to make: would I live in the past, haunted by the memory of my late wife and living in the pain her death brought to me? Or would I lay the past to rest, and choose a future with a spirited young woman who does not take no for an answer?"

Madeline let out a breathy laugh, and Arthur smiled. "I chose the latter. And I came home, anxious to tell you. But..." he shook his head, "I first went to Lily's studio to say goodbye, and to make my peace with the past."

His eyes were full of pain as he looked at her, and Madeline reached out, taking both his hands in hers.

"I was not expecting to feel such agony," he said, his voice nearly a whisper. "So many memories. So many unrealized dreams." He paused to compose himself, and Madeline gently squeezed his hands.

"You came upon me at the worst possible moment," he said quietly. "I was doubting myself and my ability to let go of the life I had planned with Lily. Seeing you there, holding her portrait, while I was in such a vulnerable state..." He shook his head. "I could not see beyond the pain to realize the implications of what I was saying."

"I knew you were hurting," Madeline said softly, "and angry. And I cannot blame you for feeling the way that you did. I am sorry for my part in causing you pain."

But Arthur was shaking his head. "You have nothing to apologize for, Madeline. Although I was curious..." He cocked his head at her. "Did you say you were creating a sketch of Lily's portrait, for Gus?"

"Yes, that is why Mrs. MacLeod let me into the studio in the first place, and gave me the key when she went with you to London."

Arthur nodded. "I see. And did you finish the likeness?"

Madeline smiled. "I did. I gave it to Gus last night, when I went to tell him goodbye."

"I would like to see it, if I may."

"Of course. We can ask Gus to show it to you tomorrow."

Silence fell between them, and after a moment, Arthur lifted her hands, kissing first one, then the other. He then moved closer, so that rather than sitting near her with their knees almost touching, he sat beside her, the length of his thigh resting against her own leg. Her heart burst into motion, pounding in her ears and causing her hands to tremble. He placed one arm around her back, tucking her close to his side.

"When I realized you had taken Winston and gone in search of the boys, I panicked," Arthur said. "Any anger I still felt evaporated at the thought that I might lose you as well. I was so relieved to find you. And that is when I knew."

"Knew what?"

"Knew that I loved you."

With his free hand, Arthur reached out and cupped her face,

tipping her head up to kiss her. The moment their lips touched, fire spread through Madeline's body, igniting her senses and causing her head to spin. Arthur pulled her close, his hand moving to the back of her head as he deepened their kiss. Madeline responded, wrapping her arms around his neck and kissing him back.

"He thinks of you as his mother, you know," Arthur murmured against her lips.

Madeline pulled back, still dizzy from his kisses. "Who?"

Arthur chuckled, tracing her jawline with his thumb. She shivered.

"Augustus," he said. "And Thomas as well, I suppose. But I was speaking of my son."

Madeline shook her head, her hands coming to rest against his chest as he sat back. "He has a mother. I am only his tutor."

Arthur leaned in until his lips found hers again. "The only thing you are, Madeline," he said between kisses, "is unexpected."

He pressed a kiss just below her ear, his lips moving down the length of her jaw. Madeline tried not to gasp for air as his mouth brushed against the softness of her throat, but she had forgotten how to breathe. Kissing Arthur was the most wonderful, intoxicating feeling. Desire stirred within her and she cupped his face, pulling his mouth back to hers.

"Miss Crawford," Arthur murmured, sensing the change in her, "what about your reputation?"

Madeline grinned, kissing him again. "I care not a whit for my reputation, sir. Only for my heart."

Arthur sat back, his look suddenly serious. "And what is your heart telling you, Madeline? Is there a place for me there, in spite of my faults?"

"Of course there is," she said, reaching up to brush a lock of hair away from his face. "As well as for Gus."

"Then you will have me?"

Her eyes brightened, but then her look turned calculating. "Hmm. A pony for my hand in marriage..." she mused, tapping her chin.

Arthur chuckled. "And private lessons. Do not forget that."

Madeline grinned. "How could I forget? That is when I fell in love with you."

Arthur responded to that by kissing her again. And again. And again. Madeline cupped his face in her hands, pulling back to look him in the eyes. "I would be honored to give you my heart, and my hand, Arthur Vanguard," she said.

Arthur closed his eyes, a soft smile spreading across his face. When he opened them again, they were bright with unshed tears. "Thank you," he said simply.

And he kissed her again.

Epilogue

Madeline urged the little pony faster, anxious to return to the house. The October wind blew the leaves across the pasture, the whisper and rustle as they knocked against one other heralding the coming winter. Winston plodded along, steady as always, and Madeline gave him a little kick to get him moving.

"Come on, Winnie," she called. "I saw Arthur's carriage come down the lane—he is home!"

Winston, of course, made no reply, and in due course they arrived at the stables. Madeline dismounted, handing the reins to the nearest groom and heading up to the house.

She hurried through the halls, smiling as she passed the paintings that had been recently rehung. Lily's artwork once again filled the house, which seemed all the more alive now they had been replaced.

Madeline found Arthur and the boys in the morning room. They all looked up at her entrance, and Gus ran over to her.

"Mother Maddie, look what Father has brought us from

London!" He held up a set of beautifully carved wooden horses, attached to a small carriage with tiny leather straps.

"How delightful!" Madeline said.

"You can even take the harnesses off and play with the horses by themselves," Thomas added, mirroring his friend's excitement. The boys headed to the corner to play with their new toy while Madeline went to greet her husband.

"Hello, Mrs. Vanguard," Arthur said, opening his arms to her.

Madeline laughed, stepping into his embrace. "I am still not accustomed to that address."

Arthur pressed a kiss lightly to her forehead. "That is understandable, considering it has only been a month since we wed."

"How did you find everything in London?"

"Excellent. I acquired two new studs at Tattersall's and was able to complete my business with Mr. Gillingham and my solicitor."

Madeline smiled at him warmly. "It was very kind of you to write Thomas into your will."

"Of course. I am his guardian, and I *did* marry his sister, after all." He bent down and brushed a kiss, soft and sweet, against her lips. "Now come," he said, "I have something to show you."

He led her over to a chair, then retrieved a parcel from the table. "What is this?" Madeline asked when he handed it to her.

Arthur grinned. "Open it and see."

Madeline untied the string and removed the paper, revealing the back of a small frame. She turned the picture over.

"Oh Arthur," she said, smiling up at him, "it is beautiful!"

She held the sketch she had drawn of Lily's likeness in her hand, an intricately carved frame now surrounding it. She looked to where the boys were playing.

"Gus, come and see what else your father has brought!"

Gus stood up and came over to her, and Madeline held the picture out to him. He gasped. "It is Mother! The drawing you did for me!" He looked up at Arthur. "Is this why you asked to borrow it before you left?"

Arthur chuckled. "Yes, it is."

"It is perfect," Madeline said, looking up at her husband with a smile. "Now it will be better protected."

Gus hugged it to his chest, then embraced his father. "Thank you, Father," he said. "Can I hang it on the wall in my room?"

"Of course," Arthur said.

Gus beamed. "It will be like having both of my mothers watching over me," he said.

He gave Madeline a hug as well and ran off to show Thomas, who had stayed in the corner to play with the horse and carriage. Madeline reached out and took Arthur's hand.

"What a wonderful surprise," she said.

"And I have one more," he replied.

Madeline laughed. "More! Arthur, you will spoil us all."

He lifted her hand and brushed his lips across her knuckles. "Is that not what a doting husband and father should do?"

Madeline gave him an indulgent smile. "What else, then?"

His eyes grew bright. "I have commissioned an artist to come to the manor in January and paint our portrait."

"Our portrait! You and I?"

"All of us—you, me, Augustus, and Thomas. A family portrait."

Madeline clapped her hands together. "That is a marvelous idea! And perhaps we can get Winnie in it, too."

Arthur laughed. "Is it not enough that you spend more time with that pony than with me?"

Madeline's eyes sparkled. "It is your own fault, you know."

He chuckled, shaking his head. "I wish I could say I regret it, but I do not. It is wonderful to see how thoroughly you have overcome your fears and taken to riding."

"And I will always thank you for forcing me into doing so," she teased.

Madeline stood, stretching up onto her toes to kiss his cheek. He turned his head and caught her lips with his, wrapping his arms around her. "Arthur!" she laughed, glancing across the room at the boys.

Arthur pulled her closer. "Will you forbid me from kissing my wife in my own home?" he asked.

Madeline pressed her lips together in mock disapproval. "In view of the children, most certainly."

His eyes moved to the corner where Thomas and Gus still played. "Hm, I see. We had better leave the room, then."

Madeline laughed, allowing herself to be pulled out the door.

The End

If you enjoyed this book, please consider leaving a review!
It only takes a moment and would be much appreciated. ♡

Acknowledgements

Writing and publishing a book is always a team effort. My deepest gratitude belongs to my Savior Jesus Christ and my Heavenly Parents, without whose blessings I could not do anything.

I am also grateful for the love and encouragement of my husband, John, who has been my biggest fan and supporter from day one. Thank you for believing in me and celebrating with me all along the way!

My children—Caleb, Elina, Audrey, and Mira—who read over my shoulder and tolerated cereal for dinner more times than I can count. I love you so much!

For the bestest bestie ever, Sally (Britton) Treanor, who has my deepest love and heartfelt thanks. There's no one I would rather talk story with than you! Thank you for all the help and encouragement, the commiseration, the chats and memes and everything in between. I couldn't do this writing thing without you.

Special thanks go to my niece Serity Odd, for whom this book is dedicated. Thank you for keeping me company while drafting, for helping me brainstorm names and descriptions, and for all the chats about Jane Austen. I can't wait to read your own book someday!

Rachel Stones, Kimberlee McCoy, Jenaca Willans, and Cherika Hedengren, thank you for reading various drafts and helping me with your edits and feedback! I am also indebted to The Society for Obstinate, Headstrong Girls and the Historymakers for answering questions and helping with research along the way. My thanks also go to Julie Donaldson for her friendship and support—I'll brainstorm with you any day!

I would also like to thank Bridget Baker and Clarissa (Kae) Wilstead for answering questions about horses and ponies. And to Rebecca Connolly, for making me laugh and helping me brainstorm when I got stuck.

And for you, dear readers, thank you. Thank you for spending your time with me and my story. Thank you for having faith in a "little old nobody" author such as myself. I love my little stories, and knowing that others enjoy them as well makes my heart so, so happy.

About the Author

Shaela Kay was born and raised near Seattle, WA. She studied Theatre and English at Brigham Young University-Idaho, but left her studies in order to be a wife and mother. When she isn't reading or writing, you can find her quilting, crafting, or working as a graphic designer. She and her husband John live in Washington with their four children, too many pets, and not enough bookshelves.